REUNION PASS

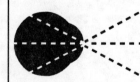This Large Print Book carries the
Seal of Approval of N.A.V.H.

REUNION PASS

EMILY MARCH

THORNDIKE PRESS
A part of Gale, Cengage Learning

GALE
CENGAGE Learning·

Farmington Hills, Mich • San Francisco • New York • Waterville, Maine
Meriden, Conn • Mason, Ohio • Chicago

LIBRARY OF CONGRESS CATALOGING-IN-PUBLICATION DATA

Names: March, Emily, author.
Title: Reunion pass / Emily March.
Description: Large print edition. | Waterville, Maine : Thorndike Press Large Print, 2016. | © 2016 | Series: An Eternity Springs novel | Series: Thorndike Press large print romance
Identifiers: LCCN 2016011404 | ISBN 9781410490117 (hardback) | ISBN 1410490114 (hardcover)
Subjects: LCSH: Large type books. | BISAC: FICTION / Romance / Contemporary. | GSAFD: Love stories.
Classification: LCC PS3604.A9787 R48 2016 | DDC 813/.6—dc23
LC record available at http://lccn.loc.gov/2016011404

Published in 2016 by arrangement with St. Martin's Press, LLC

Printed in the United States of America
1 2 3 4 5 6 7 20 19 18 17 16

To the real angel of Eternity Springs —
Mary Dickerson.

ACKNOWLEDGMENTS

I want to thank the great team at
St. Martin's Press for their outstanding
effort in giving Eternity Springs a new
home.

Rose Hilliard's fabulous editorial direction
and enthusiasm for everything Eternity
Springs make working with her a joy.

My thanks to the art department for the
spectacular cover look they've given this
series, to Kerri Resnick for her lovely cover
design, and to Tom Hallman for the
beautiful illustration.

My most sincere thanks for the support
from the rest of my publishing team at
St. Martin's Press including Jennifer
Enderlin, Anne Marie Talberg, Monique
Patterson, Erin Cox, Brant Janeway, and
Amy Goppert.

Thanks to my agents Meg Ruley and Christina Hogrebe, and the rest of the team at the Jane Rotrosen Agency for all you've done to help me achieve my dreams.

To my friends and plot group partners Christina Dodd, Susan Sizemore, and Nicole Burnham, who are always there to help with story ideas, and to plot group host-with-the-most Scott Ham for the bottomless wine glass and cookies.
Love you guys.

And to my dear friend Mary Dickerson who never fails to go above and beyond the call of friendship, who plots, critiques, edits, holds my hand, kicks my butt, and believes in me when my faith in myself is flagging. I am so blessed. Thank you!

CHAPTER ONE

Six years earlier
College Station, Texas

Lori Reese awoke to the sensation of teeth nibbling that sweet spot on her neck that invariably made her shiver. "Mmm . . ." She groaned as she opened her eyes. Her gaze sought her bedside clock and dismay washed through her. "I have class in fifteen minutes."

"Skip it." Chase Timberlake's husky voice rumbled against her ear.

Lori instinctively arched against the big hand that traced a slow caress across the naked curve of her hip. They'd fallen into her bed within twenty minutes of his arrival for a long weekend visit, his second in as many weeks, and she was in no hurry to leave it. Unfortunately, staying in bed wasn't an option. "It's my anatomy and physiology class. I can't skip it."

"Sure you can. I'll teach you everything

9

you need to know about anatomy." He nipped at her earlobe and added, "I'm an expert."

"Chase," she protested, even as she suppressed a smile. "That's a terrible line."

Swiping the rough pad of his thumb across the sensitive flesh of her nipple, he asked, "Are you calling me a liar?"

"No." She groaned.

He rolled her beneath him and his brown eyes gleamed wickedly as he challenged, "Be daring, be bold." He stroked her lower lip with the tip of his tongue. "Be bad."

"You are bad enough for both of us."

"It's a talent of mine," he quipped. "I practice."

Yet, "bad" wasn't the proper term for Chase, Lori knew. He was actually very good at what he did, though what he did wasn't ordinary. Despite having earned his business degree from the University of Colorado, Chase continued to work at what had been his summer job — guiding white-water rafting trips from April through October on the Gunnison and Colorado Rivers. Rafting had become his obsession. He had a bucket list of rivers he wanted to raft in his lifetime, and Lori had no doubt that he'd ride each one. Off-season, he led backcountry skiing tours for an outfitter out of Durango. He claimed that he was still trying to decide what to do when he grew up.

In contrast, Lori had known what she wanted to be since a school field trip to the veterinary clinic in Creede, Colorado, in the third grade. Due to the brutally competitive nature of vet school admissions, she didn't dare spend the entire afternoon rolling between the sheets with Chase. She braced her hands against his chest. "I'm not the 'bad' type. I'm responsible and boring."

"Not true. Responsible, yes. Boring? Never. You, Lori my love, are as exciting as Class VI rapids. As exhilarating as back-country skiing." He dipped his head and licked the valley between her breasts. "As thrilling as skydiving."

His lips trailed lower and weakened Lori's resistance. She tried once more. "The professor gives pop quizzes."

"I can do that. For twenty points, name this part." He slid inside her, stretching her, filling her.

"Mr. Happy."

"Half credit. Mr. Happy is too . . . perky."

"No fair. It fits." She rolled her hips and sighed. "He's perennially perky."

"Okay, three-quarter credit, then. Full credit goes to Hammer of Thor. Now, quit

11

arguing and let's get to the pop part of this quiz."

Lori was late to class. Very late. And sure enough, she walked in on a quiz. Her stomach sank and she swallowed a groan as she took her seat, hoping that today's lecture had been about something she'd already studied.

She scored a seventeen and left the classroom fighting back tears. She wanted to blame Chase, but she knew that wouldn't be fair. He hadn't tied her to the bed.

Though he'd offered to try it if she thought that was something she'd like.

The hot, muggy south-central Texas weather didn't improve her mood as she trudged across the campus toward the student center where she had arranged to meet Chase. She was so angry at herself. Chase Timberlake could tempt an angel to sin when his eyes took on that adventurous gleam and he flashed that wicked grin. And she was certainly no angel.

But she *was* a serious student. Hadn't she learned the importance of education first-hand while watching her single mother struggle? Wasn't she determined not to repeat her mom's mistake of letting hormones and a hot guy change the course she'd plotted for her life? So why the heck had she thrown all her good intentions out the window this afternoon at the first touch of his oh-so-talented lips?

"Stupid. Stupid. Stupid." Muttering softly, she rehearsed what she needed to say to him. "You've graduated. I still have years of college and professional school ahead of me. I can't skip classes. I can't neglect my study time. I have goals. I must always be on top of my game. Otherwise, I won't get into vet school and if I don't get into vet school . . ." Sudden tears flooded her eyes at the thought. She hurriedly wiped them away when she heard her roommate call her name.

"OMG, Lori," Molly Stapleton said. "I finally met your hunk. He's so hot!"

Lori's lips fluttered with a smile. "You've been to the apartment?"

"I forgot my history textbook. Chase was coming out of the shower wearing nothing but your fluffy pink towel. I told him pink was a good color for him. Makes a lovely contrast to his brown eyes. Though I admit I had a hard time tearing my stare away from his shoulders. Holy cow, Lori. He's built like a god."

"Rafting is a physical occupation. All that paddling."

"Well, all I can say is . . ." Molly gave her

auburn hair a toss and winked. "Row, row, row your boat."

Lori couldn't help but laugh. "Better not let your Andrew hear you talk like that."

Molly waved off the concern. "A little jealousy won't hurt him. I'm shallow that way. Besides, I haven't been feeling it for Andrew lately."

"I knew it," Lori declared. "You're interested in that guy who chatted you up at the post office the other day, aren't you? Your old boyfriend. What's his name? Jimmy?"

"Charlie. Charlie Malone."

Recognizing the note of interest in her friend's voice, Lori deduced that she'd seen the last of ol' Andrew.

The roommates parted ways as Molly headed for a bus stop and Lori continued on to the student center. Entering the building, she made her way to the flag room where she and Chase had arranged to meet. She glanced around, didn't see him, and decided to check the coffee shop. No Chase.

The return route to the flag room took her past the art gallery where, to her surprise, she spied him speaking animatedly with a man and woman. She glanced at the exhibit poster propped on a display easel beside the door and read: "Adventures in Photography by George Overstreet, Class of

1979. Artist reception five P.M."

The university regularly hosted special exhibits on football weekends, so she wasn't surprised to see a special event in the gallery. Nor was she surprised that the word "adventure" had pulled Chase in. It was the one thing Lori feared she couldn't compete with where her lover was concerned.

Chase's back was to her when she stepped into the room, so he didn't notice her arrival. Lori studied the couple who were the focus of her boyfriend's attention. The man was in his fifties, she guessed, with snowy, disheveled hair and a beard that needed trimming. He wore a sport coat with elbow patches, a checked bow tie, and dress boots that shone. A character, Lori decided.

The woman was the type whom Lori always found intimidating. Petite with sable-colored hair piled artfully atop her head, she was beautiful and quite a bit younger than her companion — near to her mom's age, Lori guessed — but with that rich, classy look that reminded her of Chase's mother, Ali. She wore a little black dress, pearls, and an air of sophistication that Lori couldn't pull off on a bet with a thousand-dollar budget. Moving closer, she heard Chase say, ". . . somewhere I've always wanted to visit. After seeing your photographs, I definitely want to go there."

"My husband's photography is spectacular," the woman said, looping her arm through her companion's. "You must see the rainbow he captured above Kalambo Falls on the border of Tanzania and Zambia. It's on this wall."

Lori hung back and eavesdropped as Chase admired the photo in question and quizzed the photographer about cameras and lenses and lighting and filters. Photography was a new hobby of his, and this exhibit had certainly captured his interest. She'd seldom heard this much animation in his tone.

Curiously, a wave of unease washed over her at the realization.

The trio moved from photo to photo, and Chase's attention remained focused on the art. Lori tugged her phone from the pocket of her jeans and checked the time. Almost half an hour now past the time they'd arranged to meet. He was totally and completely distracted, and Lori found herself growing annoyed. Her boyfriend needed to have more respect for her time.

Abruptly, she turned and left the gallery without making her presence known and took a seat near the entrance to the flag room. She'd give him five more minutes —

ten at the most — then she was outta here.

He showed up in eight, a sheepish grin on his face, his dark eyes gleaming with excitement. "Sorry, sweetheart. I got talking to the guy in the art gallery. Have you seen his photographs? They're fascinating. He has the coolest job ever. He travels around the world taking action photographs of people participating in extreme sports. He just returned from Bali and guess what? He has a home and studio in Vail. He's invited me to go see it."

Chase babbled on enthusiastically for a few moments until he finally noticed that Lori wasn't saying much at all. His voice trailed off, and he gazed at her a long minute. "What's wrong, Glitterbug?"

"I don't know. What could possibly be wrong?" she snapped. "I love to stand around twiddling my thumbs waiting for my boyfriend to remember I exist after I skipped class to have sex with him. And it was only one little quiz. So what if I made a seventeen? It's better than a seven."

His eyes widened, realization dawned, and then he grimaced and gave her a hug. "Yikes. I'm sorry, Lori. My fault. Coming in a day early was a bad idea. I was just so anxious to see you. I miss you so much when we're apart. October first can't get here fast enough."

Lori shut her eyes, torn in two completely opposite directions as so often happened where Chase was concerned. When she'd first gone off to college, they'd agreed to date other people. They both anticipated a friendly end to their romance. Instead, dating others only proved the adage that absence makes the heart grow fonder, and last summer, they declared themselves exclusive once again — though they'd yet to share the news with their respective families.

She'd been thrilled when he announced his intention to find a job in College Station at the end of the rafting season. Maintaining a long-distance relationship was difficult. She missed him terribly, too, when they were apart.

But at the same time, having him around complicated her life in ways she hadn't anticipated. Having him around produced seventeens on A&P quizzes. Her temper faded, replaced with despair. As wetness flooded her eyes, she abruptly shoved to her feet. "I need to walk."

He followed her, his hands shoved into the pockets of his jeans. Lori charted a course across the older section of campus toward her very favorite spot, a bench beneath the spreading branches of a huge live oak known as the Century Tree. Seated, she gripped the bench with both hands and stared at the green, sun-dappled grass in front of her.

"It's not your fault, Chase. I'm a big girl. I'm responsible for the decisions I make, the actions I take — good and bad." She drew in a deep breath, then exhaled in a rush. "I have no willpower when you are around. I can't say no to you. I don't want to say no, but I need to say no. You know?"

"I know." He picked up her hand and kissed her knuckles.

She drew a deep breath, then exhaled in a rush. "I don't think you should move to College Station." Chase dropped her hand and shoved his hands in his pockets. His fingers brushed the ring he'd been carrying for almost a week. "You're dumping me?"

"No, I'm not dumping you. I love you."

"You love me, so you don't want me around." He gave a stone at his feet a vicious kick. "Right. Makes perfect sense."

A pleading note entered her voice. "You distract me, Chase, and I can't afford to be distracted. Not this semester. Or next semester. Maybe by next year I'll be better able to handle my studies and have a life, too, but right now . . . I made a seventeen today, Chase. A seventeen!"

He could hear the fear in her voice, and even as he wanted to dismiss it, part of him wished that he'd found something to be as passionate about as she had. Another part of him resented the fact that she wasn't as passionate about him as she was about her professional goals.

Chase was in love with Lori. Flat-out, head over heels, crazy in love. She was everything he wanted, all that he needed. She was smart. Generous. Witty.

Sexy.

She made him laugh. Made him horny. She was a loyal friend with a fierce, courageous heart. His family all loved her almost as much as he did.

Yet, he wasn't blind to her faults. Lori was a whole helluva lot of work. She had trust issues. She had daddy issues. She had a head as hard as granite. Chase reminded himself that he truly believed she'd be worth the work in the end, but in the meantime, he needed to be patient. He needed to respect her anxieties, and in truth, he could see her point. He *was* a distraction. It didn't help that they were now in two different stages of life.

He'd love nothing more than to travel the world with her, but he tried not to worry that she didn't have the same sense of wanderlust as he. She was strong and steady, the kind of woman a man always wanted to come home to — wherever home happened to be.

He wanted to be with her more often than they managed now. He loved her. He missed her. Long-distance relationships sucked. Always ready to make plans on the fly, he rolled out an alternate idea he'd previously considered and discarded. "I wanted to talk to you about that, Lori. I planned to do it after dinner. I'm afraid I haven't had any luck finding anything that suits my training or degree. Lots of jobs in this town. So far, though, nothing for me."

She blinked rapidly. "You're not moving to Texas?"

He read both disappointment and relief in her evergreen eyes, and he told himself that his feelings weren't hurt, his pride wasn't pricked. "Not College Station. I was thinking of looking for something in Dallas or Houston. We could spend Saturdays together."

"I'd love that," Lori said with a heartfelt sigh, her whole body easing.

He tucked the diamond solitaire a little deeper into his pocket. *Patience, man. Patience.*

The word became his mantra throughout

the following months, the engagement ring a constant in his pocket whenever he was due to see Lori. He didn't move to Texas. George Overstreet, the photographer he'd met in College Station, hired him to be his personal outdoors guide when his river job came to a close, and by Thanksgiving, Chase had found his new vocation — outdoors photography.

George proved to be an extraordinary mentor who recognized and channeled Chase's natural talent. Despite the fact that opportunities assisting George arose and caused Chase to miss a couple of weekends with Lori, she supported and encouraged his newfound interest. "I think it's wonderful you've found your passion," she told him at Christmas when he sat working up the nerve to pull the ring from his pocket. "I think it makes such a difference in life."

You are my passion, he wanted to say. But he swallowed the words, even as he stilled his hand from reaching into his pocket for the ring. She didn't seem to notice that the gifts he gave her for Christmas lacked a one big "wow" present like he'd given her in previous years.

In February, he had the opportunity to travel with George to South America for a photo shoot to support a pitch that George's friend and former Olympic athlete Lana Wilkerson was making to the cable TV networks, so Chase missed spending Valentine's Day with Lori. Lori's trip to Australia with her mother claimed her spring break in March. Their happenstance discovery of her father, Cam Murphy, aboard a boat named *Bliss* in a marina near Cairns not only shook Lori to her soul, but also changed her summer plans. She took an internship on a horse farm in Virginia rather than return to Eternity Springs and risk further contact with the man who'd left her mother to raise their daughter alone. She was angry with her dad. Hurt at the world and not in the mood to talk to Chase about it. It drove a wedge between the two of them that summer.

Chase never did offer Lori that ring.

Inevitably, distance and different life directions created a gulf between them that neither one could bridge. They didn't fight. They didn't have an official breakup event. They simply . . . stopped.

Lori did change her name — she took her father's when he married her mother shortly before her junior year in college. She achieved her goal and returned to Colorado to attend vet school and to assume her new family role — that of big sister to a new little brother.

Chase's pursuit of his vocation took him all over the world. He had just turned twenty-eight when he finally did pull an engagement ring out of his pocket.

He gave it to another woman.

CHAPTER TWO

Present day
Eternity Springs, Colorado

Lori Murphy sat in a pedicure chair at Angel's Rest Healing Center and Spa and sank her aching feet into the heated, lavender-scented water. "Oh, that feels good. My feet are killing me."

Seated in the chair next to her, Caitlin Timberlake looked up from her magazine. "Busy day sticking your hand up a horse's rump?"

Lori smirked. "No veterinary work for me today. I did something worse. I helped Mom at the bakery. She had so many orders to fill she even dragged Dad into work. I cannot believe that after a month of holiday eating, so many people want her cinnamon rolls to serve at the breakfast buffets of their New Year's Eve parties."

"It's one final sin before starting your diet. And your mom's cinnamon rolls are as sinful as it gets." Caitlin pulled a tabloid news-paper from a stack on a small table between the two chairs. "Speaking of sin, get a load of this."

Lori noted the magazine's early December date, then read the front-page headline aloud. " 'Man's Head Explodes in Barber Chair'?"

"Page four."

Lori flipped to page four and scanned the photographs. *Chase. I should have known.*

Honestly, Lori would have preferred view-ing photos of the exploding head.

She took a moment to reinforce her emo-tional walls, then spoke in a casual tone. "Monte Carlo. Saint-Tropez. The Amalfi Coast. Glitz and glamour galore. I gotta admit, I'm shocked they're getting married in little old provincial Eternity Springs."

"The wedding is six weeks away," Caitlin said. "A miracle could still happen. Maybe you could talk to him, Lori. You know he's here in town, don't you? Skipped coming for Christmas, but shows up two days afterward. A surprise, he'd told Mom. Gonna visit three whole days. Big whoop-de-doo, if you ask me."

Lori managed to maintain her calm. No, she hadn't heard that Chase had come to town. Well, she could handle a three-day visit. It wasn't like he was moving here, after all. "I will talk to him. I'll wish him much happiness in his marriage."

"That's not what I meant." Caitlin's expression went glum as her gaze fastened on the photograph of her brother. Movie-star handsome in a black tie and three-day scruff, Chase rolled dice at a craps table, a tall, beautiful blonde resting her hand possessively on his shoulder. "I guess she's nice enough. She does make an effort with the family, and she seems to genuinely like Chase. But that doesn't make her the right woman for him. She is so wrong for my brother! Don't you see it, Lori?"

Lori would sooner kick a puppy than comment on that.

Caitlin didn't notice her lack of response as she continued her rant. "I'll bet you a hundred dollars that she gets Botox for her wrinkles. Stephen's wife says she's already had a face-lift. And of course, everyone knows she's had a boob job because that was obvious in those old *Sports Illustrated* swimsuit photos. Which, by the way, is something else I don't get. Chase was always all about nature. What's natural about boobs that lie like little Murphy Mountains on top of her chest? What is it about boobs that make men so stupid, anyway?"

Lori's mouth twisted. "Well, she is an on-air personality so her appearance is important."

Caitlin sniffed with disdain. "You'd think her wedding would be important to her. She hasn't bought a dress yet. Can you believe that? And she's turned almost all of the arrangements over to Mom."

Lori had already heard that bit of gossip from her own mother. "I'm sure it will be lovely. Your mother does everything with class."

"True." Caitlin sighed down at the casino photograph once more. "That's another reason why it's hard to believe that Chase is going to marry her. I thought men married women like their mothers. Lana Wilkerson is nothing at all like Mom."

Lori idly flipped the newsprint to another page and the photograph of a bare-chested Chase rubbing sunscreen on his fiancée's back. A memory flashed in her mind, accompanied by a twinge of regret she didn't want to recognize.

Once upon a time, Chase had rubbed sunscreen onto her back, his touch gentle and thrilling. However, the apartment pool deck in College Station, Texas, was a very,

very long way from the French Riviera.

"Your mom is the prototypical traditional mom. Chase was never one to be happy with traditional."

"If that's true, then more the fool he. Although . . ." Caitlin cut a sharp gaze toward Lori. "I don't know that I agree with that. He would have been happy with you."

"Let it go, Caitlin. That ship sailed long ago."

Just then the door swept open and Chase's bride-to-be blew inside. Porcelain skin gone rosy with the cold stretched over high cheekbones that spoke to her Slavic ancestry. The reality TV star wore her thick blond hair piled carelessly high upon her head and diamond studs sparkled in the lobes of her ears. Long dark lashes framed big blue eyes. Her red cashmere sweater clung to her curves like a second skin. A three-carat square-cut diamond glittered on her finger.

Lana Wilkerson was a vibrant force of nature — bold, beautiful, and bigger than life. As Lori buried the tabloid beneath a stack of hairstyle magazines, she felt herself shrinking and shriveling like a raisin left out in the summer sun.

"Hello, ladies," Lana said, her voice bright, her smile wide and white and perfect.

Lori's tongue automatically went to that

little space between her teeth behind her upper incisor.

"What a glorious day, is it not? Caitlin, I'm so sorry I'm late for our spa date. Chase took me skiing today, and we made one too many runs. Fabulous conditions on the mountain. Simply fabulous."

She launched into a tale about Chase's wild and reckless ways speeding down a Black Diamond hill that had Lori cringing while Lana's gorgeous eyes sparkled with excitement. Lori darted Caitlin a sidelong glance, looking to see if Chase's sister recognized how well her brother and this woman suited. If Lori had been the woman skiing with him, she'd have done so with her heart in her throat and visions of falls, broken bones, and traumatic brain injuries running through her head. Upon reaching the end of the run, she'd have lit into him like a firecracker rather than hug him with joy.

Neither one of them would have been happy.

Liar, her inner voice proclaimed. His sense of adventure and daring had been one of the things that appealed most to her about Chase.

Her mother still joked that instead of giving Lori the middle name of Elizabeth, she should have gone with "Responsible." That aspect of Lori's personality was the result of having grown up with a single mother who worked her fingers to the bone to make ends meet and atone to her parents for her Big Mistake — getting pregnant by the town bad boy before he got sent off to jail.

Then when Lori was seventeen, Chase Timberlake had walked into her grandparents' grocery store, and over the next few years, taught Lori all about temptation.

Lana snickered at something the nail technician said, and Lori realized that the older woman's laugh was as lovely as her face. Lori watched her win over the customers in the salon one by one. No wonder Chase had fallen for her. The real question was, why had the Timberlake women not?

She pondered the problem while the nail tech finished her pedicure. Family dynamics were a weird animal. Lori knew that firsthand. Wasn't her own situation fraught with tension from time to time?

She had wanted nothing to do with her father when he returned to Eternity Springs with an adoptive son in tow after years of living the good life in Australia. She'd been angry at Cam and jealous of Devin. He'd had a relationship with her father — he'd had a *father* — when she had not. Then when her parents reconciled, she'd been forced to adjust to sharing the mother whom she'd had to herself for her entire life.

Baby Michael's arrival had added more complexities to the mix. Lori loved her little brother desperately, but that didn't prevent her from experiencing moments of sibling rivalry that made her feel more like a child than an adult. As Lori Reese, she'd known exactly where she fit in the family of two. Sometimes in Lori Murphy's expanded family, she didn't know her role.

Lori's gaze drifted toward Chase's sister and she thought about his mother. She'd admired Ali Timberlake ever since she met her. The woman was all class, and according to local gossip, she never said a word against her son's choice of bride. But anyone who knew her could see she struggled with the idea of being mother-in-law to Lana Wilkerson. The age difference between Lana and Caitlin certainly didn't make a "sisters" relationship any easier, either. Lori realized she actually felt a little bit sorry for Lana — emphasis on the "little." Navigating Timberlake family dynamics would be a Black Diamond challenge for Chase's wife.

With her nails now painted a subtle rose pink, Lori moved to the drying table. A few moments later, Caitlin took the seat on her right. The two friends chatted about their New Year's plans, and Lori was almost dry and ready to leave when Lana took the seat opposite her. She slipped nails painted a tangerine orange beneath the ultraviolet light and beamed a friendly smile toward Lori. "I need to apologize. Your face is familiar so I'm sure we must have met on one of my previous visits to Eternity Springs, but I don't remember. May we start over? I'm Lana Wilkerson, soon-to-be Timberlake."

They had been introduced more than once, but Lori wasn't going to let the lack of recognition bother her. Celebrities met so many people. "I'm Lori Murphy."

"Oh. Of course." The older woman winced prettily. "We have met before. You're Chase's Lori. His 'one that got away.' "

The comment flabbergasted Lori and she fumbled for a response. Lana didn't seem to notice. She bubbled on about the New Year's Eve party she and Chase planned to attend at their producer's vacation home in Aspen the following night. "I'm sorry we're going to miss the party here, but our producer is bringing in some Hollywood movers and shakers, and he's demanded our attendance. At least we're not going to miss the bowl-game-watching party tonight at the community center. Chase is so looking forward to that. He loves watching college football with his dad. Family is so important to him. To us both."

She flashed her perfect smile toward Caitlin and added, "I've always wanted a sister, and now I'll have Caitlin."

Caitlin's smile went tight. Lana didn't seem to notice.

Lori decided her nails had dried long enough. She stood, saying brightly, "I think I'm dry. It was nice to see you, Lana."

"You, too, Lori. We will see you tonight at the party, won't we? I know it's going to be wonderful because Ali is in charge. She's fabulous. I don't know what I would have done without her to oversee wedding arrangements. She has everything organized perfectly. Chase is that way when it comes to work, you know. I depend on him for so much more than still photography."

Lori's gaze shifted to the stack of magazines where she'd buried the tabloid. *Yeah, like rubbing on sunscreen.*

"Yes, I will be there," Lori said, wondering if it was too late to change her plans. "The guy I'm dating is a serious college-football fan."

"Wonderful. I know Chase is looking

forward to catching up with people whom he hasn't seen in a while, and I can't wait to meet more of his friends."

Lori recalled that comment later that evening as she carried a bowl of guacamole to one of the refreshment tables and saw that Chase had arrived while she'd been in the kitchen helping his mother. It was the first time Lori had seen him in person in months. She watched with a reluctant fascination as he introduced Lana around the room.

They did make a glamorous pair. In keeping with the collegiate theme of the night, they wore CU colors, Chase in black and Lana in a gold lamé dress and black and gold stilettos.

"She's way overdressed." A familiar hand swooped in to snag a spoonful of guacamole for a plate piled high with crudités. Lori smiled at her undergrad college roommate, Molly Malone, and her husband, Charlie, who carried a plate filled with chips and sour cream dip.

"Of course, he is, too," Charlie added, dipping a tortilla chip into the guacamole on his wife's plate and popping it into his mouth.

Molly nodded. "Never thought I'd see your Chase wear a designer sport coat to a football-watching party and work a room like a politician."

He's not my Chase. And Lori realized — a bit to her own surprise — that she was mostly okay with that. The photos Caitlin had shown her earlier had been a graphic demonstration of just how much he'd changed from the young man she'd known and loved. "It's hard to see the river rat when he's dressed like a model. You can certainly see her influence."

Molly shrugged and wrinkled her nose. "I liked the old Chase better. I'll never forget the Aggies-versus-Colorado game when he yelled himself hoarse during the Buffalos' goal-line stand. This Chase is way too civilized and sophisticated for that much fun. What do you want to bet that he rides a polo pony? And goes on fox hunts."

"When he's not riding an Olympic athlete," Charlie suggested, his tongue planted firmly in his cheek.

Molly elbowed him in the side. "What?" He arched a brow toward Lori. "Too soon?"

"No," Lori replied with a fleeting smile. "Actually a little humor is just what I needed. Have I mentioned how glad I am that you two decided to spend your anniversary in Eternity Springs this year? You're the only people I know who aren't giving me 'poor, pitiful Lori' looks."

"Always happy to provide moral support," Charlie said.

"Not that you need it considering who you're dating." Molly patted her hand over her heart. "Brick Callahan. Capital Y-U-M in Wranglers and a cowboy hat. If I wasn't a happily married woman . . ."

"Hey, now," Charlie protested.

"You're so easy to tease." Molly flashed a grin and leaned over to kiss his cheek. To Lori, she said, "I don't know why anyone would think that you're pining away for Chase. It's been years since the two of you dated. And you were the one who dumped him, not vice versa."

"I didn't dump him." Lori shied away from the memory of the hurt, the mourning, she'd experienced when she'd realized he'd quit visiting. Quit calling. Quit e-mailing. As had she. "It was a mutual decision."

She guessed that's what it had been, anyway. She wasn't all that sure. The months following the trip to Australia and her father's return to Eternity Springs were a blur. She'd been an emotional wreck and physically and mentally exhausted due to challenges on the academic front. Chase had been . . . away.

He'd been traveling all over the world with George Overstreet and been nowhere around when she'd needed him the most. It had been all too easy for her to draw the parallel between Chase and Cam. Like she'd wanted anything to do with another man with wanderlust at that point in her life!

The ghost of remembered resentment fluttered through her. She gave her head a little shake to chase it away, then repeated her usual comment whenever asked about Chase. "We were young."

"Well . . . apparently young isn't something Chase worries about, is it?" Charlie observed. "What I want to know is, is he the trophy husband or is she the trophy wife?"

"Doesn't matter. Chase is yesterday." Molly motioned toward the door. "Mr. Today just walked in. Is he wearing shoulder pads beneath that maroon and white jersey?"

"No," Lori said, her heart warming to see that despite his allegiance to another university, Brick wore Aggie gear in what she recognized as a silent show of support. "The man has Callahan shoulders. Broad as the plains of West Texas."

And he'd come to offer her a little lean

time. Broad shoulders, a lady-killer grin, and a heart of gold.

Too bad they'd never be more than good friends.

CHAPTER THREE

On the second day of January, Chase sat in his rental car in front of his parents' home on property near Heartache Falls above Eternity Springs and wondered what the heck was the matter with him. At the New Year's Eve party in Aspen, Lana had told one of the financial backers of Thrillseekers, Inc., that Chase had never met a dare he wouldn't take. He hadn't argued the point. Nothing made him happier than going one-on-one against Mother Nature. He thrived on challenges and excelled on tests.

Why, then, was he scared to get out of this SUV and knock on his parents' front door?

Because Mom is going to tear a strip off your hide when you tell her your news, that's why.

He shivered, more at the thought of his mother's wrath than from the bitter winter chill beginning to seep into the parked automobile. Snow fell heavily now, the flakes big as quarters. Another minute dragged by. He drummed his fingers against the steering wheel, his stare lingering on the Christmas tree visible through the floor-to-ceiling windows of the great room. Christmas at the Timberlakes'. Blinking lights. A hodgepodge of ornaments collected through the years. A fire in the hearth. Warmth. Family. Love.

Timberlake family tradition dictated that the house remain decorated until Epiphany. Chase liked a later start and finish to the Christmas season — no red and green before Thanksgiving for him — and he'd lobbied for it at the New York apartment he and Lana shared. She'd had different ideas. She'd had their tree down and out of the building by sundown on December 25.

It had been a damned lonely Christmas.

Chase had missed spending the day with his family, missed his mother's traditional Christmas dinner and the boisterousness of the gift exchange with his siblings. Missed being in Eternity Springs.

He'd grown up in Denver, so this wasn't the home of all his childhood Christmases. However, this log house with its spectacular view of five of Colorado's "fourteeners" — peaks that rise more than fourteen thousand feet above sea level — had become the home of his heart from the moment his parents rolled out the architect's plans in the yurt a short hike away from here where they'd been living at the time. The family had spent the past four — or was it five now? — Christmases here, and Chase hadn't realized how much the holiday at Heartache Falls meant to him until he'd missed being part of it. Not that he hadn't enjoyed the traditions that Lana had attempted to establish in its place, and he did appreciate that she'd tried.

Nor did he blame her for his dissatisfaction with the day. After all, remaining in New York for Christmas had been his idea. He'd felt that he owed her an opportunity to create traditions that suited them both, and with a Valentine's Day wedding in Eternity Springs just around the corner, this had seemed like the perfect year to skip a holiday trip to Colorado. Mom always went a little batty at Christmas, anyway, and though she hid it well, Lana invariably went on the defensive when she got around the female members of his family.

He couldn't blame her for that, either. Despite the fact that he'd never told his family just how serious his relationship with Lori had become while she was away at school, he knew that all the Timberlakes had harbored hopes that they'd eventually

42

end up together. Caitlin, especially, wore her emotions on her sleeve, and she had made it clear to Lana at their very first meeting that she didn't measure up. Since things were dicey enough as it was between the women in his life, he'd seen no sense in adding the baggage of holiday emotions into the mix.

Of course, then the last-minute command-performance party in Aspen had come up, so they'd made a Colorado trip after all, leaving Manhattan early on the morning of the twenty-seventh. Mom had cried at the happy surprise. "Wonder if I'll make her cry tonight?" he murmured.

Focused on the blinking angel tree topper inside the house as he sat lost in thought, he didn't notice movement coming up alongside the car. Knuckles rapped against the driver's side window. Startled, Chase turned his head to see his dad.

Now in his fifties, Mac Timberlake had gone gray at the temples in a way that was fitting for a former federal judge turned small-town lawyer. His stare burned through the window, and as Mac made a rolling motion with his finger, Chase forced himself not to revert to childhood and squirm.

He thumbed the power window button. The glass slid down and bitter cold swept into the car along with the rush of falling water from nearby Heartache Falls. "Hey, Dad."

"You planning to sit out here all night?" Mac asked. "Your mother says you've been here for at least twenty minutes. She's worried you're going to freeze to death."

"Sorry. I . . . uh . . ." He gestured toward the cell phone lying on the seat beside him. It wasn't a lie. He'd been finishing up a call with the airline when he'd arrived.

His father looked at him hard. "When you left here the other day, you weren't planning to return until February."

"Right."

When he didn't elaborate, his father's stare grew sharper. "Before we go inside, tell me one thing. Do you need a lawyer?"

"What? Oh. No. I'm fine. Everything's good, actually."

"Okay, then."

Mac stepped away from the car and waited while Chase rolled up the window, pulled on his jacket, and joined him. The two men trudged toward the large log structure and entered through the back door. As Chase stomped the snow from his boots in the mudroom, the aroma of his mother's red sauce simmering on the stove drifted from the kitchen. That smell more than anything told Chase he was home.

"Michael Chase Timberlake," his mother said, a scold in her tone. "What are you doing here?"

"Begging supper, I hope." He hung his coat on a hook and walked into the kitchen. "Lasagna?"

"Veal spiedini." Ali Timberlake lifted her hand to touch his cheek, studying him intently with her blue-eyed gaze. "I fed you lasagna last week. And sent you away with leftovers."

"I polished those off for breakfast on New Year's. Veal spiedini is awesome, though."

His father scowled at him. "Hey. Your mother didn't plan for an extra mouth to feed tonight. Don't think you're getting any of my share."

"Have you used the electric broom Dad gave you for Christmas, yet, Mom?"

"Smart-ass." Mac dipped a spoon in Ali's sauce and tasted it. "That's spectacular, Alison. You've tweaked the spices again, haven't you? And I don't know why I'm catching so much grief over the broom. You said you wanted one."

"You're right. I did. I know I'll enjoy it, too. Now, talk to us, Chase. I can see that something's wrong. Why the surprise visit?"

"Nothing's wrong. Everything is great,

actually. Just a change in plans."

His parents shared a look, then his father asked in a casual tone, "Wedding related?"

"Yes." He met his mother's gaze, gave her a crooked, bashful grin, and dropped his bombshell. "We need to postpone it."

For a full half a minute, the only sound to be heard was the sizzle in his mother's frying pan. Then Ali asked, "Postpone? You're not canceling?"

Chase heard the hopeful note in her voice and tried not to feel annoyed. He knew his family thought he was making a mistake with Lana, but they didn't know the real woman beneath the public façade. In time, they'd come to see her for the wonderful woman she was. Different from Mom — about a hundred eighty degrees different — but wonderful.

"No, we're not canceling. Just pushing back the date."

"And you just made this decision now?" his father asked.

"This date has been on the calendar for months," Ali pointed out. "The invitations have already gone out."

Chase's gaze slid away from his mother's. She'd done a ton of work to pull the wedding together, all at Lana's request. The reality was that his bride would have been just as happy to elope to Las Vegas. She'd agreed to an Eternity Springs wedding for his sake. Since his mother was a pro when it came to social arrangements, turning arrangements over to her had seemed like the perfect solution. Now, Chase couldn't help but feel guilty.

"I'm really sorry, Mom. You've put a ton of work into the wedding, and I feel like a schlub. The timing is unfortunate . . ." he began.

Mac Timberlake snorted softly.

". . . but something has come up at work. It's big, something Thrillseekers, Inc., has been working on for a long time."

"Work? This is work related? Not relationship related?" His mother folded her arms, and her voice climbed an octave. "You're canceling the wedding because of a cable TV show?"

"That cable TV show is my job, Mother," Chase fired back. "It pays my bills. Very nicely, I might add."

Mac warned, "Watch it there, boyo. Respect your mother."

"Sorry." Chase dragged his fingers through his hair. As a rule, he didn't care what other people thought about his job, but his parents weren't just other people.

And they were going to hate what he had

to tell them.

So man up, Timberlake. Spit it out. Chase cleared his throat. "The government of Chizickstan has agreed to issue visas to Thrillseekers, Inc. We'll film three episodes of the show there, and then . . ." He drew a deep breath and spoke the sentence he still didn't believe was coming true. "Tibet. The monks of Kambantota Monastery have given us permission to film a white-water trip through Hidden River Gorge."

His mother, of course, focused on the part he'd known she'd hate the most. "Chizickstan?" Ali threw a worried glance toward his dad. "A 'stan' country?"

"Where is that?" Mac asked.

"It shares a border with Afghanistan."

Ali's complexion went pale and her voice trembled as she asked, "You're going to Afghanistan?"

"No, Mom. I'm going to Chizickstan. Two completely different countries."

"But both war zones," his father fired back.

"No. The part of Chizickstan we're visiting isn't a war zone."

"But it *is* tribal territory."

Chase nodded, conceding the point.

Mac asked, "How long will you be gone?"

"A couple months there. A couple months

in Tibet."

"If you ever get to Tibet," Ali said, her tone bitter.

Mac touched the small of his wife's back, offering silent support. Chase hated seeing his mother so shaken, and he was almost relieved when color flooded back into her face even though he knew from experience that her temper was about to blow.

Sure enough, anger flashed in her eyes. She lifted her chin and shot her words like bullets. "I thought the show's producers said no more filming in areas of political unrest."

"The shooting in Argentina could just as easily have happened on the streets of Atlanta," he said defensively.

"At least there are hospitals in Atlanta."

"A doctor travels with us, Mom. Our mobile medical unit is fully equipped."

"That will give us so much comfort when you are captured by terrorists."

"Mom . . ."

She picked up a wooden spoon and gave her sauce a vicious stir. It tore Chase up to see how he'd upset her. He loved his mother to distraction, and he knew she worried about him. Chase gave his father a pleading glance, but one look at the torque in his father's chiseled jaw convinced him he'd

49

find no ally in that quarter.

"So this was the reason behind the Aspen trip?" his father asked, having put the clues together.

"Yes. The producer got word on Christmas Day and made the announcement at the New Year's Eve party."

Ali looked at her husband. "You shouldn't have turned down that job you were offered in New York, Mac. If Chase had grown up in New York he wouldn't love mountain climbing and river riding so much. He'd be gambling with other people's money on Wall Street instead of gambling with his life in a war zone."

"Now, Mom —"

"No! Just no! I've been supportive of your adventures since you were a little boy, but after Argentina . . ." She drew a deep breath and exhaled harshly. "You promised me no more politically dicey areas, Michael Chase. You promised me."

"I know, Mom. And I'm sorry, but this particular project predates my promise." A note of entreaty entered his voice as he added, "It's the most famous stretch of white water in the world. It hasn't been filmed since the sixties. This is the opportunity of a lifetime. It's my Everest, Mom. It's the Hidden River Gorge!"

"Go there first then," she fired back, a sheen of moisture in her eyes. "Go raft your way to Shangri-La. Don't go to Hellistan."

Chase closed his eyes. "I can't, Mom. This is my job."

The front doorbell rang, and Ali set down her wooden spoon hard before marching out of the kitchen. Chase dragged his fingers through his hair. "That went well."

"She tries, Chase. I don't think you can appreciate just how difficult it is to parent a child who walks on the wild side, so to speak."

"I outgrew childhood a long time ago."

"And when you're in your seventies, you will still be your mother's child, and she will continue to worry about you. No sense fighting it. It's the price you pay for having such a spectacular mom."

"I know she's spectacular. I just wish she'd spread some of the worry wealth around. She doesn't give Caitlin or Stephen as hard a time as she gives me."

"Stephen is a corporate lawyer. The most dangerous thing he does is play pickup basketball at the Y on Saturday morning. As far as your sister goes . . . your mother worries about her plenty. The girl changes boyfriends as often as she changes jobs. However, emotional happiness and physical safety are two different beasts. Every time the phone rings showing a number we don't recognize, we expect it to be someone calling with horrific news concerning your safety."

"Dad, that's —"

"Reality. Look, I'm not trying to bust your balls here. I just want to explain where your mother is coming from. Her emotions are especially volatile these days. This was the first Christmas since her father's death, you didn't make it home for Christmas Day, and your wedding is right around the corner. Or at least, it *was* right around the corner."

"I love my job, Dad. I'm good at it. But I don't like knowing that I disappoint you and Mom."

"You don't disappoint us, Chase. Don't think that. We're happy that you've found a career that suits your talents and interests and allows you to indulge your wanderlust. Honestly, we are. That said, having a thrill-seeking son with wanderlust is difficult for a parent. We can't help but wish your path kept you a little closer to home — and out of certain parts of the world."

"Dad, we hire security. We don't take stupid chances. The show's safety record is unparalleled. Remind Mom of that, would you?"

"I will. But you have to do your part, too. You can't go weeks on end without checking in. When you're off in some remote corner of the world and weeks pass without a word from you, our imaginations conjure up some unsettling scenarios."

Rightfully so, Chase thought, recalling a certain gun battle in Argentina.

"You have to check in," Mac continued. "Often."

"I will. I promise."

"Don't break this promise."

"I won't, Dad."

Both Timberlake men turned toward the kitchen door to see Ali return with their visitor, and Chase's night went from bad to bad *and* awkward. Pasting on a smile, he lied, "Well, this is a nice surprise. Hello, Lori."

She almost burst out laughing when Ali told her Chase was in the kitchen. Chase, alone, without his bride-to-be. Had she known that this was what she'd find at the Timberlakes' home when she accepted Ali's dinner invitation, she'd have brought a bottle of Scotch instead of a nice Chianti along with the lemon cream pie from Fresh that her mother said Ali particularly enjoyed.

She had exchanged a few words with

Chase on a handful of occasions since their nonbreakup — always small talk, always when they both were part of a crowd, always when she'd anticipated his presence at an event and prepared herself to see him. Tonight was different.

Tonight he'd popped up unexpectedly like the clown in a child's jack-in-the-box. She'd always found that particular toy scary. Pasting on what she hoped was a bright smile rather than a fake one, she said, "Hi, Chase. I thought you went to Vail."

"No." He stuck his hands in the pockets of his jeans. "Aspen."

"Ah. That's right. More TV people in Aspen than in Vail."

"It's nice to see you. We didn't get a chance to speak at the bowl game party the other night."

No, they hadn't. She'd worked hard to make it so. Not that he'd gone out of his way to try to talk to her, either. In fact, at the time she'd sensed that he worked as hard to avoid her as she had him. "Good parties are like that."

She handed the bottle of wine to Mac who glanced at the label and said, "Nice. One of our favorites. Shall I open it?"

"Please." Lori turned to Ali. "Dinner smells delicious. What can I do to help?"

Standing at the stove, Ali glanced over her shoulder. *She looks a little pale,* Lori thought. And her voice trembled slightly when she spoke. "The veal has a couple more minutes to go, but everything else is ready. We're eating in the family room tonight. I wanted to enjoy the Christmas tree one more time before we take it down. Chase, you need to set a place for yourself."

"All right."

Judging by the clipped tone of his words and the misery on Ali's face and tightness in Mac's jaw, Lori had walked into a minefield. *Wonderful. Just wonderful. This keeps getting better and better.*

Ali's gaze followed Chase as he left the kitchen, a plate and silverware in hand. The smile she turned toward Lori was genuine, but sad. "Actually, what I'd like most of all is to think about something positive. Why don't you sit down and talk to me about what has brought you up the mountain to our home on this cold winter night. Your mother said you have a big decision to make?"

"I do. I am considering a number of fabulous offers, and one of them would mean a serious lifestyle change for me — relocating to a big city. Permanently."

"You ready to become a big-city girl,

Lori?" Mac asked.

"I don't know. I'm still weighing my options. I told Mom I wanted to talk to you about your big-city experience since you still have your place in Denver, but that's not really why I'm here today. I want to plan a special event, a surprise party, and I'm hoping you'll help."

"Of course I'll help," Ali said, her expression brightening. Actually, it more than brightened. Lori got the sense that she'd thrown the other woman a lifeline. "I assume this is a surprise party for your folks?"

"Not exactly." Lori smiled her thanks when Mac set a glass of wine in front of her. "When I graduate in May, it will be due in large part to the efforts of two people — Mom and Nic Callahan. I want to do something special to thank them and recognize them and show them how much I appreciate all they've done for me. Nobody plans a party better than you, Ali, but you are also one of the busiest women I've ever met. Between the traveling you and Mac do and running the restaurant and all of your volunteer work — I'm sure your calendar stays booked."

Ali's gaze drifted toward the family room doorway, and Lori thought she detected a hint of bitterness in her voice when she said,

"Oh, you'd be surprised about how dates can open up."

Then she gave her head a visible shake and continued, "What sort of party are you thinking about and when would you like to have it?"

"I'd like to do a dinner party. My first choice is to have it at your restaurant — you know how much I love the Yellow Kitchen — but I'm afraid I might have waited too late to make my reservation for a Saturday night in May."

"You want the private dining room?"

"Actually, I'm afraid that wouldn't be enough room." Lori smiled bashfully and added, "Once I started my guest list, I quickly realized everyone I want to invite won't fit in the private dining room. What I'd like to do is give you my budget and guest list and turn all the arrangements over to you. I've been saving my pennies."

"A surprise party for Nic and Sarah," Ali said, a smile playing on her lips. "I can't tell you how much the idea appeals to me right now." Lifting her voice, she called, "Chase, would you please bring me my tablet off my desk?"

"Sure, Mom." A moment later he returned to the kitchen and handed Ali her iPad. She pulled up a calendar and asked, "When's graduation?"

"The fifth."

"So you are looking at the seventh?"

"Yes."

Ali pursed her lips. "Hmm . . . that's right about the time the Garretts' baby is due. I may have to juggle a few things, but yes, I think we could make it happen."

"Wonderful!"

Ali made a note on her tablet, then tucked it into a drawer. Five minutes later, the four of them sat down at the Timberlakes' dining table where, unfortunately, Lori was seated directly across from Chase. For the first few minutes, the conversation centered around the party. Then it turned to Ali's veal spiedini recipe. Throughout it all, Chase never said a word, and Ali never once looked at her son.

What the heck was going on here? Did the tension have something to do with the missing bride? Lori didn't think Chase had come home to announce a broken engagement. Ali would be in comforting mode, not firing off verbal barbs and shooting dagger looks.

Once they'd exhausted the topic of the seriously delicious meal, conversation lagged. Ali's eyes grew teary, Chase looked miserable, and Mac's jaw turned to granite.

Lori wondered how soon she could graciously leave.

Mac made an effort. "So, tell us more about this decision you need to make, Lori. Your father told me not long ago that you were considering a specialization in veterinary ophthalmology."

Lori hesitated. She wasn't at all certain that she wanted to discuss her decision in front of Chase. And yet, a part of her wanted nothing more than to show him that she, too, had choices in life. She, too, had dreams and desires and goals to achieve. She wanted him to know that she most happily had roots ready to sink.

No wanderlust coating my heels. I don't need French Riviera sand. My roots are sunk deep into Colorado dirt.

The thought triggered a memory of the moment she realized that she and Chase were well and truly done. It began in her mother's kitchen. Sarah, Nic Callahan, Sage Rafferty, Ali Timberlake, and Celeste Blessing had been meeting in the living room discussing plans for the annual arts festival. Home from college to share her big news about receiving her vet school acceptance letter from Colorado State, Lori had been snatching a chocolate chip cookie from the cookie jar when she'd heard Chase's name mentioned.

"He's where?" her mother asked.

"Thailand," Ali repeated. "He landed a job with a production company shooting a pilot for a cable TV sports show."

Ali moved closer as Nic Callahan asked the question running through Lori's mind. "He's working as a river guide?"

"A photographer. It's his first professional photography job. Mac and I are proud of him, but I won't deny that I'd rather he found work closer to home."

Thailand. The cookie jar lid rattled as she replaced it. Chase was on the other side of the world — and she hadn't known about it.

"Whatever happened between him and Lori?" Sage asked.

Lori stared down at the cookie in her hand. Her mother had baked it, of course, using her special recipe — the one she'd shared with Lori as part of a Christmas gift. Lori had baked chocolate chip cookies for Chase on one of his visits to College Station. They hadn't been from scratch, but the refrigerated-dough variety. Chase hadn't seemed to mind. They'd eaten the cookies warm from the oven and chocolate had melted all over her fingers. He'd licked it off. Slowly.

Thailand.

A little sob escaped her, and blindly, she

rushed from the kitchen and into her mother's backyard. She sank onto the back stoop and tried valiantly to fight back the tears. When Daisy, one of her mother's golden retrievers, wandered over to say hello, Lori wrapped her arms around the dog's neck and hugged her close.

He's gone. He's really gone. Grief wrapped a band of steel around her chest and squeezed.

"Sweetheart." Celeste's voice floated over her like the brush of angel wings. Gentle hands gave her thigh a comforting pat. "Don't despair."

"I don't know how we got here."

"You and Chase?"

"There is no me and Chase! He's gone to Thailand."

"He didn't move to Thailand, my dear. He'll be back."

Her voice broke as she said, "Yes, but not to me. Not to stay."

"There, there." Celeste clicked her tongue, and when Daisy impatiently wiggled out of Lori's arms, the older woman enveloped Lori in hers. "My darling girl, if I may quote the Good Book. 'To every thing there is a season, and a time to every purpose under the heaven . . . a time to plant, and a time to pluck up that which is planted.' It is not Chase's time

61

to plant."

"I know. That's the problem. It's always been the problem. He's a tumbleweed who is happiest when a gale wind is blowing, Celeste. That's just not me. I'm a weed with roots that I can't get rid of. I don't want to get rid of them."

"Of course you don't, and you shouldn't. It's your roots that will give you your wings."

With Celeste's words echoing in her mind, Lori answered Mac's question. Talking about her opportunities reminded Lori of how happy she truly was, which in turn reassured her that she and Chase had made the right call. She was living the life she was meant to live. One day, she'd find a man who shared her dreams, just like Chase had found a woman to fly beside him as he soared around the world.

Yes, the what-ifs and if-onlys made her heart hurt a little sometimes, but for the most part, she was happy. Chase was happy.

Well, except for tonight. Tonight he didn't appear to be a happy camper at all.

When Ali rose to serve dessert, Lori started to stand and clear her plate, but Chase stopped her with the first words he'd spoken since dinner began. "No. You're a guest. I've got the dishes." Once both mother and son had disappeared into the kitchen, Lori softly asked Mac, "Did something happen with Chase?"

He sighed and topped off his wine. "He has a new assignment. His mother isn't taking it well."

Neither are you, Lori thought. She wanted to ask for more details, but Mac's closed expression didn't encourage them. Instead, she made small talk until Chase and Ali rejoined them, bringing coffee and pie and renewed tension between mother and son.

Mac sighed again, then did everyone a favor by launching into a story about the recent antics of the Cicero family's puppy that managed to lighten the mood and even coaxed a genuine smile from his wife. Chase followed up the dog tale with one about his neighbor's pair of parakeets that actually got a laugh from his mother. Chase answered with the flash of a familiar grin, then said, "Dinner was great, Mom. How about you let me clean up the kitchen. I promise I'll hand-wash your knives."

"That's a deal."

"The meal was wonderful, Ali," Lori said after Ali suggested they finish their coffee over by the fireplace. "It's one of my favorites."

"Thank you. I always enjoy cooking for you, Lori, and I was so happy to have a little time with you. We miss you here in Eternity Springs."

"I miss being here," Lori said as she took a seat on the Timberlakes' sofa.

Ali gave her a sly look. "Nic will be glad to hear that."

As Eternity Springs's veterinarian and her mentor, Nic had been trying for months to convince Lori to return home and join her practice. Lori held up her hand palm out. "Just because I miss home doesn't mean I'm ready to move back. Like I said earlier, I'm still weighing my options."

Ali took a seat beside Lori. "As well you should. Let me add one more thing, and then I promise it'll be the last I say on the subject."

"Okay."

Ali's gaze drifted toward the kitchen where Chase stood in their line of sight. "I don't regret leaving Denver for Eternity Springs, but I do mourn the time I missed with my father, especially now that he's gone. Family is a treasure. Don't make short shrift of its value as you weigh your choices."

"I won't." Lori allowed her gaze to follow the path of Ali's stare and took the opportunity to study her ex for the first time in forever. He stood in front of Ali's farmhouse sink with his sleeves rolled up and a frying pan in his hand. He'd matured into a ruggedly handsome man. All those hours invested in outdoor sports had filled out the frame of the young man she'd first met in the Trading Post grocery store almost a decade ago. His dark hair had sun streaks, but his eyes remained the warm, luscious brown of melted milk chocolate. He could work in front of the camera rather than behind it.

Though his frown might scare people off.

Lori finished her coffee and was about to stand to leave when two phones rang simultaneously — hers and Mac's. "It's Mom," she said, checking the number.

"And Zach Turner," Mac added.

The sheriff. Worry flared and Lori quickly answered the call. "Mom? Is everything okay?"

"It is now. I was worried about you. Are you still at Heartache Falls?"

"Yes. I was just getting ready to head home."

"Don't. A four-car pileup with injuries has the highway shut down between there and here. The sheriff's department has their hands full, and they've asked for all non-emergency traffic to stay off the road. If that's not bad enough, we're getting a mix of sleet with the snow down here in the valley. It's simply not safe for you to drive home tonight."

Lori stifled a groan. Instinctively, her gaze shifted toward the kitchen where she saw Mac speaking to his son. Chase's gaze met hers. He didn't look any happier than she.

In her ear, her mom's voice said, "I'm sure Mac and Ali won't mind having an overnight guest."

I hope not. Because it looks like they're going to have two of them.

However, one of those guests hadn't forgotten that she'd arrived in the midst of a family squabble, and her presence had delayed the settling of said squabble long enough. As soon as possible, she said her good-nights and retired upstairs to the bedroom suite Caitlin used when she visited.

She took a long, hot bath, then watched a movie, trying her best not to listen for the sound of footsteps traveling to the bedroom down the hall. Chase's bedroom.

She fell asleep, trying her best not to dream about things that could not be.

She failed.

She dreamed she sat in the bow of a canoe on Hummingbird Lake watching a pair of hot-air balloons sail above. In tandem, the pilots of both balloons fired the burners, and behind her, two young voices roared in approval. Lori glanced over her shoulder to see a little boy, with dark hair and missing his two front teeth, staring upward with wide brown eyes. His younger sister and their golden retriever puppy also looked skyward. From his position at the stern, Chase met her gaze and grinned.

Lori awoke a little after two A.M. haunted by images of a life she'd never lead. For almost an hour she lay tossing and turning, unable to go back to sleep, until finally she switched on the lamp and reached for her phone, looking for the distraction of the Internet. Her phone wasn't on the nightstand, and thinking back, she realized she'd left it on the mantel downstairs.

She hated the thought of leaving the warmth of the bed, but she desperately needed a distraction. Pulling on Caitlin's slippers and robe, she quietly opened the bedroom door and made her way downstairs guided by the faint safety lights along the staircase. The darkness shrouding the first floor of the Timberlake home was broken only by a soft glow of a light above the cooktop in the kitchen and the glow of orange coals in the hearth.

The kitchen light and Ali's admonition that she make herself at home beckoned, and she poured milk into a brown earthenware mug and warmed it in the microwave. She carried the steaming mug into the family room.

As she reached toward the mantel and her phone, a husky voice rumbled out of the darkness. "Want a shot of whisky in that milk, Glitterbug?"

CHAPTER FOUR

She almost dropped the mug of milk.

Chase watched Lori through bleary, gritty eyes and the haze of too much Scotch. Glitterbug. The old endearment he'd begun using after the first time they'd made love had rolled off his tongue like a song. Dammit.

"Chase! I didn't see you."

"Now there's a shocker. So what else is new?" A soft, bitter laugh escaped him as he lifted his glass in a silent toast. To Lori? To the past? Who the hell knew? His emotions were a jumbled mess.

"You're drunk," she said, a note of accusation in her voice.

"A little. My dad stocks a very nice single malt. Goes down smooth as silk." Unfortunately, he wasn't nearly drunk enough, though not for lack of trying. If he were, he wouldn't have been sitting here in the dark brooding about love and family and Lana and Lori. "What time is it?"

"After three. Have you been to bed at all?"

"Lana flew back to New York this morning. Or, I guess that's yesterday now. You and me . . . well . . . I thought you'd remember. But then it's been what . . . four years? Five? Do you remember the last time we went to bed? I wish I'd known at the time that it would be the last time. I'd have done something to mark the occasion."

He heard a little gasp of what? Surprise? Scandal? Or maybe even pain? "You've changed, Chase Timberlake. I've never known you to be mean."

He laughed. "Again . . . so what else is new?" He took another sip of whisky. A big sip. It burned on the way down, the only warmth within him. "You've never known me at all, have you, Glitterbug?"

"Don't call me that," she said with a hiss. "Don't you ever call me that again." She whirled around and started for the stairs, and quickly he said, "No. Don't go. Please, Lori. Don't go."

The "please" or maybe it was their shared past stopped her. She didn't turn back, but she didn't continue upstairs, either. Maybe she'd wanted to hear those words from him before. *Please, Lori. Don't go.*

She'd gone. She'd started going almost the minute she started college. "So, you've done it, haven't you?"

"Done what?"

"You've made it. Doctor Lori Reese."

"Murphy. I took my dad's name."

"You took my heart first."

"For goodness' sake, Chase."

When she lifted the milk to her mouth and gulped it back like a tequila shot, he knew he'd flustered her. "I'm happy for you, Lori. I truly am. It's what you always wanted." *Most. More than me.*

Damn, Timberlake. Have a pity party, why don't you?

"I'm happy for you, too," she replied. "Lana seems like a very nice person."

"She is. She loves me for me." Chase was glad he managed to keep the hurt out of his voice. Lori had never embraced the adventurous part of who he was. "She loves the person I am."

"She'll wander with you," Lori said softly, sadly.

He looked up at her. Their gazes met and held. He heard the note of entreaty in his own voice as he said, "I love what I do, Lori. I'm good at it."

"Yes. I know you are. I've followed your career."

"You have?"

"Of course. My mom and your mom

71

made sure I was kept up-to-date." Her mouth twisted wryly and she added, "Then there's the tabloids and celebrity news sites. Did you ever think you'd be fodder for TMZ?"

"Not in a million years. I still don't understand the attraction of celebrity, to be honest. Lana takes it all in stride — she thrives on it to be honest — but the whole thing can be a bit overwhelming at times."

"I think it would drive me crazy."

He winced. "It does me. They're like bees who suddenly swarm. They'll show up with no warning, and I won't have a clue how they found out where we are. Some of the paparazzi are excellent photographers. They could make a living doing photography lots of other ways."

"Paparazzi can make a lot of money. One of Gabe Callahan's sisters-in-law used to be one."

"I didn't know that."

Lori nodded. "Torie. Matt's wife."

"Hmm. You're pretty tight with the Callahan family, aren't you? Wasn't that guy you were with at the bowl-game party a Callahan?"

He didn't miss the subtle straightening of her spine. "Yes. Brick is Mark's son."

Chase sipped his Scotch. "Brick. That's

an . . . interesting . . . name."

"Nickname. His real name is Chris. His dad started calling him Brick because he's stubborn and it stuck."

Alcohol had dulled Chase's thought processes. "Stubborn?"

"His head's as hard as a brick."

"Ah. Yeah. Of course." Chase decided he didn't like thinking about ol' Chris Callahan being hard anywhere. "So does he live in Texas like his father?"

"No. He moved to Colorado last year. He bought into Silver Creek Ranch when the Reardons sold out."

"A local rancher," he mused. Of course she'd go for a guy with cows and horses. Suited her. "Is he good to you?"

She sipped her milk, then licked her lips. "Yes. He's a very nice man."

He's perfect for her. Just like Lana is perfect for me. "I guess it all worked out the way it was supposed to for us."

"I guess it did."

He swirled the whisky in his crystal glass and brooded a moment longer. "Do you ever wonder about it?"

"Wonder about what?"

"What might have been. If we hadn't broken up. Where we'd be in our lives right now."

"Actually, if we wanted to be sticklers about it, we never officially broke up."

"Yeah." Frowning, he thumped his finger against his glass. "That's always bothered me. We both acted badly there. Avoidance, I guess."

"I guess." Lori must have finally decided not to flee back to her bedroom because she sank into the overstuffed easy chair across from him and tucked her feet up under herself. "It's bothered me, too. Maybe we'd both feel better if we did something about it."

"Rewrite history?"

Lori lifted her mug of milk as if in toast. "Michael Chase Timberlake? Will you break up with me?"

He twisted his lips in a rueful grin and lifted his Scotch to return the toast. "Lori Elizabeth Reese Murphy, I'm honored to break up with you. Salute!"

The silence that settled over them at that point had a comfort to it rather than tension like before, and for the first time since he'd mentioned the word "Chizickstan" to his parents, Chase began to relax. "So . . . back to my question. Do you ever wonder about it?"

"About us and what might have been?"

"Yes."

"Sure. Sometimes. I think it's only natural to sometimes second-guess the choices you make in life. Especially the big ones. You were very important to me for a long time, Chase."

Just not as important as earning your DVM.

Okay, so maybe a measure of bitterness still soured his gut. Possibly his pride continued to cling to its black-and-blue marks. Perhaps he remained absurdly grateful that he'd never popped one particular question. Would he ever get over her?

Lori continued, "But I try not to look backward. 'Of all the words of mice and men,' you know?"

Chase finished the Vonnegut quote. " 'The saddest are what might have been.' Yeah, I know. But I think it's important to remember the good times, too. You and I had some great times, Lori."

"That we did." She sipped her milk, then smiled a little wistfully. "I'll never forget the treasure-hunt anniversary date. Such romance! You outdid yourself with that one, Chase. Sent my teenaged heart over the moon."

The squeak of the hinges on the kitchen door screen jerked Lori out of the argument she was making for the appropriate punishment for criminals convicted of animal abuse, the topic of her high school senior thesis. Mom was home from her Saturday-morning quilt group which meant the morning was flying by. Lori made note of the time on her computer screen. Nine forty-five. Chase was going to pick her up for their date at eleven, so she would finish this paragraph, then hop into the shower. Today was the anniversary of the day they'd met, and Chase was coming in from Boulder for the weekend. He'd planned a special date, though he'd refused to give her details of just what.

They'd both worried he wouldn't be able to make it here this weekend. With his graduation from the University of Colorado less than a month away, he was winding down projects and gearing up for finals, and the last thing she'd wanted to do was interfere with his studies. She knew he'd worked extra hard earlier this week to free up time to make a trip to Eternity Springs.

Out of the shower with her hair dried and styled and her makeup on, she stood in front of her closet debating what to wear. He'd told her casual, so she went with jeans and her favorite green sweater. Green was Chase's favorite color. The evergreen color of your eyes, he always told her.

She heard the doorbell ring precisely at eleven. Giving her lip gloss one last touch-up, she headed downstairs. She found her mom standing at the front door, gazing toward the porch with a silly grin on her face. Lori glanced out the window, but didn't see Chase.

Her steps slowed. "What is it, Mom?"

"Well, it's a puzzle."

A moment later, Lori saw what she meant. The three-foot-high stuffed animal — a giraffe — had a big bow and yellow ribbon tied around its neck. A note card and a large puzzle piece dangled from the ribbon. Delighted, Lori lifted the animal and read the note. "Roses are red. Corn is yellow. Collect the clue at the starting spot to find your fellow."

"What in the world does that mean?"

Lori giggled aloud. "It means go to the Trading Post. Remember? Chase came into the grocery store looking for work while I was stocking shelves. He opened a box of canned corn for me. He's doing a treasure-hunt date."

"Clever boy," Sarah said.

"Oh, Mom." Lori hugged the giraffe tight and turned shining eyes toward her mother. "I like him so much."

Years later in his parents' family room on a snowy winter night, Lori turned a wistful smile toward Chase. "That's the day I knew for sure that I'd tumbled head over heels for you."

His lips twisted with a crooked smile as he rose and stirred the coals and tossed a small log on the fire. "Coming up with the rhymes for those clues all but killed me."

Laughing, Lori quoted from memory. " 'My heart you've taken like my mouth loves bacon.' "

"Pure poetry." He polished off the last of his whisky, then resumed his seat. "Your moment is better than mine."

"What moment?"

"The moment I knew I'd fallen in love with you. One of the worst moments of my life."

"Well," she snapped, offended. "How sweet."

"I can't hear a John Denver song without thinking about it. Reliving it."

Summer sunshine toasted the back of Chase's neck as he walked up Spruce Street, hand in hand with Lori. Square white tents lined the street with artists and artisans selling everything from paintings to pretzels. The town was packed to the rafters with every hotel room and vacation rental in a fifty-mile radius booked. "It's a good end to the tourist season," he observed as the aroma of warm funnel cakes drew his attention.

"A great end," Lori agreed. "Mom is over the moon. She said last night that her profits were up double over last year. It's really going to help with the expenses of my going off to school."

Chase's heart gave a little twist at the mention of their pending separation. He and Lori had made the mutual and mature decision that they'd both be free to date other people once she started school at Texas A&M later this month. Having gone off to college himself four years ago, he knew that having the option to date around was an important part of the college experience. If he and Lori were meant to be, well, they'd survive it. He cared about Lori very much, and while he didn't like thinking about her dating other guys, he had confidence that their relationship would survive the test.

"In the spirit of assisting with your education, I think I'll buy a funnel cake from your mom. Want one?"

"No, thanks. Those things are evil. They have about a million calories apiece. Of course, everything my mother makes has about a million calories each."

"That's what makes them so delicious."

The singer in the cover band playing John Denver hits finished up "Fly Away" as they approached the tent where Sarah Reese sold baked goods. She had a frown on her face and Chase identified tension in her stance.

Uh-oh. Something's up.

He stepped forward and Sarah spotted them. Lori noticed her mother's troubled face, too, because she said, "Whoa, there's a frown for you. Tell me you're not all stressed out about the quilt contest?"

"No. Not at all."

"Then what's the matter, Mom? You look like you mixed up the salt and the sugar when you mixed your funnel cakes."

"Hopefully nothing, but . . . there was a guy by here that said some things that made me uncomfortable."

Chase stepped forward, his gaze scanning the crowd. "What guy? What did he say?"

"No one from around here. Do me a favor, would you? Run over to the sheriff's office and tell Zach I'd like to speak to him?"

"What guy?" Lori demanded. "What did he say?"

"Where'd he go?" Chase asked, glancing around.

"It's probably nothing, but go on now." Sarah made a sweeping motion with her hand. "Go get Zach."

She dismissed them by turning a bright smile toward a couple pushing identical twin boys in a stroller. "Oh, if you aren't the cutest little guys in town! One of my best friends has twin daughters about the same age as these boys."

Chase tugged Lori's hand and they started up the street. "That's weird," she said. "Mom works with the public all the time. She doesn't shake easily. But if she were too worried, she'd have picked up the phone and called."

"We get some strange characters coming down out of the mountains from time to time."

The sheriff's office was only a couple of blocks away from Sarah's arts festival booth, so they reached it quickly only to discover from the dispatcher that Zach had left the office a few minutes earlier to begin a foot patrol of the festival.

They explained what they needed and the dispatcher immediately attempted to reach the sheriff on the radio. They heard only static. "I swear that radio he carries is nothing but a piece of junk. We need new equipment around here desperately. I know he was headed north. If you two scoot out the back door, you might catch up to him before I can pass along your message."

Lori and Chase left the sheriff's office and jogged back toward Spruce, turning north. "There he is," Chase said, spying Zach Turner walking toward them, his radio at his ear. He waved and called the sheriff's name.

Zach returned the wave, said something into

81

his radio, then returned it to the clip on his hip. Down the street, the band launched into John Denver's "Annie's Song" as they drew within speaking distance. Zach said, "Hello, Lori. Chase. What's up?"

"My mother is looking for you. She's worried about —"

Bang!

Chase instinctively turned toward the sound. A man he didn't recognize held a handgun pointed in their direction.

Zach started forward. Chase lunged for Lori as the vocalist sang about giving his life away.

Bang!

Zach fell. Chase and Lori fell.

She gasped in pain before they hit the ground.

Bang.

Something warm and wet seeped onto Chase's arm. Blood. He smelled it. Saw the bright red horror of it. Time seemed to stand still.

Lori. Dear Lord. "Lori? Lori!"

Chase closed his eyes and shuddered at the memory. "I'll never forget it. You said 'I think I've been shot' and my blood ran cold. It's the most afraid I've ever been, before or since. You were so pale. We were both covered in blood. I was afraid we'd lose you. Afraid *I* would lose you. That's when I knew

I was in love."

For a long moment, the only sound to be heard in the room was the crackling of the fire.

"Okay, you're right. My 'moment' was better than yours. That was a frightening afternoon."

Chase dropped his head back and stared up toward the ceiling. "What happened to us, Lori? Why wasn't love enough?"

It took a long time for her to answer. "Sometimes, that's just the way it is, I guess."

"That's no answer."

Lori stretched to set her mug down on a coaster lying on the end table beside her chair. "It's the only one I've got, and frankly, I don't know that it matters at this point. You're getting married next month and —"

"The wedding's off."

Her mug rattled against the table. "Uh . . ."

"Not permanently," he continued. "We're delaying it. A work thing has come up."

"You're delaying your wedding because of work?"

The judgment in her tone put Chase's back up. "You sound like my mother."

He set his glass down hard, shoved to his

feet, and began to pace, to rant, giving voice to the words that had been piling up on him throughout the evening. "I love my mom and dad, and I hate more than anything to disappoint them, but I am who I am. They taught me to be bold. They taught me to reach for what I want. They can't complain when I do it. My mom shouldn't cry!"

"You made your mother cry?"

Chase raked his fingers through his hair and shied away from both the question and the memory. "So I live life on the edge, but you know what? It's damned thrilling. I love it! I love doing what I do and seeing new places and meeting new people and experiencing new things. Bad things can happen to a person in Eternity Springs, too, you know. I could get attacked by a bear walking from the garage to the house. I could have a tire blow at the wrong time and go plunging off the side of a mountain. Hell, I could slip on ice and crack my head open on the way into church on Sunday morning. I don't have to be overseas to encounter a dangerous situation. I don't want to look back in twenty years and regret not taking advantage of the opportunities that came my way. It's Hidden River Gorge. It's a once-in-a-lifetime ride. I can be bored and boring when I'm old!"

Lori held up her hand. "Wait a minute. Do I have this right? You postponed your wedding in order to go river rafting? And your bride is okay with it?"

"She's the star of the show. Of course she's okay with it."

"Wow. Just wow." She stared at him for a long moment as though he were a puzzle piece she couldn't figure out. Or maybe a bug. A bug in her oatmeal. Her cold oatmeal. Finally, she said, "Wow. I think I've figured it out."

"Figured what out?"

"The answer to your question."

"What question?"

"About what happened to us. Why love wasn't enough."

He shot her a bleary, wary look and waited.

Lori unfolded her legs from the chair and rose. She picked up her mug of milk. "It's like this, Chase. I love margaritas, but tequila gives me heartburn. I love bacon, but it clogs my arteries. I loved you, but you were no better for me than tequila and bacon."

"The romance of that statement overwhelms me."

"It's the truth of the statement that's important. When it came to the kind of life we wanted to live, we didn't see eye to eye."

"But we felt heart to heart," he fired back. "That should have conquered everything."

"They call it reality TV, but there is nothing real life about it. You aren't the Bachelor. I'm not the Bachelorette. We are Chase and Lori who needed something from each other that we weren't able to give and remain true to ourselves. That doesn't make one of us right and the other wrong. It's that we weren't right for each other."

She crossed the room to him and took his hand. "I'm glad we had this talk. It's been long overdue." She went up on her tiptoes to press a quick, bittersweet kiss against his cheek. "I wish you much happiness, my friend. The people who love you understand you were born to run — after all, your parents named you Chase, right? How apt was that? So go ride your white water. Reach for your stars. Chase your dreams."

Dreams, hell. Bitterness churned in his gut as Chase watched her climb the stairs. Once upon a time she'd been his dream. *It's too damned bad, Glitterbug. For a lover of animals, it's too damned bad you didn't appreciate the appeal of wings.*

Back in Caitlin Timberlake's bed, Lori heard Chase come upstairs and the door across the hall open and shut. As she drifted toward sleep, she reflected on the events of the previous half hour. The conversation with Chase had been long overdue.

Their never-official breakup had left a laceration on her heart that had never healed, but the words spoken tonight had applied a balm to the wound — a special, Eternity Springs balm. Eternity Springs–sporin. *If I could figure out how to bottle it, I'd make a billion dollars.*

Maybe now she could finally let go and move on with her love life with a whole heart. Without a hole in her heart. *You're getting loopy, Lori. You need to get back to sleep. Need to get your beauty sleep.*

Smiling, she snuggled down into the covers. Maybe she'd have a really good dream. Dream about her Bachelor. Her prince. Maybe her Brick? Could she find room in her heart for the studly cowboy to be something more than a friend, after all?

Lori drifted off to sleep with a lightness of heart she'd not experienced in ages. She slept in and awoke mid-morning to sunshine, the aroma of fresh coffee, and roads that were open.

And the news that Chase was already gone.

CHAPTER FIVE

Valentine's Day
Bella Vita Isle

Chase pressed a gentle kiss against his sleeping fiancée's naked shoulder and rolled from the bed. He pulled on his boxer shorts, opened the bedroom's French doors, and stepped barefoot out onto the verandah overlooking the turquoise waters of the Caribbean.

Below, the surf roared and frothed and foamed as it rolled onto the sandy beach. On the horizon, the setting sun painted cotton-candy clouds against a cerulean sky. Ordinarily such sights and sounds on the heels of sun, sand, and afternoon sex soothed his soul. Today, he found no peace within himself. He wasn't exactly sure why.

Maybe because today was supposed to have been his wedding day? Because the woman even now asleep in his bed had made absolutely no acknowledgment of the fact, much less expressed any regret at what had turned out to be an unnecessary postponement?

He grasped the balcony as resentment slithered through him. Immediately, he regretted the emotion. It wasn't Lana's fault that the team had experienced one delay after another for the past month. Preparing for a shoot like this one was a tremendous amount of work, and both he and Lana were doing the jobs of three people. Logistics were a nightmare. Personnel, a headache. Throw in the departure of two producers and it's no wonder they did more arguing these days than making love.

Chase was glad he'd insisted they take the weekend getaway. They'd needed the break from contract negotiations and phone calls and complaints. They'd needed some couple time. Badly. Things had been rocky between them ever since he'd returned from his visit to Eternity Springs.

He wasn't exactly sure why. He'd left Colorado tired and hungover, at odds with his parents and haunted by the late-night exchange with Lori. He'd arrived in New York with a chip on his shoulder and acid in his gut, needing reassurance about the choices he had made. Over a month later, the doubts continued to plague him. Why?

Because postponing the wedding shouldn't have been such an easy call? Because she canceled hair and nail appointments with more regret?

Because the memory of forest-green eyes wouldn't die?

Don't go there. You're with Lana now. You love Lana. You're going to marry Lana.

"Someday," he murmured.

"What a gorgeous view," observed the feminine voice behind him.

Chase glanced over his shoulder to see Lana sitting up in bed, the sheet pooled at her waist. "It's a pretty sunset."

"I'm not talking about the sky, darling."

He turned around, turning his back on both the Caribbean and his malaise. "The view's not bad from here, either."

She did take a man's breath away. Her devotion to her exercise routine combined with the physical rigors of the Thrillseekers, Inc., work kept her body toned and taut and looking a good ten years younger than her actual age.

Chase appreciated beauty as much as the next guy, but what had hooked him was her spirit. Always ready for a dare. Always game for adventure. She didn't just keep up with him. She ordinarily stayed ahead of him.

She rolled out of bed, scooped up his shirt

from the floor, and slipped into it. "That was a glorious nap. Did you sleep?"

"A little."

"Good." She joined him on the verandah and gave him a quick hug. "This was a good idea, Chase. I'm glad you talked me into this trip."

"I do have good ideas from time to time. Which reminds me. Flynn Brogan told me about a shipwreck about an hour offshore that makes a great half-day dive. I thought I might set something up for tomorrow morning. Sound good?"

"It sounds fabulous."

"Excellent."

She gave him a slow once-over, then her lips spread with a salacious smile. "Yes, you are. You absolutely are." She wrapped her arms around him and pressed her perfect breasts against his back. "So excellent, in fact, that I think we should postpone our dinner reservations."

You're all about postponing. The bitter thought flashed before he could stop it. Annoyed with himself, he smoothly turned and swooped her up into his arms and carried her toward the bed. "Have you ever known me to turn down sex?"

"Never," she said on a sigh as he laid her upon the mattress. "That's one of the many things I love about you."

He knelt, straddling her hips, and trailed his finger down the valley between her breasts, making her shiver. He knew just what to do to make her body hum. Knew exactly what it took to make her scream. He bent himself to task, but before he'd coaxed so much as a whimper from her lips, her cell phone rang. "Ignore it," he demanded when she reached toward the bedside table where it lay.

"I can't." She checked the number. "It's Amanda."

Her agent. Chase bit back a curse and rolled off her. As she launched into a conversation with obviously the most important person in her life, he pulled on his shorts, grabbed his running shoes, and quit the room. If Lana even noticed that he'd left, he couldn't tell.

Chase went for a long run on the beach, and when his legs began to give out, dove into the surf and swam until physical exertion finally drained his anger and frustration. He emerged from the water to find her waiting for him. She handed him a towel. "I'm sorry, Chase. That was poorly done of me. I should have let the call go to voice mail."

He wiped his face and torso with the

towel, nodded an acceptance of her apology, and tried to let go of his resentment. He only partially succeeded. His emotions were in turmoil. "What did Amanda want that couldn't wait until next week?"

Lana hesitated before speaking with obvious reluctance. "She wanted to know where we're having dinner. There's a rumor that a royal yacht might pull into port here, so photographers are on the island."

That bit of news didn't improve his mood one bit. Being stalked by the paparazzi and, in instances like this, courting them, was one of the things he hated most about being with Lana. "This is supposed to be a private trip."

"I know and I didn't tell her where we'll be tonight. However, since we will be out of the public eye for months while we are filming, it would be foolish to pass up this opportunity completely. I told her to set up a photo op in the market tomorrow afternoon."

Chase shot her a hard look.

"Just stop it," Lana snapped. "It's good for the show."

"Heaven forbid we do anything in life that isn't connected with the show." He slung the towel over his shoulder. "Is that why you said you'd marry me? Thought a little romance would boost the ratings?"

She sucked in her breath. "That's a horrible thing to say. I love you, Chase."

"Do you? Do you really?" He grabbed hold of her hand and asked the question that had been churning in his gut all day. "Then why didn't we get married today?"

Confusion clouded her eyes and she pulled away from him. "You wanted to get married on Bella Vita Isle?"

"I wanted to get married in Eternity Springs!"

"I know." A confused smile fluttered on her lips. "I wanted to do that, too."

"Did you? Did you really? Do you know what today is, Lana?"

"We already exchanged Valentine's Day gifts."

"We were supposed to exchange vows!"

"Come on, Chase. Be fair. When we canceled the wedding neither one of us thought that we'd still be Stateside on Valentine's Day. Is that what's been eating at you for the past month? You're upset that we canceled the wedding?"

"Yes. No. I don't know."

Damn, he was so confused. He felt like an idiot or a petulant child or both, and that embarrassed him. "It bothers me that it was such an easy decision for us. What does that say about our commitment to the marriage?"

Lana touched his arm. "Chase, I committed to you when we moved in together. I've told you all along that I don't need a piece of paper and a ceremony to be committed."

He resisted the urge to shake off her touch. "I do."

"I know you do. And that's why we decided to get married in Eternity Springs in front of your friends and family. You know, for a man who thrives on adventure, you can be very traditional."

He narrowed his eyes at her. "And what's the matter with that?"

"Nothing. Nothing at all. But two failed marriages taught me that I'm not a traditional person, and trying to pretend otherwise is a colossal mistake. You've known that about me from the first. I've always been up-front with you about what I want out of life. I haven't changed, Chase. My goals and dreams and desires haven't changed." She paused and drew a deep breath. "I think maybe yours have."

Denial formed on his lips, but when he went to speak the words aloud, another truth emerged. "I love you, Lana."

"I believe that. And I love you, too. But I am who I am. I will never be a traditional wife. I will never be a mother to any children you may decide you want. I will never be a small-town, hearth-and-home kind of woman."

"That's not what I want," he fired back, meaning it.

"Are you sure?"

"Yes! I could have had that. I *did* have it. I walked away." *I let Lori go.*

"And I wonder if you're coming to regret it."

Chase shifted his gaze away from her. He shoved his fingers through his hair and demanded, "All this because I'm unhappy that we unnecessarily put our wedding off?"

"All this because you've been unhappy ever since you returned from Eternity Springs after New Year's. What happened there that has left you so unsettled?"

"I damned sure didn't realize that I'm pining for small-town life."

She stared at him thoughtfully. "I wish I could believe that. I believe you believe it. Truly, I do. But I think it's probably a good thing that you're leaving with the advance team on Monday. You should spend this time that we're apart examining your heart."

He imperceptibly stiffened. "Are you dumping me?"

"No. I'm saying you need to make a

choice. I love you, Chase, and I want to wander the world with you for the rest of my life. I want you to be absolutely certain that you want the same thing from me in return."

I've been down this road before. "Lana, I —"

"Ssh." She rested her finger against his lips. "No more talking. Not tonight. Take me back to our room and let's finish what I so foolishly allowed Amanda to interrupt."

They spent the balance of their time on Bella Vita Isle in a state closest described as a truce and departed for New York with an underlying tension humming between them. On Monday, Chase phoned his parents before boarding the first leg of the flight that would take him to Chizickstan. The conversation was stilted from his father's end, tear-filled from his mother's, and as uncomfortable on Chase's part as any he could remember. Not quite ready to say good-bye but desperate to fill the awkward lull in their exchange, he asked what was new in Eternity Springs.

His mother answered. "The biggest news of the month is that the Callahans are expecting again and Nic wants to be a full-time mom. She has convinced Lori to take over her practice. Sarah and Cam are over the moon. Lori is coming home."

Chase closed his eyes and told himself that the ache in his chest had nothing to do with yearning.

May
Eternity Springs

Lori Murphy, DVM, walked arm in arm with her mother up Spruce Street toward Ali Timberlake's restaurant. Her father followed behind them holding her two-year-old brother Michael's right hand. Her brother Devin held the toddler's left. It was a beautiful Saturday evening in Eternity Springs with spring in all its glory. Flowers bloomed everywhere you looked. Pots of red geraniums decorated sidewalks and porches. Window boxes filled with purples and whites and pinks and yellows dressed every sill. Cascading baskets of color hung from every conceivable spot. Townspeople did love their color.

"There are the Callahans," Sarah said, slowing and lifting her free hand in a wave. "I'm so glad you asked them to join us for dinner, sweetheart."

"Me, too." The casual invitation Lori had issued to Nic when she'd called to explain why she couldn't attend the graduation had done the trick, though Ali had assured her she had backup plans for getting the Callahans there.

Lori tried to keep the excitement humming through her from bursting free. She was honestly amazed that no one had spilled the beans. Things were working out perfectly.

The Murphy family paused and waited for Nic, Gabe, and the girls. Her smile wide, Nic rushed up to Lori and gave her a fierce hug. "Dr. Murphy. I am so proud of you. I am so sorry that I couldn't make it to the graduation. It broke my heart not to be able to see you walk across the stage."

"You're the lucky ones," Devin piped up. "Graduations are a beating."

In a show of sisterly affection, Lori stuck her tongue out at her brother. Then she turned back to Nic. "I know you were there in spirit, and nothing is more important than this little guy." Lori patted Nic's baby bump. Per her doctor's orders, Nic was confined to Eternity Springs until she delivered her baby.

"I'm just as important as Twig!" seven-year-old Cari Callahan declared, scowling up at her. Twig, Lori knew, was the nickname the Callahans had taken to calling the baby after Gabe suggested naming their little boy after his father, Branch.

"Me, too!" her twin, Meg, chimed in. She folded her arms and glowered.

Oops. Lori knew better than to tread on sibling sensitivities. Didn't she have a few twinges of her own in that area from time to time? And she had almost twenty years on the Callahan twins! "That goes without saying, doodlebugs," she said. "Actually, you're more important because you are the big sisters. Being a big sister is a very important job. In fact, now that I'm going to be living in Eternity Springs, I think we should form a club. The Big Sisters Club. What do you think about that?"

Both girls' eyes lit. Meg asked, "Could we have a clubhouse?"

"I don't see why not."

"We can get Cousin Brick to build it," Cari added. "He'll do anything we ask."

The adults all laughed, recognizing the truth of that statement. Brick Callahan loved all of his young cousins, but Meg and Cari held a special place in his heart.

As the group continued toward the Yellow Kitchen, Gabe and Cam talked about the latest shipment of fishing rods to arrive at Refresh, her father's sporting goods store. Devin regaled the women with a story about a friend who'd decided it was a good idea to adopt a Saint Bernard puppy and keep him in his college dorm room, while the Callahan girls made silly faces at Michael that made him laugh.

The Yellow Kitchen's front door opened as they approached, and as arranged, Celeste Blessing stepped outside. She wore a white tunic over a broomstick skirt, and when Lori noticed her earrings, she did a double take. Instead of her customary angel's wing earrings, gold dog bones dangled from her earlobes.

"Well, if it isn't Dr. Murphy!" Celeste said, her delight genuine, the surprise not so much. She held out her arms for a hug. "Congratulations, sweetheart. We are all so proud of you."

"Thank you, Celeste." Lori stepped into the older woman's embrace and returned the hug with enthusiasm. Without Celeste and the economic turnaround her decision to open Angel's Rest had brought to Eternity Springs, she honestly didn't know if she would have managed to complete her undergrad degree, much less vet school. "I couldn't have done it without all the support from family and friends."

"I know that family and friends helped to clear some of the obstacles in your path, but I firmly believe that you would have achieved your dream in any case. You are a determined young woman, Lori Elizabeth. Such a trait is a blessing. It is something you'll be able to call on throughout your life when circumstances require strength of resolve."

Celeste moved to hug first Sarah, then Cam. "Careful there, Mr. Murphy. All that pride filling your chest . . . if you're not careful you'll pop your buttons."

"It could happen." He bent down and gave her a kiss on the cheek. "Watching my daughter receive her diploma was one of proudest moments of my life."

"As is only right. You know, when I was living in Charleston, my next-door neighbor graduated three children on the same day. A horrible-weather day it was, too. Why —"

While Celeste held the Murphy family politely captive with her tale, Lori murmured, "Excuse me," and slipped into the restaurant. She'd wanted to be in position to see her mother's and Nic's faces when they entered, and Celeste had been charged with the task of making it happen. Ali met her at the door and handed her a glass of champagne, asking, "So, did we pull off the surprise?"

"Completely! Oh, Ali, thank you so much." She gave Ali a quick, hard hug.

Lori knew that Ali had worked hard to

keep the party secret from Sarah and Nic — not an easy feat in a town the size of Eternity Springs, especially when all of their close friends were in on the surprise. But Ali had pulled it off, and as Lori took in the scene — the restaurant filled with dear friends and the banner she'd requested hanging on a wall — joy filled her heart. "I am so blessed."

The door opened and Celeste led the guests of honor into the room. Sarah and Nic were chatting with each other, so it took them a moment to notice that this was no ordinary evening at the the Yellow Kitchen.

Nic's gaze scanned the crowd — all of whom were staring at her. "What in the . . . oh!"

Sarah covered her mouth with her hands as she read the banner. "My dream came true because of you. Thank you, Mom and Nic!"

A wide smile spread across Cam's face as his gaze shifted between his wife and daughter. Ali signaled the waiters, who handed champagne to the newcomers and sparkling grape juice to the children. "Oh, Lori," Sarah said, her voice choked. Tears spilled from her eyes when Lori stepped forward and raised her flute of champagne. She'd been planning what she wanted to say for weeks, but now that the moment was upon her, emotion pushed her speech right out of her mind. So, she spoke from the heart.

"Nic. Mom. From the bottom of my heart, thank you. Nic . . . when you moved back to Eternity Springs and allowed me to hang around your clinic and indulge my love of animals, you changed my life. I don't have words to explain how much I value your encouragement and support. You've been my teacher, my confidant, my friend. I can never repay you, but I will promise to try to fill a similar role for Meg and Cari and Baby Branch as they grow up. I love you."

"Oh, Lori. Thank you. I love you, too."

Lori drew in a deep breath, then turned to her mother. Tears blurred her eyes and her throat went tight. "Mom, where do I start? You are my hero. By both word and deed, you taught me every important lesson I've learned in life. From you I learned the power of dreams and the necessity of hard work. I learned the value of family and friends. I learned how to love and be loved. You are the best mother in the world and I'm so proud to be your daughter."

Sarah's audible sob tipped the scales for Lori. Blubbering, she rushed into her mother's arms. As they opened their embrace to include Nic, Cam lifted his champagne glass and completed the toast Lori had been unable to finish. "To Nic and Sarah."

When the women broke apart, Cam lifted his glass once again. "That was lovely, Lori. Now, I'd like to offer a toast. Do you mind?"

She gestured for him to proceed.

"All right, then. I have a few things I'd like to say publicly to my beautiful daughter, Dr. Lori Murphy."

"Aw, Dad," Devin Murphy protested in a long-suffering voice. "Are you going to get mushy, too?"

"Probably." Cam met Lori's gaze and smiled warmly. "Definitely."

"Obviously left your man card at home."

Lori elbowed Devin in the side and teased, "Deal with it, squirt."

"For a guy who finished high school as an afterthought, I'm still in awe at the idea that my firstborn has earned the right to use 'doctor' before her name. I'd like to be able to claim some credit for her accomplishment, but we all know that would be a lie. This is Lori's accomplishment. Lori and Sarah's. I'm so proud of you, Lori, and of your mother, too. I'm also grateful more than I can say to this awesome little town who kept my girls safe for me until I found my way back home. So, to my girls. I love you dearly."

Then, the party got started.

Ali served Lori's favorite pasta Bolognese as the entrée, the house Chianti, and pizza for the children — of which there were many. Very many. Lori gazed out toward the back patio where the usual tables and chairs had been cleared out to make room for picnic benches and a bounce house. Two high-schoolers had been hired to babysit — another example of Ali's excellent planning. Although, in another year, the increased munchkin population among their friends would probably require a need to hire three. Lori leaned toward Brick Callahan who was seated next to her and said, "I think we might have to change the name of the town to Maternity Springs."

Brick sipped his wine. "That's an idea. Maybe if Celeste's angel theme ever needs a reboot, they could consider it. It'd be a great marketing tool. I can picture it now. Spend the night at Fertility Falls and nine months later, visit Maternity Springs."

Lori laughed and Brick shot her a grin. Then, unexpectedly, he leaned over and kissed her cheek. "You done good with this, Lori. It's the perfect pick-me-up for Nic. Gabe, too. They've been a bundle of nerves

106

since her early-labor scare. It's nice to see them relaxed and enjoying themselves."

"Yes, it is."

When Maggie Romano brought out her famous Italian cream cake at the end of the meal, the guests all cheered, and Lori decided that the whole evening had been just about perfect.

Two beloved faces were sadly missing. Her maternal grandparents, Frank and Ellen Reese, had been irreplaceable influences in Lori's life during her childhood and early teens. Both were gone now and their absence left a hole in her heart.

So did the absence of another.

Chase.

Her gaze drifted to Ali and Mac, who were seated at the table across from her. She'd spoken to Ali a number of times since her visit after New Year's, but she'd never brought up the subject of her son. That was nothing new. Since the relationship ended, any conversation about Chase between her and his parents had been awkward.

Of course, the postponed wedding had been quite the topic of conversation in Eternity Springs for a time. Publicly, Ali had said little more than what Chase had told Lori during their middle-of-the-night meeting — that work had interfered. However, Caitlin hadn't hesitated to give Lori the lowdown when the two met for lunch in Denver in late March. "You walked into the middle of it," she'd said. "You deserve the truth."

Caitlin also shared the tidbit that Chase had left for Chizickstan a month later than originally scheduled, which meant that he and Lana need not have postponed the wedding, after all.

"Seriously, they could have married in Eternity Springs and honeymooned in Chizickstan. I mean, how many people could say they spent their honeymoon camping in the wilderness of a third-world nation?"

Lori smothered her sigh with a bite of cake. Chase had been on her mind more than usual during the past week, the what-ifs and if-onlys chirping like crickets in the night in her mind.

She was listening to Brick and Gabe tell a story about the Callahan family Christmas yard display when she noticed one of the waiters approach Ali with a worried look on his face. Was there a problem? She turned her head to look out at the children on the patio. No obvious problems, just lots of smiles and laughter and happy kiddos.

Lori looked back in time to see the waiter hand Ali a telephone. Lori couldn't hear what Ali said, but she could read her lips. *Hello? Lana?*

Every drop of color drained from Ali's face. Lori reached for her mother's hand at the same time Ali shot to her feet. In a loud, fearful voice, Chase's mother said, "What do you mean, he's missing?"

She listened for another interminable ten seconds, then Ali Timberlake collapsed.

Chapter Six

Five days earlier

In the large tent that served as Thrillseekers, Inc.'s field office in the staging area on the edge of a Chizickstan village, Chase exploded in frustration. "That's a stupid move, Lana. Why are you being so hardheaded?"

Of course, he knew the answer already. She confirmed it with her next words.

"It's for the good of the show!" She braced her hands on her hips and lifted her chin. "I'm doing my job. I'm doing what Thrillseekers pays me to do. Quite handsomely, I'll add."

Chase had said the same thing to his mother not long ago. *I should have listened to her.* "Tell me that's worth it after you're taken prisoner by these effing zealots and turned into a sex slave. Although, since you're a celebrity they're liable to go the rape-and-beheading route. Makes for better

110

Internet fodder, I imagine."

She inhaled sharply, drawing back as if his words had been a physical slap rather than a verbal one. Then her eyes narrowed, and when she spoke, she did so in a quiet voice. "I'm not stupid. I know we need more security, and I'm arranging for it."

More security? Didn't she realize that "more" wasn't the issue? What mattered was the *type* of security. This was not an area to bring in a bunch of Hollywood bodyguards whose experience was with managing paparazzi and obsessed fans. This was the real deal. "You don't need security to go into those mountains. You need an army."

"That's ridiculous. This isn't Afghanistan or Syria or Yemen. People here have been wonderful to us. They like Americans. What would be stupid would be to go forward with the Hidden River shoot under these conditions. It's been our bad luck that they've had a biblical-type flood."

"Then we should pack it up and go home." He had a bad feeling about this whole thing.

"We can't! We're committed. We still have two shows to produce and Thrillseekers has invested all of this money. We'd go way over budget, which we might be able to weather, but we simply don't have time! Between the delays at the beginning of the schedule and the delays here — we have no choice but to go forward with an episode from Markhor Pass. If we don't, they'll cancel the show."

"Would that be so bad?" Chase asked, his tone quiet and deliberate.

"Yes! It would be a disaster!"

"Or an opportunity for something new." Chase touched Lana's arm. "Maybe that should be the next adventure, Lana. Think about it. For you and me, life is about the adventure, right? What if we jumped off and did something seriously wild and crazy? Something you never thought you'd do?"

"Like what?"

"Well . . ." He hesitated, then floated the trial balloon that had been on his mind for weeks. "How about we go live in Eternity Springs for a little while?"

She jerked away from him. "Seriously? Now? You want to have this discussion now when I have to phone New York in" — Lana checked her watch — "fifteen minutes? I've been trying to get you to talk to me for the past two weeks! Ever since you had that close call and almost drowned I knew this was coming. No. I am not going to move to Eternity effing Springs and I am not going to cancel the shoots at Markhor Pass, and if you don't like it you are welcome to take yourself home to your cozy little mountain burg. I am going to save this show with you or without you!"

"You can be a real bitch sometimes, Lana."

"We're a fitting pair, then, because you can be a real ass sometimes, yourself."

A muscle worked in Chase's jaw, and frustration churned inside him. Afraid he'd say something unforgivable, he turned to leave.

The sunrise cast a golden glow upon the eastern sky, a scattering of clouds adding a splash of pink and purple to the dawn. The mild temperatures of the early morning would disappear with the sun's ascent, but for the next few hours, the heat would be bearable.

Good thing, too, because Chase was plenty hot as it was. He decided he needed a good long run to burn off his temper, so he changed clothes and headed out, taking his usual route.

As his shoes pounded the ground, anger and frustration burned in his gut like acid. The woman's damned ego was going to get them all killed. Just when had the damned show become the be-all and end-all for her? When had she gone from being a woman lucky enough to make a living from her play to a woman for whom the job played the primary role in life?

And why had he refused to talk to her? She'd been on the mark with that shot. Was it because he simply wasn't sure about her anymore? About *them* anymore? He sucked at breaking up. Look what had happened with Lori.

Lori. Was that the problem? Was *she* the problem? Surely not. They'd settled their unfinished business that night at his folks' house. Hadn't they?

Maybe not.

No, Lori wasn't the problem. Lana was the problem. He and Lana together were the problem. He'd sensed the change before the trip to Chizickstan, but the weeks of filming here had left no doubt. Lana displayed an intensity, almost a desperation, about remaining the star of the show. She said he'd changed? Pot, kettle there.

He'd known she wouldn't take well to the idea of moving to Colorado, but for the crew's sake, he'd had to try. She was completely ignoring the reports they'd heard from some of their local guys that bad stuff was happening in the Markhor Pass region. It would be beyond stupid to go forward with her plan. His sixth sense was screaming at him that it was so.

Someone higher up the food chain than Lana needed to know the truth about what was happening here. If he picked up the sat phone and reported what they'd been told, the powers that be would probably pull the plug. He'd put those odds at seventy percent. The chances that his making that call would end his already tenuous engagement with Lana stood at a firm one hundred percent.

He'd do it if he had to. Better to lose the show than to lose their lives.

He had one day to convince her to change her mind, but he knew her well enough to know she needed time to cool down. No sense even trying to talk to her for the rest of the day.

He'd been an idiot to throw out the Eternity Springs suggestion. If he'd taken half a minute to consider the idea after it popped into his brain, he would have bitten it back rather than roll it out. Where the thought had come from, he didn't know. He'd never before considered the notion himself.

Not *exactly* like that, anyway.

As he headed back toward town, he heard a voice call, "Hey, Timberlake."

He glanced over his shoulder to see his best friend in camp, helicopter pilot Bradley

115

Austin, striding up behind him. "What's put the torque in your jaw?"

"Don't ask." Spying the knowing look on his friend's face, he quickly asked, "What's on your docket for this afternoon?"

"Same thing as what's on yours." A grimace flashed across his face. "Boss wants us to make another run up toward Markhor Pass."

"Why?"

"She wants more photos."

"What's wrong with the ones I already shot?"

"Don't have a clue. I don't think the call to New York went well. She gave me a list of what she wants. She said if you refuse to go, I should tell Frank he needs to do it."

Frank was a great video guy, but his still shots sucked. "Let me see the list."

Bradley handed it over and Chase scanned it. "Seriously?"

Bradley held up his hands, palms out. "Hey, she's your lady. You ask her. She's in the office working on her script now. I should warn you, though. She is on a tear."

Yeah, well, so am I.

He almost went back to argue with her again. He'd given her damned good pictures the first time. This was Lana's way of pulling rank.

In the end, he decided he didn't have the energy for Round Two right now. He'd go take her blasted pictures and they'd be the best damned photos he'd ever shot.

Twenty minutes later, with his camera bag on his shoulder, he climbed up into the helicopter as Bradley flipped switches and powered up the helo. They were just about to take off when David Whitelaw, one of Lana's assistants, came running up. Chase couldn't hear him, but he read the younger man's lips. "I'm coming, too."

Once they were airborne, Chase sat back, shut his eyes, and tried to find some inner peace. He brought his mood to the photographs he took. Professional pride wouldn't allow him to give anything less than his best.

Markhor Pass was a two-hour trip over a mountain ridge by air, but about a million miles by land and hundreds of years back in time. Some of the roughest country in the world, it was starkly beautiful and so remote that it made isolated little Eternity Springs look easy to get to. Under different circumstances, he'd be stoked at the notion of donning a wingsuit and BASE diving off those mountains.

Lana thought he'd lost his nerve after he came perilously close to drowning during a recent white-water rescue of a crew member. That wasn't it. There was nerve, and then there was stupidity. This crossed the outright stupid line. The men who'd reported the intrusion of jihadists into the Markhor Pass area had been well and truly shaken by the stories they'd heard.

He brooded about the situation for the better part of the next two hours, listening with only half an ear to Bradley's yammering on about his South Beach hookup over Christmas. Chase was glad to let Whitelaw keep the conversation rolling — until a light on the instrument panel flashed red and the emergency horn sounded.

"What's wrong?" asked Whitelaw, sounding panicked.

"Not sure." Bradley's tone was all business as he immediately began the autorotation maneuver in order to make a controlled landing. He lowered the pitch, reducing rotation and drag, and the helicopter began to descend.

Chase was confident in his friend's piloting abilities, however, they would need a full measure of good luck to locate a suitable landing zone in this locale. A landing zone needed to be flat, firm, and free of debris. Staring at the rocky, mountainous terrain below them, he muttered, "Wish we were in Kansas."

"Iowa would be good," Bradley added.

They had maybe half a minute at the outside. Chase studied the mountain ridge rising immediately ahead of them intently. Mentally, he sent up a short but heartfelt prayer.

Time seemed to slow to a crawl even as the ground came up fast. It was the longest half minute of Chase's life. Bradley remained calm, cool, and professional — and yet still himself. Rather than say "brace yourselves" or "prepare for crash landing," he drawled, "Pucker up, boys."

Chase realized then that they weren't going to make the valley floor, and a fog bank hid the mountainside below them, obscuring the view of any accessible landing spots. It'd be the luck of the draw, but the surrounding terrain that was visible didn't look promising.

Chase thought of his parents, his brother and sister. He thought of Lori and wondered if this was the "life flashing before his eyes" thing. Then, as if an angel blew a breath at precisely the right moment, the clouds parted, revealing a miracle below — a relatively flat rectangle of ground. "Ten o'clock."

"Got it," Bradley said.

"Chances of reaching it?"

"Sixty/forty."

With Bradley on the throttle, Chase would take those odds. Behind them, Whitelaw made a garbled noise.

The ground was a hundred feet away. Five or six seconds. *We're gonna make it.* Bradley was a damned fine pilot and fate had wrapped up this landing area like a gift.

Filled with new confidence, Chase nevertheless held his breath as at twenty-five feet Bradley initiated an aggressive flare by pitching the nose up and reducing the collective. The rotor rpm increased significantly. At ten feet, he leveled the helicopter and applied the collective.

The helicopter hovered and touched down gentle as a butterfly. "Holy Moses," David Whitelaw breathed.

Chase shot his friend a grin. "Sick flying, dude."

"What can I say? I'm a sick pilot." He released a heavy breath and added, "Now we gotta hope I'm a sick mechanic. Otherwise, we'll be spending the night here."

"Here" was a natural, unspoiled pasture of high grass that all but swallowed the helo. A behemoth of a mountain rose sharply to the south and west. The absence of cliff faces to the north and east suggested the downward slope not obvious from the direction of their approach.

"Spending the night?" Whitelaw repeated, anxiety returning to his voice. "We have a satellite phone on board, don't we? We can contact camp."

Alarm skittered along Chase's nerves when he saw his friend wince.

"I screwed up. Lana's sat phone wouldn't power up today for her big call, and she took mine. I didn't think to ask for it back. I do have my ex-wife, though," he added, using his personal nickname for the pocket-sized GPS tracker that was a standard part of his gear.

"Good. I have mine, too, so we have a backup. You make the call, Bradley. Do we activate the emergency signals now or do we see how we make out with the engine first?"

"The engine. I'm a decent mechanic. With any luck I'll figure out what's wrong and have us airborne in ten minutes. No sense scrambling the forces if we can get ourselves out of this jam."

"Then let's get busy and fix this bird."

"What can I do?" Whitelaw asked. "I don't know anything about helicopter engines, but I'm a great assistant. Want me to hand you tools?"

"Sure."

They went to work on identifying the problem. Chase knew a little about engines, but he ran through that basic knowledge quickly. The fast, easy fix they'd all hoped for didn't happen. Bradley kept at it longer, and after half an hour of trying one thing after another, he threw in the wrench. "That's it. I don't know what else to try. Sorry, boss."

"I'm not your boss," Chase muttered. It was an old argument, and one he figured both men found comforting at this juncture.

"What are we going to do?" Whitelaw asked, subdued.

"Engage the GPS beacons and get to work setting up a camp, just in case."

"Just in case," Whitelaw repeated, his voice glum. The kid shoved his hands in his pockets and turned in a slow circle. "Do you seriously think we'll have to spend the night here?"

Chase pulled up the GPS function on his phone and checked their position. "I think it's a fifty/fifty proposition." To Bradley, he said, "You have a paper map?"

"In the pocket on the side of my seat."

A longtime map aficionado, Chase appreciated the ease of electronic maps, but when he needed to study one, he liked to stretch out a physical version.

He pinpointed their position and whistled beneath his breath. "If we hadn't made it over that ridge, we'd have been screwed. We were damned lucky to find this spot."

"It's because you were with us. You have the damnedest luck, Timberlake. That's why I like piloting for you when shooting the show."

Chase's mouth twisted and his thoughts flashed to Lori. "A friend used to say I have an angel on my shoulder."

Bradley snorted. "I wouldn't go that far. I don't see an angel coexisting with those horns on the top of your head."

Chase flipped him the bird, then folded the map and absently stuck it in the pocket of his camera case. "How much water do we have on board?"

Bradley leaned into the helo and flipped open a cooler. "Four."

"You have your pack?" he asked Bradley, recalling that Whitelaw had boarded the helo without one.

"Of course."

Chase never went anywhere without his pack, so they were well equipped for an overnight on this high flat if they needed to access their water filtration supplies. "We need to recon a water source."

Whitelaw asked, "Want me to do it?"

123

The kid was like a puppy, Chase thought. Eager to please, but clueless. He recalled an incident during a shoot in Switzerland when the poor guy came close to walking off the side of a cliff. He was definitely no mountaineer.

Bradley's thoughts ran along the same line as Chase's because he shook his head. "Let Timberlake look. He'll find water faster than either one of us. Gonna pick a campsite for us, too, or do we stay with the ship?"

"We need to shelter at the base of the mountain within reach of higher ground. Hard to know where the run-off goes in a place like this if we were to have a toad-strangling thunderstorm."

All three men looked at the sky where ominous dark clouds built to the west. His tone subdued, Whitelaw asked, "What do you want us to do?"

"Gather whatever we might need or be able to use from the helo and be ready to move when I come back."

Chase grabbed his pack and slipped it onto his back. Out of habit rather than conscious thought, he picked up his camera bag, hooked it over his shoulder, and added, "Hopefully, this won't take long."

He started to strike out through the waist-high grass toward the mountain looming like Mordor in front of him, but after half a step, he paused. "Any weapons on board, Bradley?"

His friend shook his head. "Just my knife. You?"

"Knife." Chase would have liked something with a trigger.

"Weapons? Why would we need weapons?" Whitelaw jerked his gaze around frantically. "Oh, jeez. You think there're wild animals up here? Are we in danger from tigers?"

"I'm more concerned about animals of the two-legged variety," Bradley observed.

Whitelaw's brow knotted. "Why?"

"There is some bad mojo going on in this part of the world."

"Not in Chizickstan!" Whitelaw protested. "The locals love Americans. This isn't Afghanistan."

"No wonder you get along with Chase's lady so well. Let me give you a piece of advice, son. You need to start thinking for yourself."

Whitelaw turned a worried gaze toward Chase. "Chase? Do you agree with him?"

Chase thought of the warnings that had precipitated today's argument with Lana. They were still over a hundred miles away from Markhor Pass, and the last village they'd flown over had been in a valley over five minutes ago by air. This wasn't a spot any mujahedeen were likely to be wandering around while they waited for the searchers to arrive. And yet . . .

"Chase?" Whitelaw repeated.

Damn, he looks young. And scared. Chase attempted to reassure him. "Considering our particular landing spot, I suspect that the most dangerous thing we're liable to encounter while we're here is a mountain goat. That said, they can be inquisitive sonsobitches. Don't forget they own the trail. Go at least fifty yards away to piss."

"Fifty yards? Why?"

"They like the salt."

With a wave, he headed out. Just before he disappeared into the high grass, Bradley called out. "Hey, Timberlake."

He glanced over his shoulder. "Yeah?"

"I decided what I want as my prize for whipping your ass in darts last week."

"Oh, yeah?"

"I want a pan of your mother's lasagna."

Chase grinned. Bradley had accompanied Chase on a visit to Colorado a year ago, and of course, Mom had cooked for them. Bradley hadn't stopped talking about her lasagna since — especially once he learned she sometimes sent frozen lasagna packed in dry ice to Chase in Manhattan.

"I can probably beg her to send some."

"No. I want your mom's lasagna fresh. I want to go to Colorado and have it there. With salad and hot bread and tiramisu for dessert."

"Sounds like a plan." It would make his mom crazy happy, Chase knew. She always loved it when he brought friends home to visit.

With a final wave, he moved into the grass. He traveled as quickly as was safe, physical exertion helping to chase the chill from his bones. The cold wind whipping across the grassland easily penetrated the T-shirt he'd pulled on that morning. Like him, Bradley would have a survival blanket in his pack, but with two blankets shared by three men, it likely wouldn't be a pleasant night. He'd need to pick a spot out of the wind — and hope the direction didn't shift in the middle of the night.

The grass was thick, difficult to penetrate, and higher the closer he got to the cliffs. Progress proved slower than he'd antici-pated. He completely lost sight of the helo. The grass finally ended about twenty yards from the rock face, but the stretch of cliff directly in front of him offered less than ideal shelter.

He followed the perimeter of the grassland over truly horrible terrain and eventually identified a viable shelter and source of water. He turned around and wasn't surprised to see that he would need to climb higher to view the helicopter and chart the best way back to it.

He needed to go about twelve feet up. No big deal. He identified a path up, but when he lifted his boot to take the first step, he hesitated. What the heck? Chase had climbed hundreds of mountains in his life, scaled his share of sheer rock faces. Relatively speaking, making this ascent would be a piece of cake. But for some weird reason, the climb filled him with dread.

"Don't be stupid, Timberlake," he muttered. And he climbed. Two feet. Six. Ten. A glance over his shoulder. Nope. The slight rise at the center of the grasslands meant he needed to take it a little higher.

Four feet would have done it, but he spied a ledge at six. Gaining it, he found his balance and turned around.

Oh, God. No.

CHAPTER SEVEN

Mac and Ali went home to Heartache Falls. The Callahans, Murphys, Raffertys, Davenports, and Celeste went with them.

The phone call from Lana had ended before she'd provided more than bottom-line information. Local search-and-rescue officials had needed to speak with her, so she'd promised to provide more details via Internet phone call in two hours.

They were the longest two hours of Lori's life.

She hadn't spoken one word since hearing Ali say that Chase was missing. In Chizick-stan. It wasn't like he'd gone off the trail on Murphy Mountain. He was in a part of the world where bad things happened. Really bad things.

The fear that gripped her was unlike any she'd ever experienced. Her insides had turned to ice, and she felt as if she stood at the very rim of Lover's Leap, waiting for news that would push her over the edge. Conversation remained muted. Tension thickened the air in the Timberlakes' family room where they'd all gathered, waiting for the call. Lori was inordinately grateful when her mother sat down beside her on the sofa and silently took her hand.

The two-hour mark finally came — and went. The computer remained despairingly silent. Finally, eight and one half minutes after the appointed time, the laptop signaled an incoming call.

Lana's face came into view, and seeing her, Lori gripped her mother's hand even harder. The woman looked haggard. "Mr. and Mrs. Timberlake, I'm so sorry. I —"

"Wait," Mac interrupted. "Please repeat what you told Chase's mother for my benefit."

Lana visibly swallowed hard, and then in a shaky voice, she spoke of a helicopter trip into a remote mountain wilderness carrying Chase and two other men. No phone was on board, but at some point, they activated their emergency beacons.

"Miscommunication at camp meant that nobody was concerned when they didn't return by dark," Lana said. "I had left shortly after Chase, so I wasn't there. I returned after dark and didn't realize the helo wasn't in the LZ. Nobody noticed the emergency signal until late the following afternoon, and by then, it was too close to dark to track them."

"You didn't notice?" Cam muttered.

Lana rubbed her brow, then shoved her fingers through her hair. "We took off at first light and followed the beacon right to the helicopter. It's in a high meadow. It didn't wreck. They obviously landed safely. Only —" She closed her eyes. "It's burned. It's burned and there are no bodies inside, but my men are not there." Her voice broke. "There's no sign of them."

Mac dragged his intense gaze away from the computer screen long enough to look at his wife. "That's good news, honey. If anyone knows how to survive in the wilderness, it's Chase."

Ali held her hands steepled over her mouth. She still didn't speak, but nodded.

"What's being done to find them?"

"We are searching by air, and we currently have twelve people on the ground searching the plateau. We have located the nearest villages and we have people looking for locals who are familiar with that area, but it is extremely remote. So far, we've struck out. Although . . ." She drew a deep breath and exhaled sharply.

A wave of dread rolled over Lori. She didn't like the sound of that sigh one bit. Mac's subtle stiffening told her that he sensed the same thing.

Lana continued. "I'm not sure they're telling the truth. My crew members have picked up some rumors about the presence of strangers in the mountains. A completely different part of the mountains, mind you, but if Chase was right —"

"About what?"

"Outsiders. Chase believed that outsiders from other countries might be coming into the more remote areas of Chizickstan."

Outsiders, Lori silently repeated. What did she mean . . . oh. Terrorists? *No. Please God, no.*

"So, what? My son decided to climb onto a helicopter and check out the rumors himself?" Mac snapped.

Lana opened her mouth to reply, then hesitated. After the pause, she shrugged and continued without responding directly to his question. "We haven't substantiated any of the rumors. No one in the villages is talking about it, but we sense a threatened undercurrent. It's as if they've been silenced."

Ali swayed and Mac reached out to steady her. He continued to stare at the computer screen, and Lori could tell he hadn't dragged his mind beyond the horrific possibility Lana had just presented. When his hesitation became obvious, Jack Davenport stepped up and asked, "Are you using dogs?"

"No. Not yet. We have to fly them in, and to be honest, I don't think they'll be able to help. This area has had a significant amount of rain in the past few days. Any trail they left has likely been washed away."

"You will try, though," Davenport fired back.

"Yes. Of course. They're on their way as we speak."

Mac finally found his voice. "What can you tell us about the fire? Was it set?"

"I don't know. None of us here have the knowledge base to determine that. Again, I'm waiting on an expert to arrive."

"Lots of waiting going on," Lori's father muttered.

"You need to send the coordinates of the position to me at this number immediately," Jack said, then rattled off his telephone number.

That's when Lori remembered that Jack had government connections. He'd *been* a government connection himself not too long ago. *Bet he can get access to spy satellites.*

Hope flared inside her at the thought.

And she couldn't forget about Gabe's family, either. His brothers ran a security business of some kind. Mac and Ali Timberlake had many people on whom they could call for help.

Jack asked a few more terrain-specific questions, then nodded to Mac, indicating that he was through. Mac asked, "Did Chase —" He broke off when his voice choked. He cleared his throat and tried again. "Did Chase have his backpack with him?"

"I'm sure he did," Lana responded. "He never left camp without it and his camera bag, and neither one are in our tent. The helicopter pilot always carries one, too."

Good. Lori knew he'd be prepared for wilderness survival.

With that, Mac appeared to have run out of questions. He turned to Ali. "Anything you want to ask, honey?"

She closed her eyes and nodded, then took a deep, bracing breath. "How was his mood?"

Lana's tone held an ocean full of sadness. The tears that had pooled in her eyes this entire time swelled and overflowed when she replied, "Actually, I think he was ready to come home. I think he missed Eternity

Springs."

At Lana's words, Ali let out a little whimper and her knees buckled. Mac grabbed her, supported her, wouldn't let her fall. She buried her head against his chest and sobbed. Through the blear of her own free-falling tears, Lori saw that Lana and every other female in the Timberlakes' great room had joined in the weeping. The men all looked carved from granite.

They ended the call to give Lana the opportunity to send Jack the coordinates he needed. His phone dinged a moment later, and he stepped outside to phone his contacts.

Mac stood holding on to Ali, his head buried against her blond hair. Watching their despair, Lori wanted to curl up in a fetal position and bawl. Instead, she leaned over and rested her head against her mother's breast, taking comfort there.

After probably ten minutes on the phone, Jack reentered the house and approached Mac and Ali. "I have some people pulling up satellite imagery, and they're going to give it a thorough going-over. We're also gathering intel about any possible movements into the country from bad actors. I spoke with your brothers, Gabe. They'll have S and R wheels up within the hour."

"Good," Gabe said decisively. "Mac, Callahan Security has access to people who can track a flea across the Grand Canyon. The search couldn't be in better hands."

"Okay. Good. That's good. Whatever it takes. Whatever it costs. I can cash out some investments and mortgage —"

"Don't worry about that," Jack interrupted. "It's already been covered."

Ali lifted her head and spoke softly. "How?"

Jack's lips twisted in a secretive half smile. "I have my ways, Ali. Seriously, costs are one thing you don't have to worry about."

She nodded and softly said, "Thank you."

Mac cleared his throat and said, "Sweetheart, we need to call Stephen and Caitlin."

"Yes. Will you do it, Mac? I should put together some refreshments for —"

"No," Sarah and Nic said simultaneously. Nic continued, "We know our way around your kitchen. We can do it. Besides, we're all still stuffed from dinner."

When she looked as though she'd protest, Mac said, "They're right, Alison. Why don't you go up and take a hot bath. You'll feel better after a soak in the tub."

Her eyes flooded with new tears. "I won't feel better until we find him."

"I know, baby."

Celeste stepped up and wrapped an arm around Ali's waist. "Here, dear, I'll walk you up and wait with you until Mac is off the phone. Do you still have some of the bath salts I gave you for Christmas? The custom fragrance our Savannah created for the Angel's Rest spa product line is so soothing. A little time with it will do you a world of good."

Celeste continued to prattle all the way up the stairs. Once they'd disappeared from view, Mac turned to his friends. "You guys have kids you should get home to. You don't need to stay."

"Sure we do," Sage said. "We want to be with you."

He swallowed hard, then nodded once. "Okay. Thanks. You guys are the best." He rubbed the back of his neck and added, "I guess I'd better make those calls."

When Mac disappeared into his study, Nic turned to Sarah. "Let's see what Ali has in her pantry. You know her. She won't stop fussing if there's not food on the table."

"That's not going to be a problem," Sage's husband, Colt, said from his position beside one of the front windows. "Word has gotten around town. People have been setting food on the front porch. At the rate they're coming by, we'll soon have enough to feed a small army."

Sarah said, "God bless Eternity Springs."

Following a short discussion about how Mac and Ali would prefer to handle the gathering crowd, the women directed their men to set up the folding banquet tables Ali kept stored in her garage on the large, covered front porch. Once that was done, they set out the food and invited those congregated in the yard to help themselves.

Mac's phone calls to Chase's siblings took half an hour. When he emerged from his study, Lori thought he looked as if he'd aged ten years. Gabe approached him and the two men spoke softly for a moment, then Mac walked over to the front window and gazed outside at the gathering crowd. His lips twisted in a sad half smile. "This will touch Alison's heart."

He turned to look at his closest friends. "And to think that once upon a time, I wished Ali had never heard of Eternity Springs."

He went upstairs to check on his wife. A few minutes later, Celeste came downstairs. "How's she doing?" Nic asked.

"Better. Never underestimate the power of a nice, hot soak. You know our girl. Courage is a muscle that's strengthened by use, and she needed a little time to mentally prepare for the test that's upon her. She knows she has faith, family, and friends at the ready to offer a boost when her bravery begins to flag. That's a comfort to her. She's putting on her makeup, and I expect she'll be downstairs soon. She knows that Mac, Caitlin, and Stephen need her to be strong, and Ali will not fail them."

"No, she won't."

Needing something to do to keep herself occupied, Lori offered to be in charge of brewing coffee. One skill she'd learned from working for her mother at the bakery was to make excellent coffee in large quantities, and Ali's kitchen had everything she needed to get the job done.

It proved to be a demanding job, because with every hour that passed, the crowd outside the Timberlakes' mountain home grew. By midnight, the public campground nearby in the national forest was filled to capacity. Local businesspeople, friends from church, legal clients of Mac's, and customers of Ali's restaurant came to wait for word with Chase's family in a silent show of support.

Since so many of Mac and Ali's closest friends had young children who needed tending to, they organized a watch rotation with moms and dads taking turns at home.

Lori told her parents she was there for the duration. Chase's two siblings arrived together at three A.M., and while Mac and Stephen spoke together in his study, Ali and Caitlin shared a good cry.

Nobody slept much or very well throughout the course of the night. Sarah returned at six A.M. with more coffee beans for Lori and enough baked goods to feed everyone gathered at the Timberlake home. Devin arrived at eight A.M. looking for Lori.

"Thought you might appreciate a break about now. I brought fishing gear. Want to go dip a hook and relax for a little while?"

She opened her mouth to refuse, then second-guessed herself. It would do her good to get away from the house for a little while, and they could stay close. "Sure. Thanks, Dev."

She told her mother where they were going, ducked into the family room to see if Caitlin wanted to join them, but found her dozing with her head in her mother's lap. Lori nodded to Devin and they exited the house through the back door.

As a vet, Lori was accustomed to getting her hands dirty. Nevertheless, she'd never gotten over the "ick" factor of putting a worm on a hook, so she fished with salmon eggs. In the way of brothers everywhere,

Devin liked to give her a hard time about it. Today, however, when they reached the fishing pier that stretched into the small alpine lake a short walk from the Timberlakes' house, he refrained from teasing her and simply handed over a fishing rod and plastic container of neon-pink eggs.

Lori sat cross-legged and lowered her baited hook into the water. For a good ten minutes, they fished in companionable silence. Lori's mind was blessedly blank when Devin finally spoke. "One thing you shouldn't forget is that Chase stays calm and collected during a crisis. Remember that time the three of us went on that picnic up on Murphy Mountain? You were home from college and Chase came to visit. He and I went for a hike and you got mad because we were gone longer than we'd intended?"

"Oh, yes. I remember that. You not only invited yourself along on my picnic, you monopolized my date."

"Did Chase ever fess up about what happened? Why we were gone so long?"

Lori lifted her gaze from her fishing bobber and shot her brother a sharp look. "No."

Devin's lips twisted in a crooked smile. "I begged him not to say anything. I figured that everything had turned out okay, so why bother worrying everybody? He agreed. He especially didn't want me to tell you."

"About what? What happened?" Lori asked. "All I remember is that you both came back dirty and you jumped in the lake. The freezing lake."

"I was stupid and careless. I told Chase I wanted to do some rock climbing. I'd never done that. Chase knew about a spot not too far from the picnic area that he said would be an easy climb for a first-timer. He was taking me to see it."

Devin had come to Colorado under protest and with a chip on his shoulder the size of Ayers Rock. He didn't like the way these Colorado women were pushing his dad around.

"What do you see in Lori Reese, anyway?" he asked Chase. "She's a stuck-up b."

"Careful. I get that you and Lori don't have the smoothest of relationships . . ."

"Now there's an understatement."

". . . but I won't listen to insults about her."

"But —"

"Can it, Oz," Chase replied, using the nickname he'd given the Australian native the first time they'd met. "She's in a tough spot. You don't know how hard she and her mother have struggled without Cam in the picture."

"Well, Cam is here now, and he's doing

everything he can think of to make things right with Lori. Shoot, he bought her a car!"

"That particular bribe was a good one, but you have to admit that the family dynamics here are tough. Cam has made some gains and Lori's heart has softened toward him a little, but she's stubborn. You and Cam are both going to need to be patient."

"I'm not very good at being patient."

"Then you damn sure don't need to be rock climbing. Look." Chase pointed toward a sheer rock face that rose probably fifty feet above them. "If you're going to climb that, you need to be patient and deliberate or you're going to fall and bust your ass."

"That's it?" Devin's eyes went round. "I thought you said it was an easy climb?"

"I said it was a good beginner climb and it is. Handholds are plentiful and well spaced. Look. There." Chase pointed toward the rock face. "There. There."

"Hmm . . ." Devin said, trying to identify the handholds Chase had pointed out. He'd done some climbing on a wall at a gym back in Cairns, but he'd never gone rock climbing out in the wild, so to speak. He wasn't exactly sure what he was looking for.

His gaze fixed on the cliff rising above him, Devin walked sideways, attempting to get a better view. Eventually, he saw the route up based on Chase's description. He never spied the old, rotted boards covering the entrance to the mine shaft until his boot went straight through it. His body dropped and darkness closed in.

He fell no more than three or four seconds, though it felt like three or four hours. He hit solid rock and it knocked the breath from him. Even as he fought for breath, his descent continued because the shaft sloped at a thirty-degree angle and was covered in loose gravel. The spasm in his chest ended and he managed to draw a breath. He dug his heels into the ground and grabbed for something — anything — to hold on to and halt the slide.

Finally, his left foot found purchase against a crevice in the rock and slowed him down long enough so that he managed to stretch his arms and wedge himself against the walls of the shaft.

His pulse pounded. His mouth was dry as a bone. Fear unlike any he'd known before made his blood run cold.

He couldn't see a damned thing.

Chase's voice called, "Oz? Let's hear you say something, Oz."

His voice emerged thin and reedy. "Help!"

"I'm here. It's okay. It's going to be okay. I'll get you out of there."

"Hurry."

"I will. We need to be smart about it, though, and not make the situation worse. How far did you fall?"

"I don't know. Seemed like forever."

"Can you see daylight?"

"I'm afraid to look up."

"I need you to look up. I have a rope and you're going to have to tell me if it's long enough."

A rope. Thank you, God. "Okay. Okay."

"I'm shining a flashlight down at you. Can you see the light?"

"No. No!" The words emerged as a little wail. "I don't see it. It's not . . . oh, wait!"

Devin spied a light about the size of his fist bobbing above him. "I see it. I see it."

"How far above you?"

"I don't know. Forty feet, maybe?" Fatigue pulled at Devin's muscles. Hurry, Chase. Please. "I don't know how long I can hang on. If I start sliding again, I'm afraid I won't stop."

"Can you see what's below you?"

He was afraid to look. He was afraid to move. "No."

"All right. Stay calm, Oz. I'm coming to get you."

Devin heard the skitter of gravel above him. Seconds later, rock pinged his fingers. Ow. Ow. Ow. That hurt. "Don't fall, Chase."

"I won't fall."

If he fell, he'd knock Devin down, too. They wouldn't stop until they hit China. "Please hurry. But don't fall."

"We've got this, Devin. It's going to be okay."

"Okay. That's good." Chase sounded so calm, so in charge. "You're not nervous? Why aren't you nervous? I'm scared to death. I don't think I can breathe. I'm running out of air. Oh, jeez. That's what happens in mines, isn't it? The canary runs out of air and falls over dead. I'm going to fall to China."

"Enough!" Chase demanded, his tone filled with command. "You are being nonsensical, Oz. You dive in the ocean. With sharks. That's a hundred times more dangerous than falling down a mine shaft. What you should do is grab hold of the flashlight I'm lowering your way and shine it around. I wouldn't be surprised if you managed to stumble on a vein of gold or silver. Lots of people think this area isn't completely played out, you know."

"Gold?" Devin repeated.

Chase's diversion worked. "My great-something grandfather on my mother's side was one of the original miners who hit it big in Eternity Springs. Your dad is a descendant of another one. Did you know that?"

Chase kept up the patter about the history of Eternity Springs and the big Silver Miracle strike, and Devin grabbed hold of the distrac-

146

tion like a lifeline. The combination of Chase's soothing, confident tone and the sounds of his approach eased Devin's fears.

Until his leg cramped, his muscle contracted, and he lost his grip on the sides of the shaft.

Devin screamed as he slid another thirty feet before the tunnel narrowed enough that he managed to wedge himself to a precarious halt.

"Sound out, Oz," Chase called.

"Here. I'm still here. Oh, Jesus. Oh, Jesus. I shouldn't have argued with Dad about going to church last Sunday. I swear, I'll never do it again."

"Hold it right there, Oz. I have a thing about bargaining with God. You don't do it, especially not in the middle of a situation. It adds some bad mojo to the whole process. You wait until we get you out of here before you start on that. Okay?"

"Okay. Is your rope long enough?"

"I need you to not fall any farther."

"I won't do it on purpose!"

"Don't do it by accident, either. I'd rather not have to call in the cavalry for help. I think we're both better off if we can keep this little escapade to ourselves. Something tells me that letting you tumble into a mine shaft would play hell with my love life."

"Love life? I thought you and Lori were just friends."

"Yeah, well, we tried that. It didn't take."

"Huh. So how is that gonna work? You live in Colorado. She's going to school in Texas. You into long-distance romance?"

"Not my preference, but . . ."

Devin caught his breath as he heard Chase slide and gravel rained down upon him.

"I love her," Chase continued, as if nothing had happened. "The real, honest-to-God, forever kind of love. I haven't told her yet. I've been waiting for the right moment. But it's the real deal. I'm in love with your sister."

"Wow. This is great. I know before she does. That gives me so much ammunition in the sibling wars."

"Only if you want me to leave your clumsy ass down here in this hole."

"Forget I said that. My lips are sealed. Are you getting close?"

"Almost there."

He did sound close. Devin's bone-deep fear eased to where he felt more anxious than afraid.

Then, suddenly, Chase was above him. A rope dangled before Devin's eyes. "There's a loop in the end. We need to get it over your shoulders and around your chest without you sliding any farther down. Think you can manage that?"

Oh, man. Jeez. His heart felt like it was about to pound out of his chest. "Well. I just. Yeah. I hope."

"You've got this. I'm going to hold it a little taut. That'll make it easier."

"Okay."

Devin tried to reach for the rope, but he couldn't make himself release his death grip on the side of the shaft. "I'm afraid to let go."

"You can do it, Devin. I'm right here. I won't let you fall. Let's do it on three, okay? One. Two. Three!"

Devin grabbed for the loop and managed to get it over one shoulder before he lost purchase and his feet began to slide. Immediately, Chase tightened the rope. "Gotcha. Use your legs, Oz. Plant those boots of yours. There you go. That's good. Now, I'm going to give you just a little slack and you wiggle that other shoulder in. Here we go. Yeah. Yeah. Atta boy. Okay, the hard part is done. You're secure. I'm heading up, and when I'm out of the tunnel and ready, I'll give two hard pulls on the rope as the signal for you to start climbing. Okay?"

"Okay."

It seemed like forever before Chase gave the signal, but once Devin started climbing, he ascended the mine shaft fast. The first sight of blue sky above him filled him with hope. The warmth of sunshine on his face felt like a kiss straight from heaven.

Years later, as Devin baited his hook and let it fly into the small, natural pond that Mac and Ali had dubbed Reunion Lake, he explained his reasons for sharing that story at this particular time. "He was ice, Lori. Calm, cool, and confident. Later he told me he knew of a teenager who had fallen down a shaft in that same general area and died from gases. The only reason he was able to get me out of there was because he supplied his pack like a survivalist. He always took deliberate care with what he brought with him into the wilderness. Wherever he is, you can count on the fact that he's equipped both mentally and physically for the challenge."

Lori looked at him with tears in her eyes. "He told you he loved me that day?"

"Yeah."

"He didn't tell me for another couple of months."

"You were pretty hot about us being gone so long that day. Guess he figured to give you time to cool off."

"Guess so," Lori repeated, her gaze locked on her bobber floating undisturbed on the surface of the lake, a sad half smile on her lips as she thought about her brother's revelations.

How like Chase to have blabbered about his feelings. He was open, honest, and as straightforward a man as she'd ever met. She'd always appreciated that about him. He could keep a secret when necessary — she'd made him promise not to share the fact that they'd become lovers with their families — but it wasn't his first instinct. Not like it was for her. They'd discussed that difference between them on more than one occasion, and concluded that each was a result of their individual family circumstances. Chase's family was large and loud and loving. Lori's had been small and secretive, though just as loving in their own way.

Of course, her world had changed when Cam came home to Eternity Springs with an adopted son, a brother Lori had fiercely resented at first. They'd had a rocky beginning, but now . . . "I'm glad you're here, Dev. Thanks."

"Hey, it never hurts to remember reasons to think positively. If anyone can survive in the wilderness, it's Chase Timberlake."

Lori held on to those words like a talisman during the course of the next five days while the whole town of Eternity Springs waited anxiously for word from the other side of the world. Word that never came.

With every day that passed, tension mounted. Ali grew wan and fragile. Mac walked as if the weight of Murphy Mountain rested on his shoulders. Caitlin and Stephen Timberlake tried to present a positive front, but Lori knew them both well enough to see through the façade. They were scared.

Lori herself was petrified.

She slept fitfully, haunted by nightmares starring Chase and monsters and mountains filled with rock slides and raging rivers. It took near constant vigilance not to drift into daydreams that could be even worse.

The one bright spot in an otherwise gloomy week came on Wednesday evening when Shannon Garrett was safely delivered of a healthy daughter following a twenty-hour labor. Daniel Garrett broke down and bawled like a baby when he introduced Brianna Kathleen to friends and family.

Lori spent as much time up at the Timberlake home as she could manage. Between her mother, father, Devin, and herself, at least one Murphy stood by 24/7 to offer support. Each day upon finishing the baking she did for Fresh, Sarah made an extra batch or ten of baked goods to help feed the crowd of supporters. Some days she sent cookies, other days bread or muffins or cinnamon rolls or a mixture of both. On the sixth day after news of Chase's disappearance reached Eternity Springs, Lori answered a phone call from her mother shortly before noon. "Are you still planning to go to Ali's house today?"

"Yes. I have two more appointments this morning. I figured I'd head up there when I finish. I'll leave here in probably forty-five minutes. Do you want a ride?"

"No. I'm not going to make it. Michael has a tummy ache and Dad has an appointment at the store this afternoon. I have rolls in the oven now for the crowd up there. Would you run by Fresh on your way and pick them up?"

"Sure. What's wrong with the Squirt?"

"I think he caught that stomach bug that Racer Rafferty had over the weekend — either that or he sneaked too many cookies when I wasn't looking."

"My little brother takes after Dad's dog."

"I know. We should have named him Mortimer II instead of Michael. Speak of the devil dog," Sarah added. "He's scratching at the door. I better let him in before he eats it."

"See you in a few, Mom."

After hanging up the phone, Lori reviewed the file of the ten-year-old black Lab who was her next appointment, due in for his annual exam and shots. After seeing to him, she treated a Persian calico for an eye infection, then flipped her open sign to closed and swept up the blizzard of hair the cat left behind. She turned off the clinic's lights and stepped out into the warm May sunshine.

When Lori decided to move home and take over Nic Callahan's veterinary practice, she'd chosen to relocate the clinic. She'd leased space in a building on Third Street between Cottonwood and Pinion and her father had overseen the renovations. Due to the clinic's location just down the street from Ali's restaurant, each time she arrived or departed, Lori couldn't help but glance down the street. Ali hadn't put in an appearance at the restaurant this week, but the Yellow Kitchen continued to open every evening for dinner. Ali didn't want her staff to lose their jobs. At precisely five P.M., her manager updated a sign in the window with the day's news — or lack thereof — from Heartache Falls.

Lori's heart twisted as a black thought sneaked into her consciousness. Would the Yellow Kitchen ever serve Ali's famous red sauce again?

"Don't go there," she cautioned herself,

then she dug in her bag for her car keys and clicked the lock to the SUV that had come to her as an asset of Nic's practice. It was a short three blocks to Fresh, and ordinarily she'd walk it, but Mom could easily have a dozen rolls to send up to Ali's place.

She should have asked her mother exactly how many rolls she was sending. She'd rather take her car — the sweet little ride that had been a birthday present from her dad — but she'd yet to unpack it completely since her move home, so she couldn't fit too much inside. Sighing, she blinked away sudden tears. Nothing about her first week of work as Dr. Lori Murphy had gone the way she'd anticipated. She had a million things to do and only one place she wanted to be — with the Timberlake family when word arrived that Chase had been found safe and sound.

She started the SUV and drove to the bakery where she entered through the side door that led directly into the kitchen — where her grandmother's handwritten recipe card waited like a rattlesnake on the counter, the aroma that curled through the air its venomous strike that knocked her back into the past.

Her flour-coated hands rolled dough into logs a half inch around and about ten inches long. In a movement learned at her grandmother's side, she flipped the dough into pretzel twists. After she filled a baking sheet with rolls, she brushed them with melted butter, sprinkled them with cinnamon sugar, and set them aside to rise while she rolled out another tray of rolls.

She had one pan in the oven when she heard a key in the lock. Glancing at the wall clock, her heart skipped. "Molly," Lori called when she heard the front door open. "I'm so glad you're home. Chase's plane will land in an hour. I need to hop in the shower. Would you listen for the timer and switch out my rolls, please? Feel free to sample."

Knowing her roommate would have her back, she didn't wait for a response, but headed for her bedroom, stripping off her clothes as she walked. She switched on the shower, soaked her head, and lathered up her hair with the apricot-scented shampoo that Chase loved.

She didn't hear the shower door open, so she jumped when the large hand cupped her soapy breast. "Chase!"

His dark eyes gleamed wickedly, though his tone sounded innocent as an angel. "I hurried to catch an early flight. Didn't have time to shower. Mind if we share?"

"Chase!" she repeated, her heart filled with

joy as she turned into his welcoming arms.

They kissed and his hands strayed, stroking over her. Lori had never had shower sex before. Thrill zinged along her nerves until a stray thought occurred. She pulled back. "Wait. My rolls."

"I heard you. I tended them. We have ten minutes before the next tray needs to come out of the oven. That's enough time for us both to get . . . clean."

She let her hands drift teasingly down his belly. "Better make it five. The hot water heater in this apartment won't last that long."

"In that case . . ." He dropped down onto his knees and licked her where she ached. They finished just as the water began to run cold.

The timer dinged as he laid her across the bed. Lori groaned. "I forgot about my rolls again."

"Then I have done my job right. Stay where you are, Glitterbug. I'll get them. I'm guessing these are the Swedish rolls you've been telling me about? Your one specialty."

"Yes. My grandmother's coffee bread. Her kringlor."

"They smell fabulous. I can't wait."

He wrapped one of her thick pink towels around his waist and disappeared into the kitchen. A few minutes later he returned with two paper napkins holding hot rolls fresh from the oven. He'd brought three for himself.

They sat propped against her pillows, snuggled close, with Lori's lavender sheet pooled across their laps. His expression reverent, he lifted one of the rolls toward his face and inhaled deeply. "Wow, I do love this smell."

"It's the cardamom," she observed.

"Cardamom, yeast bread." He turned his head and gazed into her eyes. "Apricot shampoo, and the scent of sex on your skin. It's heaven. My heaven." Without looking away, he took a bite of roll. "Mmmm . . ."

Lori smiled with pleasure. "You like it."

"No. I love it. I really love it."

"I'm so glad."

"Are you? Then I guess this seems like a good time to go all in. I love you, Lori. I'm in love with you."

In her mother's bakery kitchen in Eternity Springs, the aroma of hot kringlor heavy on the air, Lori remembered the moment and broke.

Her knees turned to water. Grief erupted from her heart and sobs tore through her throat. Keening, she sank onto the floor and wept.

CHAPTER EIGHT

Sarah Murphy remodeled her childhood home for the first time when she opened her bakery, Fresh. As a single mother to Lori and with Alzheimer's disease slowly claiming her own mother's mind, Sarah had needed a means of support that allowed her be "on site" as much as possible. Converting half of her home into a bakery had accomplished the goal. Fresh became a rousing success.

The second remodel and expansion occurred after she married Cam when they learned that Michael was on the way. She loved the convenience of basically working from home — especially on days like today when illness upset their schedule.

Having checked on her sleeping son moments ago, she was halfway down the staircase headed back toward the bakery when she heard the door from the garage open and the familiar squeak of Cam's favorite summer footwear — flip-flops — against the tile floor of the family kitchen. She wasn't surprised he'd cut his meeting at his sporting goods store short. Since hearing the news about Chase, both she and Cam tended to hold Michael a little tighter, and hug Lori and Devin a little longer and more often. Cam was a nervous father anyway. News of Michael's having a stomachache never sat well.

She met her husband at the bottom of the staircase. Lines of worry creased his brow as he asked, "How is he doing? What do you think is wrong with him? He was fine this morning when I left. Should we take him to the doctor?"

"He's asleep. I think it's just a bug, but I went ahead and made an appointment at the clinic at four."

"Good. I —" Cam broke off abruptly as the sound of a wailing child broke the quiet of the house.

Except, the keening wasn't coming from upstairs. It was coming from Fresh. Even as Sarah realized what she was hearing, a second wail sounded, this time from up in Michael's room. "We have two crying children," Sarah murmured. "This is a first."

"Lori? That's Lori in the bakery?" Cam's eyes went wide with panic.

"Yes. You go see to Michael. I'll check on Lori."

Relief flashed in Cam's eyes as he nodded. As uncomfortable as dealing with a physically ill child made him, supporting an emotionally devastated daughter went way beyond his comfort level.

Sarah knew that's what she'd find when she entered Fresh. She'd been watching her daughter for days now, seeing the fear grow more brittle with every passing day. Lori still had feelings for Chase. Exactly what feelings and how deep, she wasn't sure, but if the past week had taught Sarah anything, it was that Chase still owned a piece of Lori's heart. And that piece, small though it might be, was breaking.

Sarah hurried into Fresh, spied her sobbing daughter in a crumpled heap on the floor, and her heart sank. She went down on her knees and gathered Lori in her arms. "Oh, baby. Sweetheart. Shush, now. I'm here. Mama's here."

"I'm so scared, Mom."

"I know, baby. Me, too."

An ocean of tears and fears swam in Lori's big green eyes — eyes so much like her father's. "Where is he? Why haven't they found him yet?"

Sarah had no answers to the questions, so

161

she voiced the litany she'd repeated to herself for days now. "We have to keep the faith, Lori. Chase is better equipped to survive in that part of the world than most."

"I know. I just . . ." Fresh sobs tore at her throat. "I'm so angry at him!"

"Angry? Why?"

"Because he went there to begin with. With her. With that beautiful, blond, Botoxed . . . because he's going to marry her. Not me. He loved me. I was his heaven. Cardamom and apricot shampoo and the scent of sex on my skin."

The scent of . . . oh, dear.

"I would have married him, Mom. I loved him, but I wasn't enough for him. Why wasn't I enough for him?"

They'd been sleeping together. I should have known. Why didn't I know? "You were sleeping together."

"In college." Emotion flashed across Lori's face. Wistfulness and pain and regret. "He visited me in Texas. I wanted to keep it a secret. He was my first. I made him kringlor when he came to see me. It's the only thing I can really bake, you know? That and premixed cookies. But he loved my kringlor and I loved him. I should have known better. He's a lot like Dad. Handsome and outdoorsy and athletic. Only they ran Dad out

162

of Eternity Springs. Chase left of his own accord. I wasn't enough for him. Eternity Springs wasn't enough for him. He chose her and she took him to Terroristbuktu and now his helicopter is burned and he's disappeared! Why couldn't I have been enough, Mom? Why couldn't he love me enough? Why didn't he wait for me? We could have had a life together. I really wanted that. I just wanted him to wait. Why wasn't I important enough to wait for?"

Erupting in fresh tears, Lori buried her head against her mother's breast. Sarah held her, rocked her, her heart breaking; she was at a loss to comfort her daughter. She wasn't really surprised to learn that Chase had been Lori's first. She'd recognized the stars in her daughter's eyes.

Sarah clicked her tongue, then stretched to grab a tissue from a box just within reach. "Oh, sweetheart. Shush now. It's okay."

She wiped tears from her daughter's cheeks. "I'm sure Chase did love you, but you were both so young. And, at different stages of life. That's a huge mountain to climb — bigger than you realize when you're in the middle of it. You put your education first and that's okay. I know it had to hurt when the romance ended. When did you break up, honey?"

163

"We didn't really 'break up.' It was like we . . . stopped. He just kept wandering and I kept studying and here we are. Except, he isn't here. He's missing and I'm falling apart and I don't even have the right to it, do I? He's hers now."

"You have every right to be upset and worried. Even if he's not still your lover, you still care about him. You probably always will."

"I do care. You can't just stop loving someone because they move on."

"Oh, I know, honey. Believe me, I've traveled that same road myself. I wish you had said something to me. I've been down that road. I would have walked along with you."

"I couldn't tell you when I was sleeping with him. That would have been awkward for you and me and for you and Ali, too. I sure couldn't tell you when we stopped sleeping together. My pride wouldn't let me. I was devastated, Mom. I just wasn't enough. I was rooted and he wanted to fly. He flew right to her. I tried to be an adult about it, but when I heard he was engaged . . . oh, I was so jealous. Now . . . I swear, I don't care about that. As long as he comes home safe and sound, that's all that matters. Shoot, I *want* him to marry her. Here in Eternity Springs like they'd planned. I'll bake kringlor for their reception. I'll volunteer to be a bridesmaid if she needs one. As long as he comes home!"

Sarah gave her daughter another hug as movement at the doorway to the hallway that led from the bakery to the house caught her notice. She looked up to see Cam standing with a sleeping Michael snuggled in his arms and a stormy expression on his face. His voice a low-pitched growl, Lori's father said, "I hope that kid comes home so I can tear his ass apart."

Her head still buried against Sarah, Lori emitted a thready laugh. Lifting her gaze, she looked at her father. "You might have gotten a late start on active fatherhood, but you've picked up the clichés nicely."

"Damned straight." Cam crossed over to his women and placed a supportive hand on Lori's shoulder. "I'll beat him up for you the first chance I get, sweetheart."

"Thank you, Daddy."

With that, Lori pulled away and stood, gathering both her dignity and her emotions. "Enough of this. I came by wearing my delivery girl cap. Do you have the kringlor all boxed up and ready?"

"I do." Sarah used the pad of her thumb to wipe a tear off Lori's cheek. "Are you sure you want to make the trip up to Heartache Falls?"

"Yes. I'll be fine now. I think I just needed a good cry."

"You know what Celeste says: 'Tears are raindrops from Heaven that dilute one's sorrow and nourish the healing process.' "

"She's a wise woman, our Celeste."

"That she is."

Lori dusted stray cookie crumbs off her jeans, then asked, "How's my man Mikey doing?"

"I've diagnosed a stomach virus." Because Sarah recognized that her daughter's need for emotional support was higher than her son's need for his mother at this particular moment, she said, "Your father is taking him to the doctor in a little while, which frees me to run up to Heartache Falls with you."

Lori and Cam spoke simultaneously. Cam's voice held a note of panic as he asked, "Are you sure, Sarah?"

Sarah didn't miss the gratitude in Lori's. "Are you sure, Mom?"

"Positive." She kissed her sleeping baby's head, then kissed Cam's cheek. "You've got this, Daddy. Lori, the boxes are on the counter if you want to start loading the car. I'm going to run upstairs and change my shirt. Michael rubbed banana all over it when he tugged at my shirttail."

With marching orders issued, Sarah hurried up to her bedroom and into the master bath where she ran a comb through her short hair, and took two minutes to indulge in a good cry of her own. She cried for Lori and for Chase and for what-might-have-beens. Then she splashed her face with cool water, changed her shirt, and hurried back downstairs where she gave Cam a couple more dealing-with-a-sick-child instructions and headed to Fresh to finish helping load the SUV. To her surprise, the task was completed. "Sorry, Lori. I guess I took longer upstairs than I thought."

"I had help." Lori gestured toward the passenger seat of the SUV. Celeste finger-waved toward Sarah. "Celeste said she wanted to spend the afternoon at Ali and Mac's."

Sarah climbed into the SUV's backseat and addressed Celeste. "I thought you had a meeting you couldn't miss at Angel's Rest today."

"I rescheduled. I want to be with Mac and Ali this afternoon."

Something in her friend's tone caught Sarah's notice. She darted her a sharp look, but Celeste's expression remained its usual serene self. Nevertheless, unease fluttered through her stomach. All of a sudden the drive had a sense of anticipation to it that she had not noticed in previous trips up the mountain, and it was why upon reaching Heartache Falls, she asked for help distributing the rolls from a couple of teens in the crowd. Slipping her arm through Lori's, she suggested, "Let's hang with Celeste for a bit, shall we?"

Lori gave her a questioning look that said she'd sensed the strange undercurrent, too. Sarah shrugged, and she and Lori followed Celeste inside.

Mac, Ali, and Caitlin stood at their dining room table where a large paper map lay spread across two-thirds of the table's surface. Jack Davenport spoke softly to the family as he marked on the map with a pencil. Sarah tuned in to hear Jack say, ". . . and expand the search grid tomorrow."

Mac asked, "How many men did they estimate again?"

Solemnly, Jack replied, "At least a dozen."

Ali grimaced and closed her eyes. Caitlin brought her hand up to cover her mouth. Mac's voice sounded harsh and hopeless as he said, "It would take a miracle . . ."

Celeste joined the family at the table and spoke in a voice filled with comfort and confidence. "If I've said it once, I've said it a dozen times. Thank God we do miracles here in Eternity Springs. Now is not the time to lose your faith, my dear friends." She turned her head and her gaze met Lori's as she added, "Chase will come home to you."

With that, Sarah took her first easy breath in a week.

She wasn't even all that surprised when Gabe Callahan's cell phone rang ten minutes later. He checked the number and sucked in an audible breath. "Hello, Mark."

Instantly, the room grew as quiet as a snowfall. Ali and Mac reached for each other's hands. Lori took a half step closer to Sarah.

Gabe exhaled a heavy breath. "Okay. Just a moment."

He extended his phone toward Ali. "They found him. He's safe. Ali? Mac? Chase wants to talk to you."

Through watery eyes, Sarah watched her daughter react to the news. Lori swayed a little bit and shut her eyes. She sighed in relief, and like many others in the room, she offered up a soft prayer of thanks and gratitude.

Sarah added her own prayer of thanks, and then said another one on behalf of her daughter. Because when the Timberlakes finished their phone call, Mac summarized what he'd learned and finished by saying, "Chase said he and Lana are on their way home to Eternity Springs."

Had her gaze not been on her daughter, she wouldn't have seen the brief look of pain that flashed across Lori's face. Something in her own expression must have revealed that she hadn't missed it, because Lori winced.

Sarah reached over and patted Lori's hand. "It's okay, honey. I won't tell anyone about the bridesmaid thing."

Lori laughed. "I love you, Mom."

"Love you, too, babycakes. Love you, too."

Nine days later

Chase sat staring out the passenger seat window of the SUV Lana had rented at the Colorado Springs airport. He was marginally aware that as she drove, Lana kept up a constant barrage of chatter. It was noise. He wanted to ask her to be quiet, but to do so meant he'd have to speak. Speech required more effort than he had within himself to manage at the moment.

The Callahan Security team had flown him out of hell to a military base in Afghanistan where he'd been debriefed by a couple of suits who had dropped Jack Davenport's

170

name. He'd told them the truth of what had happened, though not all of the details. Some things didn't bear repeating.

Some things he couldn't bear to remember.

Lana had joined him at the base. She'd run toward him, wrapped her arms around him, and hadn't seemed to notice that he couldn't hug her back. Then she'd started spitting out questions like bullets and he'd had to physically walk away from her. She, like everyone else who asked, got the bottom-line version — Bradley Austin and David Whitelaw hadn't made it out alive. Their bodies were nonrecoverable.

From Afghanistan, they'd flown to the States where they'd paid private, soul-wrenching visits to South Carolina and Alabama, the respective homes of the Austin and Whitelaw families. He'd told them expurgated versions of the truth. It was the last time he intended to repeat his tale to anyone.

Hearing Lana take responsibility for the decision to send them on the ill-fated trip had helped ease some of the fury he felt toward her. Of course, nothing would ease the fury he felt toward himself.

They'd flown into Colorado this morning and passed through Eternity Springs ten minutes ago, taking the road past Cemetery Hill, which seemed appropriate. Now his parents' house was only minutes away. Chase had mixed feelings about coming home. On one hand, he needed to see his mom and dad, his sister and brother. And yet . . . he didn't know if he could manage to look them in the eye.

He was on a kind of autopilot like he'd never known before. It had switched on the moment he'd watched the bastards set the helicopter on fire and it hadn't switched off yet. He was numb and grateful for it. If he started feeling . . . if he started thinking . . . he might start talking and say the unspeakable.

Beside him, Lana rattled on. ". . . people want to welcome you home, but I told them you'd probably prefer to keep everything low-key. Was that okay?"

He offered no response. He knew she didn't expect one. Not at this point. At some point in the past nine days, she'd finally figured out that her efforts to engage him in conversation were futile.

"Your father said that the townspeople were wonderful. Super supportive. I told him you might be ready to have a thank-you party in a few weeks, but that you need some time to . . . well . . . chill."

Chill. Yeah. He had chillin' down pat. He was cold, cold through to his bones. He didn't know if he'd ever be warm again.

The car approached the turn to the house. Chase felt detached from the moment, wrapped in a cocoon of numbness. Lana pulled up in front of his parents' home and parked in the same place that Chase had parked in January when he'd come to deliver news of the impending trip. He gazed into the front window and remembered the Christmas tree. He thought of the comfort of his mother's kitchen, his dad's booming laugh. The heat of the hearth. The warmth of family life.

He didn't deserve warmth. He deserved to be stone-dead cold. Like David and Bradley.

Lana switched off the engine and opened the driver's side door. Chase remained seated, unmoving, as reluctant to exit the car today as he'd been that bitter winter day. Even colder today despite an outdoor temperature that was sixty degrees higher.

"Chase?" Lana stood beside the passenger door. "Darling?"

He stared at the house, gazed into the big picture window and remembered the Christmas tree. He'd thought about that tree and that window a lot during those god-awful days. He'd remembered his mother's voice. Her warning. Her fear. *"That will give us so much comfort when you're captured by terrorists."*

Mom was right. Mom was always right.

And here comes Mom.

Ali rushed out of the house, Mac close on her heels, Stephen and Caitlin right behind him. Chase knew an instant of relief at the sight of his mother, then the cold returned. He could never tell her what he'd seen, what he'd done, who he'd become. NEVER. Despair rose up within Chase. He swallowed the lump in his throat and blinked away the watery film that suddenly obscured his vision at the sight of his family.

His mother began to run, her arms open wide. A tidal wave of yearning swept over him, and Chase finally moved. Out of the car, he took three big steps and then she was there.

"Chase. My Chase. Oh, Chase," Ali said, flinging her arms around him.

He closed his eyes and lowered his head against hers, inhaling her familiar scent, indulging in the comfort of her embrace. Then his father joined them, Mac's big arms engulfing them. "Son. You're home. Thank God, you're home."

Caitlin and Stephen joined the group hug,

and for a few short moments, Chase allowed himself to bask in the warmth of his family's love. All too soon, reality intruded. Caitlin asked, "Oh, wow, Chase. What happened to your neck?"

He stiffened and, in his mind's eye, saw the flash of sunlight on the knife blade. The thaw begun by his mother's embrace ended in a flash of frost. *Stone-dead cold again, just like I deserve.* He pulled away from them, saying, "I need to help Lana with the bags."

Ordinarily, Lana never touched the bags. She was the boss, the star of the show. Today she had one in each hand, a guilt-ridden woman doing penance.

Chase vaguely noticed the worried look his parents shared, but he simply didn't have it in him to try to ease their minds. He pulled one of Lana's three suitcases from the back of the SUV and grabbed his backpack.

Chase's mother said, "Are you hungry? I made lasagna and Maggie Romano sent us an Italian cream cake for dessert. I thought we could have a big lunch and a lighter dinner. Is that all right, Chase?"

Lasagna. Oh, God.

In his mind's eye, he saw Bradley's grin. *"I want your mom's lasagna fresh. I want to go* to Colorado and have it there. With salad and hot bread and tiramisu for dessert."

"That's fine, Mom."

He didn't care about dinner. He hadn't been hungry since he saw David and Bradley forced onto their knees.

The family filed into the house, chattering away in a manner unfortunately similar to Lana's. Chase wanted to scream at them all to be quiet. But he couldn't begrudge them their happiness, so he pasted on a smile that he knew didn't reach his eyes and soldiered on through the afternoon.

He ate his mother's lasagna despite his lack of appetite. He offered to help with the dishes because he knew that was a normalcy she would grab onto like a lifeline. When the doorbell rang and he heard the Raffertys and Callahans and the Davenports and the Murphys — Lori included — sweep into the house, their voices filled with concern and caring and gladness and joy, he did the only thing he could bear.

Chase grabbed his pack and ducked out the back door. He hiked away from his parents' home, away from friends and loved ones. Away from comfort and community. Away from *warmth*. He didn't belong there. He couldn't bear to be around it.

He hiked a familiar path through the forest away from the falls, but toward a spot that offered a scenic view of the valley that cradled Eternity Springs. Upon reaching it, Chase sat cross-legged on a wide, flat boulder and gazed down at the sleepy little town. He tried hard not to think.

Chase wasn't surprised when his father joined him a few minutes later. Mac sat beside Chase and pulled a couple of beers from his pack. Silently, he offered one to his son. Chase eyed the can and debated. *If I start drinking, I might never stop.* "I think I'll stick with water."

Mac nodded, popped the tab on his beer and took a long sip. "Want to tell me what happened over there?"

Chase let silence be his response.

"Okay, then. If not me, then someone else? A professional?"

"I don't need a shrink, Dad. I need . . ."

When he didn't finish, Mac prodded. "You need what?"

"I wish I knew." Chase scooped up a handful of loose pebbles and began tossing them one by one off the side of the mountain. "I thought maybe I could come here and Eternity Springs would work its mojo on me. I'd hoped that I'd get here and life would be normal again. I'd feel normal again. But that didn't happen. Dad . . . I

177

can't stay."

Mac frowned. "You've only been here a few hours. Give it some time. I'll be honest, your mother needs you to stay, Chase. *I* need you to stay. For a few days, at least. These last few weeks have been very hard. We need to spend some time with you."

The old me, perhaps. They didn't understand that the Chase they knew and loved had died in the mountains of Chizickstan as surely as had Bradley and David.

He gestured down toward the town. "Look at it, Dad. A pretty little town in a pretty little valley. Your house may sit up on a mountain, but it's still part of that world. Eternity Springs is an oasis of light in a really dark world. I like looking at it. But, I'm outside. I'm apart. I don't belong there. I can't sit in your kitchen with Lana and eat Mom's lasagna like everything is the same as it was before. Nothing is the same. I'm definitely not the same. I don't want to hurt you and Mom any more than I've already hurt you, but I can't stay at Heartache Falls."

Mac mimicked his son's actions by gathering up a handful of pebbles and tossing them out into space. "First, you need not worry about hurting your mother and me. We love you and we want what's best for

178

you. If what's best for you is being by yourself in order to get your head on straight, then we will deal with it. We do understand the concept, after all. That's why your mother came to Eternity Springs the first time.

"However, I might have a solution that would suit us both. We didn't rent out the yurt this summer. Why don't you go stay up there? I'll run interference with family and friends and see that you get the space you need. At the same time, your mother and I will feel better knowing you're only a short hike away."

Chase grew still. When his father bought the acreage for their Heartache Falls home from a local character named Bear a few years ago, the purchase had included the yurt — a circular tent that already had all the comforts of home. Mac and Ali lived there while they planned and built their dream house and, in the process, added amenities that made the yurt downright luxurious. The Timberlakes often loaned the yurt out to friends for romantic getaways, and in recent years, they'd rented it out to summer tourists. The yurt was isolated, but within hiking distance of his parents' house.

"People have to make an extra effort to drop by the yurt," Mac continued. "It might be just the ticket for you."

"Yes. It's a great idea, Dad. Thanks."

Mac visibly relaxed and, for the first time since joining Chase, smiled. "If Lana has any objections, your mother will be happy to assure her about the comfort of —"

"No," Chase interrupted. Everything within him rebelled at the idea of sharing the yurt with Lana. It was too small a space. She was too . . . noisy.

He needed to be alone. He should send her away, tell her to go back to New York, but he simply didn't have the energy to do it. He sucked in a deep breath, then asked, "Could she stay at your place?"

Mac hesitated only a second. "Sure."

"Okay. Thanks. Okay."

Mac threw the last of his pebbles over the cliff. "I can't begin to tell you how much support our friends and neighbors gave us while you were missing. Lots of prayers sent up on your behalf. I know they're anxious to see you. You up to going back to the house and saying a quick hello?"

Chase knew it was the right thing to do, but the thought of being in a crowd of well-wishers overwhelmed him. "Will you give them my regrets?"

Mac hesitated. "Our friends are one thing, but you need to have a conversation with

180

your lady. It's not my place to tell her she's not welcome at the yurt."

No, he didn't suppose it was. Chase dropped his head back and lifted his face toward the sky. "You're right. Lana is my responsibility." He might as well go back to the house and face the whole damned symphony. "I'll come back to the house with you now."

The process was excruciating. Chase returned to his parents' home, accepted hugs and handshakes from friends, and expressed his thanks for their prayers and support of his family. Lana remained at his side throughout.

Lori kept her distance.

She approached him only once as the gathering broke up and visitors began to make their way back to their cars. He recognized the bracing breath she took before she walked up, nodded to Lana, and met his gaze. "Welcome home, Chase."

A lump of emotion clogged his throat, and he cleared it. "Thanks."

She turned a smile toward Lana. "I love your sundress."

"Why, thank you. Yellow is my favorite color. It's so happy, don't you think?"

The words triggered a memory that had Chase's gaze dropping to Lori's breasts.

It was during the first summer that they dated.

They lay upon an old tattered quilt spread out on a hidden alpine meadow dotted with wildflowers. A picnic basket anchored one corner of the quilt, Chase's hiking boots another. Lori's dark hair lay fanned around her head. Moisture glistened on her kiss-swollen lips. When his nimble fingers slipped the last of her shirt buttons free, he caught his first daytime sight of her full, luscious breasts bound by a silky bra of transparent yellow silk. "Yellow is my favorite color."

Today, Chase jerked his gaze up from her chest, past her blushing cheeks, and momentarily lost himself in the mountain forests of her green eyes. *She remembers, too.*

Thinking about those eyes had kept him sane once or twice in the past month.

Lana took a half step closer to him and possessively slipped her arm around his waist. "Thanks for coming, Lori. I know Chase appreciates it. Right, darling?"

Instead of answering Lana, he asked Lori, "Did you graduate?"

"Yes."

"Good. Congratulations."

"Thanks. Now, I'd better hurry or I'll miss my ride back to town."

When Lori followed her mother out the front door, Chase shook off Lana's hold and his own steps headed for the back. The need to be outside, alone, away from all the smiles and looks of concern and . . . touches . . . overwhelmed him.

Lana hurried after him. "Chase? Sweetheart?"

Oh, damn. He still had to deal with her. Halting abruptly, Chase lifted his gaze toward the mountain trail that led to the yurt. "Lana, I need something from you."

"Anything, darling."

"I need you to let me be alone."

"You mean tonight?"

"Tonight. Tomorrow. However long it takes. I'm going up into the mountains. By myself. You can stay here with my parents. You can go home to New York. Whatever you'd rather do. I just need . . . I've got to go. Let my mom or dad know whatever you need. They'll help. You can always count on them."

Too bad he couldn't say the same about himself.

Lori cleaned her hemostat and sent Sage Rafferty a reassuring smile. "That was the last one. We will keep Snowdrop until the anesthesia wears off and make sure she's doing well, but I don't expect any ill effects. You can pick her up after lunch."

Sage pulled her worried gaze off her bichon frise. "Porcupine quills are not a good look on her."

"I do like her in her little Easter bonnets better," Lori agreed.

"With Racer being such a live wire and now that Ella is crawling, we're going to have to rethink our approach to picnics in the woods. Snowdrop has always been such an easy dog. I think my children's bad habits are rubbing off on her. She's never before wandered away like she did today. I've wondered if she's testing us just like the kiddos do."

"Maybe. Sometimes bad behavior in a pet is a demand for attention — just like it is with children. However, I doubt you'll have to worry about her tangling with a porcupine again. Snowdrop has always been a quick learner."

"Good. I never want to go through that sort of trauma again. The only good thing I can say about it is that she made an impression on Racer. He won't try tangling with any porcupines he might run across."

Lori gently lifted the anesthetized dog and carried her to a crate where she would sleep off the effects of the drug. Lori made notes in Snowdrop's chart, then put check marks beside services rendered on the clinic's billing paperwork and handed it to Sage. "I heard Myra come in a few minutes ago. She will check you out."

"How is she working out?"

"She's wonderful." Myra Thomas was a recent Eternity Springs newcomer with fifteen years' experience in a medical clinic's billing office. Her desire for part-time work made her a perfect match for Lori's office needs. "It was my lucky day that she knocked on my door before she tried the medical clinic. They'd have snapped her up, and I'd still be struggling with paperwork."

After Sage left, Lori vaccinated and chipped Eloise Martin's new puppy, then filled a prescription for Dale Parker's cat. She took Brick Callahan's call, pulled up the pictures he'd e-mailed to her on her tablet, and gave him her honest opinion of the fabrics his designer had recommended for the tree house he was building up at his camp. "It's too busy, Brick. You want elegance and peacefulness. These fabrics say South Beach on Friday night."

"Seriously? South Beach?" He sounded horrified at the idea.

"Seriously."

"Huh."

185

While Brick griped about interior designers in one ear, the other picked up the sound of voices in the waiting room. She glanced at her clock. Ten after twelve. She had no appointments until two. Leaning from behind her desk in order to get the angle, she was surprised to see Caitlin Timberlake. Surprised and a little bit wary.

In the eleven days since Chase had come home, he'd not come into town once. Lori didn't know if that fact concerned anyone who'd seen him up at his parents' house on the night of his homecoming. All the talk at the chamber of commerce meeting the day before yesterday had centered on how good he'd looked and how he'd appeared to be no worse for wear — except for the big scratch on his neck. Lori wasn't so sure. There'd been something in his eyes that disturbed her, a distance. A detachment. It was as if his body resided in Colorado, but his heart hadn't made the trip home.

Only once had life flickered in his eyes. It had been that instant when Lana spoke of yellow, and her and Chase's gazes had briefly connected. She'd had the sense that in that moment, they both recalled a certain high country picnic.

"Hello? Earth to Lori?" Brick's voice said in her ear. "You still there?"

"Yeah. Sorry. What did you ask me?"

"Are we still on for Memorial Day weekend?"

Brick had cajoled her into joining him on a trip to the Durango area where he had an appointment with a rancher to look at some trail horses he was considering buying for his camp. "Sure. I can't leave until after noon. I have appointments in the morning."

"Not a problem. I have rooms reserved for us at a B and B my mother loves. She said to tell you the truffle eggs are spectacular."

"Yum. Okay. Pick me up at twelve-thirty." Lori waved a silent hello to Caitlin, now standing in her office doorway. "I gotta run now. See you Saturday."

Lori disconnected the call, then asked, "What's the matter?"

Misery wreathed Caitlin's face. "Oh, Lori. I'm so worried about Chase."

Everything within Lori tensed. She realized she'd been anticipating this visit for days. "What's happened?"

"Nothing. Absolutely nothing!" Caitlin waved a dramatic hand. "He won't leave the yurt. He won't talk to us when we visit. It's like he's become this reclusive mountain man who spends all his time sitting beside the creek throwing leaves into the water.

Mom and Dad are worried sick, but trying to pretend everything is okay. We all tiptoe around the fact that something is terribly wrong. I'm worried I'm going to go up there one day and find him missing or worse. I never see him without a gun within reach. Not a shotgun or a hunting rifle in case a rabid bear wanders up, either. A handgun. He's so quiet and sad and . . . damaged. I even feel sorry for Lana!"

Now that was a first. Caitlin really must be concerned. "He treats her poorly?"

"He doesn't treat her at all! She's living at my parents' house. He won't let her stay with him at the yurt. When he first came back, I thought he was angry at her, but now . . . he doesn't seem to care. About her. About us. About himself. About anything. I don't know what happened to him over there, but it's obvious it was bad. I think he has PTSD."

Lori closed her eyes, hurt for Chase twisting her heart. *Sounds like it's even worse than I imagined.* "Sounds like he needs to talk to someone."

"I know. I overheard my parents talking about that this morning. Apparently, Dad has tried to bring the subject up more than once, most recently yesterday. Chase is having none of it. Mom is going to reach out to

Sage because, apparently, she has fought her way through PTSD. I don't know the whole story of that."

Lori did. Sage had been volunteering with Doctors Without Borders in Africa when terrorists attacked the camp clinic where she worked. It had taken her a long time and a good dose of Eternity Springs to heal from the experience. "That's a good idea."

"It's not a bad idea," Caitlin said. "I don't think it's the only one that might help. That's why I'm here. I think you should try to talk to him."

"Oh, no." Lori pushed her desk chair back. "No, no, no. We've been down that road before. You've been pushing me in that direction for months."

"Wait a minute. Hear me out."

"I don't need to hear you out."

"He's in trouble, Lori. The two of you have always had something special between you. I have a feeling that you could cut through his defenses like nobody else."

"You're wrong. It's not my job. It's not my place. He's engaged to marry another woman."

"It's never gonna happen," Caitlin said flatly. "She missed her chance with him when she put off the Valentine's Day wedding."

"Now, Caitlin."

"Don't. You sound like my mom. She told me to stay out of it, too. But I can't. I won't. I'm too worried about him. Look, Lana isn't part of this discussion. I'm not asking you to talk to him as a girlfriend. You guys were friends. That doesn't have to stop and he needs a friend right now. Be a friend to him. He needs that. He needs you."

Further protest from Lori was interrupted when Celeste swept into the clinic with a whimpering ball of golden fur in her arms. "Lori, this poor little guy needs your help."

CHAPTER NINE

Mac and Ali Timberlake's yurt sat nestled against a mountain with a spectacular view of Murphy Mountain. Powered by a generator, its amenities included a wood floor, a full kitchen, indoor plumbing complete with a whirlpool bathtub built for two and a walk-in shower, a stone fireplace, and a king-sized bed.

Most nights, Chase slept outside beneath the stars. Though in truth, he did little sleeping. A guilty conscience kept him tossing and turning on a mattress full of the nettles of regret all night long.

He should have listened to his gut. He could have stopped it. He should have stopped it. He was as responsible as Lana.

His gaze drifted toward the boulder where she sat with a pen in her hand and a journal in her lap. After leaving him peacefully alone for the first five days of his time up at the yurt, Lana had shown up on the afternoon of the sixth. She stayed a couple hours, fixed supper for the two of them, then left. The following day, she'd arrived around the same time and stayed just about as long. Having her around hadn't bothered him enough to take the effort to make her leave. She hadn't interacted with him much at all. He quickly noted that during the hours of her visit, none of his family popped in. They arrived at other times. One or two quick visits every day.

He was being babysat.

Whatever trips their triggers, he thought. He didn't care.

Today Lana sat in a lawn chair writing in a journal. Her fingers flew across the page as she filled it with words. It occurred to him that she wasn't the same person as before, either. Before the Chizickstan trip, he rarely, if ever, saw her still. That Lana was flash — all motion and energy and intensity — like lightning from a summer thunderstorm. He'd liked that about her. He'd been attracted to it.

Now, the flash was . . . well . . . maybe not gone, but definitely muted. Nevertheless, she was not peaceful.

Dear God, right now, he craved peace.

Lana sat not ten feet away from him. Just when she'd started talking to him, he couldn't say. He hadn't noticed. However, when she said his mother's name, it caught his attention.

". . . a house in town. It's a cute cottage with lots of potential. It has good bones. You must know Shannon Garrett? She wasn't at your homecoming gathering because she's just had a new baby. Anyway, I met her when I went to lunch at your mother's restaurant yesterday. She remodeled the darling little red and white house in town called Heartsong Cottage. Do you know the one I'm talking about? It's so cute. Anyway, she's not doing that sort of work herself anymore, but she told me she knows all the subs to recommend if we decide to tackle it."

"What are you talking about?" Chase asked.

Momentary surprise flashed across her face. Obviously, she hadn't expected a response from him. "Our house in town, darling. We can't keep living with your parents after we get married, and your mom says the yurt is rented for hunting season. We need to get our own place."

Chase simply looked at her. Was she seriously talking about living in Eternity Springs? Now?

Whatever. He didn't have the mental

energy to engage in conversation about it. He didn't have strength to even think about it. After all, the question had been part of the argument that god-awful day, had it not?

"No. I am not going to move to Eternity effing Springs and I am not going to cancel the shoots at Markhor Pass and if you don't like it, you are welcome to take yourself home to your cozy little mountain burg. I am going to save this show with you or without you!"

The show. Always, the show. What was she doing about the show now? Had anyone mentioned it to him? He couldn't recall. He certainly hadn't cared enough to ask.

"I told your mother I want to be part of the wedding planning this time around," Lana continued. "She says it won't take too long to put together. We just need to pick a date. I think she and I and your sister are going to make a quick trip to Denver tomorrow and shop for a wedding gown. I'm really excited."

Noise. It was all babble and noise with a measure of desperation.

"You should go," he told her.

Lana brightened. "All right. I will!"

Chase frowned. He hadn't meant she should go to Denver to shop for a wedding dress. He'd meant she should leave here.

194

The yurt. His parents' house. Colorado, entirely.

Before he'd worked up the words to clarify, she'd scrambled off the boulder and was walking in his direction. She threw her arms around him and pulled his head down to hers for a kiss.

Chase stood as still as Murphy Mountain. It was the first advance of any kind that she'd attempted since he'd failed to return her embrace when she'd arrived at the base during his debriefing. Like then, today he didn't push her away, but he didn't respond to her, either. He had nothing inside him to give to Lana or to anyone.

She stepped back, then pasted on a bright smile just shy of sincere. "Your family has been so nice to me. It's especially nice of your mother to have taken me under her wing. I'm so glad I've had this time to get to know everyone better." Giving a little laugh, she added, "Even Caitlin has warmed up to me."

A sheen of moisture flooded her eyes and she blinked rapidly. Chase was no more moved by her tears than he had been by her kiss. If anything, the sight of tears only made him colder.

In his mind's eye, he saw the tracks of tears

on *David Whitelaw's* face as his knees hit the ground.

"So," Lana said, her voice crisp and way too perky. "I should probably get back to the house. You mother said she'd teach me to make Bolognese sauce, and I need to make a run to the grocery store. Can I get you anything while I'm in town?"

He shook his head. He wished she would leave. He wanted her to leave. Her voice today had a sharp note to it. Sharp like a knife blade.

"Okay, then. Well. I guess I probably won't make it up here tomorrow. Ali said we'd leave early."

"Drive safely," he said, picturing his mother, sister, and Lana at the summit of Sinner Prayer's Pass.

"I always do." She blew out a little breath, then went up on her tiptoes and pressed a kiss against his cheek. "See you later, hot stuff."

She'd taken maybe ten steps away, and he'd begun to breathe a little easier, when she suddenly stopped and turned around. "Chase, what should I say when your mother asks about our new wedding date?"

"I don't care."

Her smile faltered, then she lifted her chin and beamed her television-star smile. "Then

I'll tell her the Fourth of July."

He didn't protest. He turned his attention to the bubble and rush of the cold mountain stream. He'd always loved the sound of white water. The rush and crash and whoosh. Now he thought of the natural pool down closer to his parents' house. Reunion Lake, they called it.

Still water didn't make sound. Still water offered quiet. Peace. Peace and quiet. Oblivion. He imagined sinking slowly into Reunion Lake, cold water closing over his head. Deeper. Deeper. Quiet. Stillness.

Peace.

Lori had rented a two-bedroom bungalow on Fifth Street that had a porch swing in front where she liked to sit and drink an after-work glass of wine. The glider on the back patio was the perfect place to drink her morning coffee and read the national news on her tablet each morning. Twice a week, she took an extra ten minutes to peruse the *Eternity Times.* Bucking the national trend toward shrinking subscription rates, the little local newspaper was thriving. People here were not only slow to change their ways, they actively supported local businesses — and local gossip.

Today, Lori had company on her patio

that distracted her from the New Books in the Library column she was attempting to read. Her golden-haired guest sat huddled between the back steps and a pot of red geraniums. He had to be most skittish dog she'd ever encountered.

"What happened to you, baby?" she asked, her voice soft and gentle as she set down her coffee on the patio table. She judged the mixed-breed pup to be three to four months old. He had some retriever in him, obviously, and maybe some bird dog. He had big paws and floppy ears. He'd be a large dog someday, but right now he was a needy little too-skinny bundle of cuteness.

Celeste had told her that one of Angel's Rest's housekeepers had found the stray hiding beneath a porch swing at the carriage house apartment. He'd worn no tags or collar, and Lori's scan for an ID chip failed to turn up anything. Nor had inquiries around the resort and in town produced any clues about his ownership. What they had was another dumped dog who had probably been on his own for weeks. *What's wrong with people?*

Just as she silently asked the question, his ears perked up. Seconds later, Lori heard the sound of her mother's voice at the back gate. "Lori? Are you in the back?"

"Hey, Mom. Yes. Come on in."

The gate latch clanged open and Sarah Murphy walked into Lori's backyard carrying a paper cup bearing Fresh's logo. "Good morning, love. Have time to share a cup of coffee?"

"With you? Always."

"Oh my gosh. Is that the puppy Celeste brought to you yesterday?" When Lori nodded, Sarah added, "He's the cutest thing ever. Now I see why you didn't take him straight to the shelter. You'll find a home for him right away."

"Yes, it shouldn't be a problem."

Lori set aside her tablet as Sarah took a seat beside her. She read both uncertainty and hesitancy in her mother's expression, and since she knew her mom, she braced herself for unwelcome news. *What now?*

Apparently, Sarah had to work up to her subject because she said, "It feels good to sit down. We had a busier morning rush than usual. A big group of Campisis were taking a cycling tour this morning and they came in for cinnamon rolls."

"Campisis?"

"The reunion family at Angel's Rest this week. Anyway, your dad was in the bakery getting coffee, and he actually asked one of them who had recommended they carb-load

199

with gut bombs before they exercised."

"Gut bombs?" Lori's brows arched. "He called your cinnamon rolls gut bombs? Does my father still live?"

"Yes, but it will be months — maybe years — before he gets to enjoy one of them again. I'm considering cutting him off from muffins, too."

"Would serve him right."

"So how was your trip to Durango?"

"We had a good time. It's been a while since I made that drive. The views are simply spectacular. Brick bought three trail horses and I talked him out of two others. He's determined to make this camp of his a raging success."

"Well, I think he's onto something. From everything I read, glamorous camping is hot. Heaven knows I enjoy our getaways to Ali's yurt. If Brick's facilities are going to be that luxurious, I predict a rousing success." Sarah hesitated, visibly braced herself, then said, "Speaking of the yurt . . ."

Lori stiffened. "Is Chase okay?"

"As far as I know, he is. Based on what I'm hearing, he must be improving."

"I'm not going to like this news, am I?"

Sarah winced. "Am I that easy to read?"

"You're asking me?"

"Right. Stupid question. Okay, well. I

thought I should be the one to tell you. Savannah Turner also stopped by the bakery this morning. She had some news. Lana Wilkerson shopped at Heavenscents yesterday. She told Savannah that she's put her Manhattan apartment on the market, and she's looking for a house in town for her and Chase to live in. She's considering the old Carpenter place, but it needs a lot of work."

Lori's stomach did a slow flip. "Oh. That would be quite a change for her, wouldn't it?"

Sarah's teeth tugged at her lower lip. "Yes. But the last time I talked to Ali she did say that Lana is like a different person. She's really being kind and patient with Chase and with the situation. As a result, Ali wants to be supportive of her. However, she — Ali, that is — is terribly worried about Chase's state of mind. She says he won't talk to anyone about what happened. He won't talk to anyone, period, and he stays holed up at the yurt. So, I don't know if moving to town is simply Lana's wishful thinking or if Chase has had a breakthrough, or what, but after everything that happened when he was missing, I thought I should give you a heads-up that she's apparently planning an extended stay in Eternity

Springs."

"I appreciate your concern, Mom, but you don't need to worry about me. Chase is alive and that's really all that matters."

Sarah studied her with a long look, then nodded once. "Okay." She drained the last of her coffee, then stood. "I should be getting home. Dad might try to sneak into Fresh and score a cinnamon roll if I'm not there to stop it. You have a good day, honey."

"Thanks. I intend to."

"Do you have a full slate of appointments?"

Lori carefully chose her words. "I have a full day."

The puppy let out a series of whimpers, drawing the attention of both women. "What a little doll. However, since I'm your mother I have to caution you —"

"I'm not going to keep him, Mom. I know better."

The years of working as Nic's assistant before Eternity Springs established a city animal shelter had taught Lori the pitfalls of a vet practice being adoption central for the town's lost and abandoned animals. Together with the best practices guidelines she'd learned during vet school, her experience made her determined to draw a definitive line between her clinic's boarding facilities and the town's shelter. She'd had every intention of performing an exam on this little guy, then delivering him to the shelter. Somehow, on the way there, they'd ended up at home.

Sarah gave Lori a quick kiss on the cheek, handed over her empty coffee cup for the recycle bin, then departed. Lori watched her mother go, then shifted her gaze toward the puppy. "I won't think about Chase or Lana or love nests. I'll think about you. What am I going to do with you?"

Oh, quit lying to yourself. You know exactly what you're going to do with him. You've known it since the moment you looked from the puppy, to Caitlin, to Celeste, then back to the puppy. Mom's news doesn't change anything.

She was just working up the nerve to follow through on the idea.

Lori closed her eyes and surrendered. "Well, if we're going to do this thing, Little Bit, I need to get my butt in gear. I have appointments this afternoon."

She climbed the back steps and opened her screen door. The puppy bounded inside the house and went straight to her bedroom where he burrowed beneath the bed. He'd spent most of the previous evening in the same spot since last night's huge fireworks show at Angel's Rest. It wasn't unusual for dogs to be afraid of fireworks, but her house was far enough away from the resort that it ordinarily wouldn't be a problem. That wasn't the case for Mr. Skittish. He was such a poor, pitiful thing.

She showered and took a little extra time with her hair and makeup. She pulled on jeans and reached for her yellow sweater, then hesitated and chose a purple one instead. She donned her hiking boots, then loaded up a box with the required supplies and carried it to the SUV. It took some coaxing to get the puppy out from beneath her bed, but finally they headed out.

As she drove up Cemetery Road, Lori told herself there was no need to be nervous. She made her living diagnosing the health issues of animals. Animals who couldn't talk to her to tell her where it hurt. Accordingly, she'd learned to trust her instincts.

Those instincts now were clamoring that this was indeed the right thing to do.

Twenty minutes later, she turned onto the private road leading to the yurt. "Okay, boy. Ramp up your cute meter. It's time to shine."

She switched off her engine, inhaled a bracing breath, and when the yurt's door opened muttered, "Showtime."

She stepped out of her SUV. Her heart gave a little twist at the sight of him. He hadn't shaved in days, and though he wore the look well, the Chase she remembered had hated letting his whiskers grow. He'd always complained about the itch of anything over a three-day beard. He was tanned, shirtless, barefoot, and the red gym shorts he wore hung low on his hips. Lori drank in the sight of him, the woman in her appreciating the maturation of the young man she'd known and loved into a man in his prime.

There wasn't an ounce of fat on him. His shoulders were broad, his abs cut, and his muscles chiseled. The Chase Timberlake glaring at her from the doorway of his parents' yurt was all grown-up.

When he saw who'd come to call, his eyes narrowed. "Lori."

"Hi, Chase." She lifted her chin and pasted on a smile.

"What are you doing here? Who sent you? My mother? My sister? It was Caitlin, wasn't it? She won't leave me the hell alone."

Okay, this is off to a good start.

Rather than respond, Lori opened the passenger side door and removed the puppy from the carrier in which she'd transported him. She set the dog down and was pleased to see that instead of scrambling under the vehicle and whimpering, he put his nose down and started to explore.

"Nobody sent me," she told him honestly. "I'm here on a mission. You still owe me for the bet you lost for the Cotton Bowl. I'm here to collect."

He blinked. Gave his head a shake. "Excuse me?"

"Our bet. I won. You lost. I had Alabama and you took Texas Tech. The Crimson Tide won thirteen to ten. The stakes were a favor to be named later. At the time I intended to make you help me move but then . . . well . . . it didn't work out. So, now I need a favor and I'm calling in the bet."

"Lori. That's crazy. That was a million years ago."

"You may have changed in a lot of ways, Timberlake, but you don't squelch on a bet."

His brow lowered and his eyes narrowed to slits. "So what's the favor?"

She pointed toward the dog. "He needs a foster home. Celeste brought him to me yesterday, and he's the most pitifully afraid dog I've ever seen. The immediate problem is that it's tourist season in Eternity Springs, which means it's fireworks season. The show last night at Angel's Rest almost drove the poor thing insane. You're the perfect solution."

"Oh, no." He held up his hands, palms out. "No. No. No. I am not adopting that dog."

"I'm not asking you to adopt him. I need you to give him a foster home until we can find the perfect forever home for him."

"No. Absolutely not."

Matter-of-factly, she continued as if he had not spoken. "Someone will want him. He's a puppy. Puppies are easy to place. But right now he's simply too skittish to qualify for adoption. He needs basic care and some time to grow up a bit away from the hustle and bustle of town."

"Hustle and bustle. In Eternity Springs. Right."

Lori ignored his protests. Strategically, her best bet was to get out of here ASAP, so she walked around to the back of her SUV. Hinges squeaked as he opened the door of the yurt. Before she'd opened the SUV's back door and removed a wire crate from inside, Chase exited the yurt again. She quickly set the crate on the ground, and as she reached for the box of supplies, the crunch of gravel beneath his feet warned of his approach.

He'd added sandals to his attire.

Another man might look foolish dressed only in worn leather sandals and baggy shorts and wearing a scowl. Chase made Lori think of a mountain lion, sleek and graceful and dangerous. Without hesitation, she shoved the box into his arms. "Here're food, bowls, a leash, puppy pads, toys, and a bed. Oh, and three boxes of treats. He's partial to the bacon ones."

"Dammit, Lori."

He took a step backward, but he didn't drop the box. Quickly, she slammed the SUV's door shut. Wouldn't do to give him the chance to redeposit the box in the back.

"He doesn't have a name yet, so you need to choose one. That's the way our system works. We will use the name you choose for tracking purposes." The puppy scampered back toward them and weaved his way around her legs. Lori bent down and scooped him up. "Of course, the family who adopts him will be free to change it, though we've discovered that oftentimes they don't. So choose wisely."

"I'm not taking care of this dog!" Chase insisted. He set down the box. "I'm barely managing to take care of myself!"

Tough love, Murphy, Lori told herself.

"Then it will do you good to have someone else to think about, Timberlake. Have him sleep in his crate. He'll feel safer, and you'll sleep easier knowing he's not getting into mischief." She shoved the pup at him and let go. As she'd known he would, Chase caught him. "I'll be back in a week to check on him. You two have fun."

She hurried to climb into the SUV, and as a precautionary measure, she locked the doors. Just in time, too, because he tried the passenger door as she fired up the engine.

"Dammit, Lori!" he repeated. He banged on the window with his fist.

Lori grinned and finger-waved, put the van in gear, and spun her tires as she left. Just before she made the first curve that obstructed her view of the yurt, she glanced in her rearview mirror. Chase held the wiggling puppy out at arm's length, and he appeared to be lecturing the dog. Even this far away, she could see the red scratches on his chest. "That's what you get for parading around bare-chested where any trespassing female can see."

She fastened her attention on the road ahead, though her thoughts remained on the man — and mutt — she'd left behind. All in all, it had gone better than expected. Maybe, just maybe, Celeste's little found dog would prove to be the medicine Chase Timberlake needed.

What had just happened?

Chase stared from the wriggling puppy he held to the dust stirred up by Lori Murphy's spinning tires. What *the hell* had just happened?

"She dumped a dog on me. That's what just happened."

Without taking his gaze from the curve where Lori had disappeared, he set the dog onto the ground. Anger flared like a match strike. That woman had more nerve than a root canal. Who did she think she was? What kind of veterinarian was she? Dumping puppies on unsuspecting men! Did she do this sort of nonsense often? What made her think it was all right to waltz in here like nothing was wrong, dump a dog on him, then give a little smart-assed finger wave and speed off?

Chase slowly straightened, his anger abruptly draining away. He absently rubbed the scratches on his chest. "She waltzed in here like nothing is wrong. Huh."

She didn't ask how he was doing. There'd been no questions about what had happened or why he was living at the yurt or why he refused to leave it. Huh.

She'd treated him . . . normally. Nobody had treated him normally since he had crossed paths with the Callahan search team while making his way out of hell.

Chase glanced down at the mutt, who had begun to climb his ankles. "The least she could have done was trim those razors that are attached to your paws."

He gave his leg a gentle shake, dislodging the dog, and eyed the box she'd unloaded. He didn't have to let this stand. He could carry the supplies and Captain Claw here to his parents' house and return the whole enchilada to Eternity Springs within the hour.

Except, Lori had treated him normally. She didn't spend long minutes searching his expression with eyes filled with worry like his father. Her voice wasn't choked with emotion when she spoke to him like his mom. She hadn't acted perkily out of character like Lana.

She'd trusted him to care for the mutt.

From Lori Murphy, DVM, that showed a phenomenal amount of trust.

Her stubbornness was the stuff of which legends were made, but then, so was her compassion. Lori had a gold-plated healing heart when it came to four-legged animals. She wasn't Mother Teresa with the two-legged variety, but she was still more caring than just about any female of his acquaintance. With the exception of her response to her father during those early months following his return to Eternity Springs, Chase couldn't think of anyone whom Lori treated with anything less than kindness.

She hadn't been kind to him just now . . . or had she?

She'd believed in him.

He clung to the thought like . . . Captain Claw's paws.

"A week," he murmured. She'd said she'd be back in a week. He imagined it would be easier to keep the damned dog a week than to make a trip into town where he'd have to speak to people.

The dog scratched his calf. "No!" he said, giving the pup the stink eye. The little floppy ears perked up. A little pink tongue slid out of his mouth and his tail wagged a mile a minute. The cute factor was ridiculous.

With a heavy sigh, he picked up the supply box and carried it into the yurt. The puppy followed, right on his heels. The first thing he did upon entering the structure was pee on the wooden floor. It was a warning of things to come.

By noon, Chase was considering abandoning the name Captain Claw in favor of

Captain Havoc. The puppy could give Lori's dad's dog, Mortimer, a run for his money. Right under Chase's eye, he'd managed to chew up the grip of a fishing pole, pee on one of Chase's running shoes, and rip a five-inch tear in the bedsheet. After a lunch of the leftover pasta primavera his mother had brought over last night, he put the pup in the crate and crawled into bed for his afternoon nap.

The past few days, Chase had indulged in long afternoon naps — following an extended morning nap. He'd had trouble getting out of bed at all during the day. For some weird reason, the nightmares didn't plague him as much when he slept during the day.

He pulled his pillow over his head to drown out the pup's whimpers and whines. It didn't work. After a good five minutes of the nerve-grating noise, Chase jerked the pillow aside, lifted his head from the mattress, and glared at the mutt. "I'll bet Edvard Munch used one of your ancestors for inspiration for *The Scream.*"

He rolled out of bed and decided to take the dog for a walk. "You can call me Drill Sergeant Timberlake. I'm going to march you until you drop."

Despite the threats, that's not what happened. After hiking for the better part of an hour, the dog continued to go strong. He made Chase tired just watching him.

The exercise did Chase good. Despite his weariness and the lack of sleep, when he took a seat at a spot with a nice view of the valley and Eternity Springs below, he felt more rested than he'd felt in weeks. When the pup climbed up onto his lap and settled down to sleep, a sniffy little snore coming from his snout, Chase absently scratched him behind the ears and let his mind drift.

Lori had sure looked pretty this morning. She'd always been appealing, but the girl-next-door look she'd had about her in high school had matured into a natural beauty that made a man think about snuggling in a sleeping bag at sunrise.

She wasn't as in-your-face beautiful as Lana, and he couldn't picture her wearing an evening gown and standing at a craps table in Monte Carlo. But honestly, that whole scene had lost what little appeal it had had for him in the past. Not that Lana had dragged him into it kicking and screaming. High-stakes gambling on the French Riviera was a thrill sport of its own, and Chase had enjoyed the experience. Once. He couldn't imagine doing it again.

But then, he couldn't imagine doing much

of anything. Except maybe hiking over to Lover's Leap and taking a running jump off the cliff. Or going for that swim in Reunion Lake that sounded so tempting.

It would be the easy way out. Too easy. He could never do that to his family and friends. He'd already caused them enough grief as it was. He'd assured his father of that just yesterday when Mac came by the yurt, rousted him out of bed to go fishing, and eventually confessed his concerns about Chase's mental health.

Captain lifted his head, looked at Chase with solemn brown eyes, and licked his hand. Chase took a ridiculous amount of comfort from the little pup's action. He realized that sometime during the past few hours something within him had started to thaw.

"Leave it to Lori," he murmured. His little healer. Except, she wasn't his any longer, was she?

The thought gave his heart a twist, which was downright sorry of him. After all, he was still engaged to marry another woman — on the Fourth of July, apparently. He'd better begin working up some enthusiasm for the idea. After all, she was ready to change her whole life for him, wasn't she?

Because she feels guilty. Almost as guilty as I do.

That thought led him right back down the road to hell.

He awoke to a bloodred dawn and the certainty that he'd screwed up. After four days and three nights of near constant movement, he'd sat down and slept. Hard. Cautiously easing out from behind the boulder that had provided concealment, he looked around. It was quiet. The stillness was different. It was as if he were the only living being left alive.

They'd moved out during the night. He'd slept right through it. Oh, God, I've lost them.

On a mountainside in Colorado, Chase fought nausea that suddenly churned in his stomach. Abruptly, he set Captain down on the ground and stood. "We've sat on our asses long enough. Time to get back and chop some wood."

Never mind that he already had a wood-pile tall enough for three winters — long, bitter winters — he found that swinging an axe and sweating battled off the daylight nightmares as good as just about anything.

He ended up carrying Captain two thirds of the way back to the site of the yurt. The dog explored the clearing while he chopped his wood, and when Chase went inside to shower, he put him in the crate so that he wouldn't emerge from the bathroom to discover he'd clawed his way through the yurt's canvas.

The sound of the water almost drowned out the puppy's cries. Almost.

The rest of the day and the next passed in a haze of puppy care, proving to Chase that his parents had always been right with the advice they gave to potential dog owners — get one that's at least a year old. He solved the crate-crying problem by letting Captain sleep with him. The pup didn't move once he snuggled up against Chase, who got the best night's sleep that he'd had in weeks.

And his heart thawed, just a little bit.

Lori had included a couple of tennis balls in the supply box, and on the afternoon of the seventh day Captain's retriever blood showed itself. He figured out how to play fetch.

The pup's delight in the game was contagious. Something a little magical happened.

Chase laughed aloud.

CHAPTER TEN

With the Memorial Day weekend behind them and the summer tourist season in full swing, Lori's schedule at the clinic kicked into high gear. The steady stream of appointments kept her so busy that she rose early in the morning and fell asleep late at night and didn't have a moment to spare to fret about Eternity Springs's newest citizens.

Until late in the week when a no-show appointment finally gave her time to grab a bite of lunch and check her messages, and she found a long, bombshell text message from Caitlin on her phone. So, Chase's sister was on her way to Denver with Ali and Lana to go wedding-gown shopping because a new wedding date had been set.

"July Fourth," Lori murmured. Huh. First Valentine's Day, now the Fourth of July. Lana must really have a thing for holidays.

Of course, Chase liked holidays, too. Lori would never forget how silly he got about the community Easter egg hunt in Davenport Park. The man always volunteered to be in charge of hiding the eggs, and like a general preparing for battle, he would devise detailed plans for each of the three different age classes of hunters. He had a baseball cap equipped with tall, pink and white rabbit ears that he'd wear during the hunts. He'd wander the field helping the little ones and giving the older kids a hard time.

He'd been in Chizickstan on Easter this year. She wondered if he'd spared a thought for rabbit hats and plastic eggs and chocolate bunnies. Her freshman year at A&M he'd sent her a three-foot-tall chocolate bunny.

Yes, the man should marry on a holiday. *Except, he shouldn't be marrying a reality TV star.*

The chime on her office door announced the arrival of her next appointment. Lori was glad for the distraction. However, at the end of her workday, she decided she needed to spend a little time with her own unsettled thoughts, so she loaded her kayak into her SUV and drove to Hummingbird Lake. She found time spent on the water both relaxing and soothing, and in light of the day's news, she could use a dose of both. She needed to make peace once and for all with the fact that Chase was getting married.

She launched the kayak from the fishing pier and began to paddle the circumference of the lake. Immediately, the water began to work for her and her spirit began to settle.

What a weird start she'd had to this new beginning of hers. When she'd decided to accept Nic's offer regarding the practice and move back to Eternity Springs, never in a million years would she have thought that Chase would be living here, too. Two streets down and one block over from her, if they moved into the old Carpenter place like rumor had it.

Not that Lori expected they would be there for long. Chase had come home to heal, but he'd get his mojo back and then they'd be off again. In the meantime, Lori had to figure a way to move beyond any awkwardness that would arise from running across Lana or Chase at a mutual friend's house or in the grocery store.

The thought startled her, and that quickly, her calm disappeared. Oh, jeez. She'd first met Chase in the grocery aisle at the Trading Post. Her teenaged heart had fallen a little bit in love with him at first sight. What if she ran into him among the canned vegetables again?

Fresh is best anyway. Just don't buy canned.

You don't even like canned veggies. Stay in the fresh produce aisle! Or if you're desperate, go frozen! Everyone should have a bag of peas in their freezer to use as an ice pack if needed. It's basic first aid!

First aid? She blew out a sigh of self-disgust and dug her paddle into the water. *Seriously, get over yourself, Murphy.* Avoidance only made the situation worse. She *needed* to run into him in the canned vegetable aisle. Face the problem and deal with it.

"Like a vaccination," she murmured as the orange kayak glided silently forward. That's how she would think of it. She needed to deal with the situation — with them — in short little shots. That was how vaccines worked. A person took little doses of dead virus so that the body developed antibodies and thus immunity to them. She could think of it as the C&L vaccine.

Pitiful, Murphy. You're just pitiful.

She paddled hard for a few minutes, chasing off her demons, and searching once again for that elusive peace until a familiar voice hailed her. "Lori! Careful, dear! There's a submerged log about ten feet from your bow."

"Yikes! Oh, wow!" Lost in her own thoughts, Lori hadn't noticed Celeste pro-

221

pelling toward her. The older woman paddled a sparkly gold kayak that was uniquely Celeste Blessing. As usual, just seeing her made Lori smile. She dug her paddle in the water and changed course, avoiding the submerged log and steering toward her friend. "Thanks, Celeste!"

"You're welcome. I just happened to notice it. I'd have hated for you to bump it and tip over. Hummingbird Lake stays unbearably cold all year long. Remember that Fourth of July after your father came home? The kayak race?"

Lori laughed. "Oh, yes. I'll never forget that day. Mom and Dad both ended up in the drink." And she'd ended up a basket case after discovering that her mother was sleeping with the enemy — Cam Murphy.

Without verbal communication, the two women turned their kayaks and began to paddle in the same direction. Lori idly thought that spending time with Celeste was like a double dose of being on the water. The woman soothed just by being near.

"You had a terrible frown on your face before I hailed you, sweetheart. Want to talk about it?"

No. She absolutely didn't. That didn't explain why she suddenly ran on from the mouth. "You know that Chase and I were . . . close."

"He was your first love."

My only love. "Yes."

"You are a little nervous about him and his wife living in Eternity Springs."

"Yes!"

"You are trying to figure out how to approach the situation."

"Are you a fortune-teller?"

Her laughter rang out across the sapphire blue of the lake. "I'm simply observant."

Not simply observant, Lori thought. Uncanny. Prescient. Wise. So ridiculously wise. "How do I handle this, Celeste? Eternity Springs is my home. If it were a big city I could go about my business and not worry about running into him when we both reach for a can of corn. But it's not a big city. It's a small town. I can't avoid them. I don't *want* to avoid them. I want it to be easy and natural and not tear my heart in two."

"Completely understandable."

"So, what do I do? How do I make that happen?"

"Oh, darling. You don't need me to tell you this. You know."

"I don't —"

"Sure you do. Robert Louis Stevenson said it best: 'A friend is a gift you give

223

yourself.' "

Out of the blue, tears stung Lori's eyes. She blinked them away. "I should have taken the job in Seattle."

"Bosh." Kindness and compassion gleamed in Celeste's blue-eyed gaze. "No one ever said that being a small-town girl was easy, but I have total faith that you will rise to the challenge, dear. Look at your forebears. You are both a Murphy and a Reese. Your roots are sunk deep into the soil of Eternity Springs, and you will stand as strong as the mountain that holds your family name. Don't doubt yourself."

"It's hard."

"Life isn't meant to be easy." Celeste pulled her paddle from the water and rested it across the kayak. She waited until Lori met her gaze to add, "But at the same time, you must draw upon lessons of the past and stand strong against the winds of adversity. Generosity of heart provides nutrients to the soil in which grow the roots of strength."

Lori wished she had a piece of paper and pen to write the sentiment down. Sometimes Celeste's advice took study to thoroughly understand. This, she feared, was one of those times. Winds of adversity. Generosity of heart. *I hope I remember.*

"Now, I must paddle on. I'm meeting the

Turners for a burger at Murphy's Pub tonight. Enjoy the rest of your evening, love."

"You, too, Celeste," Lori said absently.

She watched the older woman paddle away at a speed that belied her age. Lori could only hope that she was half the athlete that Celeste was when she was her age. *And just how old is she, anyway?*

Old enough to have stored up enough wisdom to fill Hummingbird Lake and the charm to impart it without coming across as lecturing. Funny. If her mother had said exactly the same thing as Celeste, it probably would have made more sense — but it wouldn't have made nearly as big of an impression. If her dad had said it . . . forget it. No way would Cam Murphy use any sort of language that even brushed upon lyrical.

Celeste managed to say just the right thing in exactly the right way. Because even though her advice today was a bit convoluted and less than clear, she'd managed to help Lori figure out how to solve her problem.

She needed to continue what she'd begun by taking the puppy to Chase. She needed to be Chase's friend. Chase *and* Lana's friend. Period.

Lori filled her cheeks with air then blew

out a harsh breath. Lovers to friends, rather than the other way around. Not the usual story twist, true, but doable.

Necessary.

Maybe in the next couple of weeks or so Chase's recovery from his ordeal would have reached the point where he was ready for a double date with her and — well . . . hmm. She hadn't been on a single real date since moving home. Brick would step up and fill in if she asked him, but she hated to use the man. Besides, from a couple of comments he'd let slip on their trip to Durango on Saturday, a newcomer to town had caught his notice.

Probably what she should do is begin by inviting Lana to lunch or maybe for happy hour at Murphy's Pub.

Happy hour. That sounded like a better idea. *I could arrive a little early and belt back some liquid courage.*

A wry smile on her lips, Lori dipped her paddle back into the cold, blue waters of Hummingbird Lake. Friends with Lana Wilkerson. Who'da thunk it? Excluding anything Timberlake related, could they possibly find any common interests? Was Lana an animal person? Lori had never heard any mention of Lana and pets. Wonder what she would think about Chase's new position as a temporary foster dad?

Maybe they could talk about the outdoors. Except, Lana would probably find this kayak ride as boring as could be. For Lori, it was just about perfect. Lana made a living challenging nature. Lori found contentment in experiencing it.

Okay, so maybe another subject might work better. Wonder if Lana was a foodie? Lori didn't bake like her mother, but she loved to experiment in the kitchen. In the past few years, she'd grown to be an excellent cook. And she knew her cheeses, too. Wines, to a point. Okay, she had somewhere to start.

Friendship with Lana Wilkerson soon-to-be Timberlake.

"If I pull this thing off, I'll have earned a feather for my angel's wings."

Two feathers, she decided at the end of the week when she started up to Heartache Falls in order to keep the promised visit with Chase and the dog. Caitlin had called this morning to confirm the dinner they'd planned for this evening, and she'd hesitantly asked if Lori would mind if Lana tagged along.

"I never thought I'd feel sorry for her, but I do," Caitlin had confessed. "The whole bridal gown shopping trip was just sad. She got a gorgeous dress and she looks fabulous, but . . . I don't know . . . she's a little desperate."

Lori had pictured herself in her kayak on Hummingbird Lake and told Caitlin she'd love to have Lana join them.

She played Celtic spa music during her drive, which turned out to be a good thing because when she made the second-to-last hairpin turn before the turnoff to the yurt, she discovered a car pulled over on the side of the road.

Lana. With a flat tire. Looking a bit perplexed. *The woman parasails off the side of mountains. Surely she knows how to change a tire.*

Well, Lori couldn't very well drive right by her. It was time to meet her demons and wrestle them into submission. She braked to a stop behind Lana and opened her car door. "Need some help?"

"Hi, Lori." Lana looked relieved. "I have a flat tire. I was just trying to decide if I should change it myself or ask Chase to do it. I thought it might be good to give him something to do. I worry about him. He doesn't seem to have much . . . energy. What do you think?"

Lori hesitated. "From things Caitlin has said, I think he sounds depressed."

"I know. I've tried to talk to him about seeing a counselor. So have his parents — more than once. We thought we'd give him some time, but if this lethargy lingers too much longer, I think we'll insist."

And under the circumstances, you think it's a good idea for him to get married right away? But that wasn't a question Lori had the nerve or the right to ask aloud. Mac and Ali must think it's okay or Ali wouldn't have taken Lana wedding-gown shopping. Instead, Lori said, "Caitlin told me she worries that he sits and broods. That's why I brought a stray dog up here for him to foster. I thought having a puppy around might pull him out of his funk."

"I've met the dog." Lana's lack of enthusiasm was obvious. "I'm not a pet person, I'm afraid."

That's just plain sad.

"Fostering is temporary." Lori explained about the pup's skittishness and the fireworks in town, then added, "I think changing your tire might do Chase some good. I'm headed to the yurt to check on the puppy. Why don't you ride with me?"

"Okay. Thanks."

As they climbed into the car, Lori could almost feel feathers popping onto her wings. A few minutes later, they pulled up to the parking area beside the yurt. "I hope he's not still in bed this time of the day," Lana murmured.

"I don't think so," Lori replied, and the sound of yips and yaps reached her ears. "Listen."

They followed the happy puppy noises toward a nearby rise, beyond which stretched a rolling alpine meadow. What they found there surpassed even Lori's hopes.

Chase wore boots, jeans, and a flannel shirt over a T-shirt. Sometime since her last visit, he'd shaved. And now he drew back his arm and threw a yellow tennis ball into the meadow. The puppy raced after it. Retrieved it. Returned it to Chase. "Attaboy, Captain!"

"Oh, my God," Lana murmured. "He's smiling. He just laughed! Is that not one of the most beautiful sounds you've ever heard?"

"Yes, it is," Lori agreed.

Score one for the veterinarian.

Movement to his right caught Chase's attention and he was startled to see his visitors. He'd expected Lori to show up sometime today — she always kept her word — but he didn't anticipate that she'd arrive with Lana. He didn't like the disappointment he experienced when seeing them together.

Lana rushed toward him, her expression filled with delight. "Oh, Chase. It's so wonderful to hear you laugh."

She threw her arms around him, hugging him hard, and Chase stiffened. He put his hands on her upper arms, not returning her embrace, exactly. Something closer to gently pushing her away. "I thought you went to Denver?"

"We got back last night. It was a great trip. I had a really nice time with your mother and sister."

"That's good."

She explained about her flat tire and told him the car's location. He said he'd change it, then turned his head and met Lori's gaze. "You came to pick up your dog? You've found a home for him?"

"No. Just checking to see how you and your foster are doing. So, you've named him Captain?"

Chase's lips twisted. "More or less."

"Any problems? He's eating and sleeping okay?"

No way did he intend to admit that he let the dog sleep in his bed. "He never shuts up. Did you bring a muzzle for him?"

231

"What? Are you afraid his barking is disturbing the neighbors?" She took an exaggerated look around. When he narrowed his eyes and scowled at her, she laughed and knelt beside Captain who bounded over to her and started licking her hand. "Aren't you the cutest thing? Smart, too. How long did it take you to teach him to fetch the ball, Chase?"

"No time at all." It was ridiculous how much pride he felt at the answer.

"He is cute for a dog," Lana said, making an obvious effort. "Look at all the shades of gold in his coat. Wish my hairdresser could copy that look."

Lori smiled. "That would be one expensive hair appointment. Long, too."

Chase shifted uncomfortably. Something about seeing Lana and Lori together and acting friendly bothered him, but he couldn't put his finger on exactly what. He was glad when Lori stood and faced him.

"Seriously," she said. "Do you have any issues or questions about his care?"

He shoved his hands in the back pockets of his jeans. "Actually, I'd like you to take a look at his left front paw. He got into some brambles yesterday. I think I got all the thorns out, but he's been favoring that paw some."

While Lori examined all of Captain's feet, Chase asked a few other questions about puppy care. He hunkered down beside her to point out a concerning bump he'd noticed on Captain's belly, and as she explained away the bulge, a sudden gust of breeze brought the scent of her wafting over him. Her shampoo, her soap, the fragrance that was uniquely Lori. The familiarity of it all but knocked the breath right out of him.

Yearning washed over him. Yearning for the life, for the love, he'd once had. For the person he'd been before events on the other side of the world changed him forever.

Lori's gaze met his and something of what he was feeling must have shown in his eyes because she suddenly looked startled. Abruptly, she shot to her feet. Chase slowly rose, his stare never leaving hers.

"I'm glad Captain is doing well," she said, her voice sounding a little tight. "I need to be going."

Captain bounded toward Lori, then got distracted by his tail and turned in a circle. Ignoring the dog, Chase reached out and touched her arm. "Lori, I . . ."

I what? Don't want you to go? Don't want to hurt like this anymore?

"Thanks for the ride, Lori," Lana interjected, using that damned falsely perky

233

voice that grated so on his nerves.

Lana. Chase shut his eyes. Guilt washed over him. Craving Lori right in front of Lana? Is that the sort of jerk he'd become?

Maybe. He didn't really know who the hell he was. Jerk? Failure?

Killer?

Reflexively, his hand formed a fist and he could all but feel the knife hilt in his grasp and the drag of flesh against the blade as he sliced and plunged. Jerk. Failure. Killer.

Avenger.

God, help me. When he opened his eyes again, Lori was gone and Lana stood cuddling the puppy, watching him with a stormy expression. She hated dogs. What the hell was she doing here? Damn, he was tired. Exhausted. He wanted to crawl into his bed and sleep . . . forever.

Instead, he made his first effort with Lana since they'd fought about the Markhor Pass shoot in Chizickstan. "So, how was Denver? Did you find your dress?"

Storm clouds dissipated and she offered up a hesitant smile. "I did. Your mother is such a sweetheart. You are awfully lucky when it comes to parents, Chase."

"Yeah. I know that."

"I found a gorgeous dress and picked out one for your sister to wear — she'll be my

234

maid of honor, of course. We also found a cake topper. Your mother isn't going to make our wedding cake. She and Caitlin convinced me that I should take up Maggie Romano's offer of an Italian cream cake."

Chase's throat suddenly tightened. The famous cake. Was there anything that better symbolized an Eternity Springs wedding, Eternity Springs's relationships, than Maggie Romano's cake? He murmured, "It's why I wanted to get married in Eternity Springs."

"A cake? Seriously, is it that good?"

No, not the cake. The promise of it. The community, the ideals, the sense that no matter how crazy the world has gone elsewhere, in Eternity Springs, honesty and integrity and responsibility matter. Compassion and forgiveness and generosity are on display daily. And the thing that keeps the world of Eternity Springs spinning? Love.

Love that isn't always perfect, but one that endures.

Enduring love, like what you feel for Lori.

Damn. Chase rubbed the back of his neck. He was so screwed up.

"I have an appointment with Celeste Blessing later today." Captain began to wriggle and Lana set him on the ground. "She told me she has a storeroom full of antiques that would be perfect to furnish our little cottage in town."

Antiques? The woman who furnished their entire Manhattan apartment in European Modern was talking antiques? Talk about screwed up. This wasn't the Lana Wilkerson he knew and, yes, loved.

Because he did love her. Maybe not in the same way he had before . . . everything. Maybe not the way a man should love the woman he promised to marry. Chase thought it entirely possible that he never could love anyone with a whole heart again. To love with a whole heart, one's heart must be whole, correct?

"What are we doing, Lana?"

She misunderstood the question. "Well, your mom mentioned that they keep mountain bikes up here. I wouldn't mind going for a ride. First, though, we should probably go change my flat."

For an instant, he hovered at the edge of the conversational cliff, ready to make the leap. In the end, cowardice won out. Again. "You're right. I'll take care of it, though. You don't have to come with me."

"I want to help. Besides, I have something for you in my car. I picked up a gift and I'm totally excited to give it to you."

She started down the road. Burying a sigh,

Chase fell in beside her, his thoughts in turmoil. He needed to get his crap together. He couldn't let this fairy tale Lana was building continue, and not because of the complicated feelings he had for Lori, either. He needed to get his head on straight because he did still care about Lana, and this "happy small-town housewife" thing she had going on concerned him.

Caring. Concern. Love.

Whoa. Those were emotions. He didn't want to feel emotions. He couldn't. He needed the ice around his heart. It was protecting him. If the ice melted, what would hold off the guilt? The grief?

Chase's stomach made a slow, sick flip. Hell, maybe he'd been wrong about this whole thing from the git-go. Maybe he shouldn't be anywhere near Eternity Springs and its magic. Maybe after he changed Lana's tire, they should load up and return to Manhattan. He'd drop the dog off at Lori's on the way.

Upon reaching the car, Chase made quick work of changing the tire while Lana continued to rattle on about wedding plans. She never once mentioned Thrill-seekers, and for the first time since leaving Chizickstan, Chase found himself wondering about it. Out of the blue, he asked, "Has the show been canceled?"

Lana stiffened and darted him a glance. "We're officially on hiatus. The crew needed to work, and we couldn't leave them hanging."

"Everyone found work?"

"Yes."

"That's good." He stowed the jack in the trunk and pushed the lid shut. Glancing at Lana, he saw that her expression had grown pensive. Was she thinking about the loss of her show or the loss of two of her crew? She wasn't a cold woman. The events in the mountains had not left her emotionally unscathed. Chase had been so wrapped up in his own trauma that he hadn't spared her psychological state any thought until today.

She's as screwed up as I am. After all, she's picking out bedspreads for a house in Eternity Springs.

Catching his look, Lana gave her head a little shake, then beamed a bright smile his way. "Thank you. I have to admit that tire-changing is not on my list of favorite things to do. Gift-giving, on the other hand, is something else entirely."

She opened the backseat of the car and removed a square gift box tied with a ribbon and sporting a big red bow on top.

Excitement and anticipation glittered in her eyes.

It's wrong. This whole thing is wrong.

"There was a shop just down the street from the bridal salon your mother took me to," she said. "I thought it was a sign. The owner was extremely helpful and I'm fairly certain I got the right things. Once I decided to do it, I called around to people we know and got recs, but it will be no problem to exchange anything that isn't what you want."

"Lana —"

"Open your gift, Chase."

She shoved the box at him, and coward that he was, he allowed the distraction. He tugged the ribbon, opened the lid, looked inside and froze.

A camera. She'd given him a damned camera.

Blood. Warm and thick and pungent with the scent of copper, it soaked his clothes, his hands, even his hair. His breath came in harsh, shallow pants and his heartbeat continued to thunder. The physical exertion of the past hour and a half had been beyond anything he'd ever experienced. Now, as he stood at the precipice of the rocky cliff, the victorious predator over his kill, he lifted his face toward the sky and roared out his pain, his

x

239

grief, his fury, and his triumph.

Then with one last heave, one final shout, he threw his camera off the cliff.

Chase hurled the gift box away. "No!"

Then he turned and walked — ran — away.

CHAPTER ELEVEN

Running in hiking boots and blue jeans was almost as foolish as attempting to outrun his demons. What Chase needed to do was to stop, turn around, and give those demons hell.

Yeah, well. He needed to turn back time, too. That was just about as likely.

His friends wore jumpsuits. Blood orange. Orange and bloody. Shutter click. Shutter click. Shutter click. Hands tied behind their backs. Was Bradley limping? Shutter click. Shutter click. Shutter click. Faces bruised and swollen. Broken noses. Busted lips. Focus on the mouth. Shutter click. Shutter click. Our Father who art in Heaven.

Chase muttered an expletive and stopped in the middle of the dirt road, panting hard, sounding like an out-of-shape tourist trying to pedal a bike up Sinner's Prayer Pass. He bent over, resting his hands on his knees, as Lana caught up with him. "Don't you dare run away from me," she challenged, a sharp edge to her voice. "I've just about had it with you, Michael Chase Timberlake."

She'd said the same damned thing to him that fateful day in Chizickstan. Hearing it now pushed his temper over the edge.

Chase whirled on her and exploded. "Then go! Leave. I didn't ask you to come here. I didn't ask you to stay. I damned sure didn't ask you to buy a house in town and become BFFs with my former lover!"

The color drained from Lana's face, and from the corner of his eyes, he saw Captain dart away from him and crawl beneath a nearby bush. Both things served to stoke his temper.

She'd had it? Well, so had he! It was always about her, what she wanted, what she needed to accomplish, what she required. Hype, photo ops, ratings. Always the damned ratings.

"You should have listened, Lana," he yelled, his hands fisting at his sides. "You never listen to me. Why don't you listen to me! They'd all still be alive if you'd listened to me!"

"Don't you think I know that?" she fired right back. "It haunts me!" Tears flooded her eyes and slipped down her cheeks. "I know it's my fault and I'd change it if I

242

could, but I can't bring them back! I've been doing what I can. I'm living in Eternity Springs."

"And what the hell does that have to do with anything?"

"I'm trying to fix what I can fix. I'm trying to be what you want. What you need."

"You don't know what I need. You always assume you do, but you don't. You bought me a damned camera. The very last thing I need is a camera."

"Why? I don't understand. Talk to me, Chase. Tell me what happened to you!"

To me? Nothing had happened to him. The blood wasn't his. Not the blood he'd watched erupt from the safety of his hiding place, through the magnified power of his camera lens. Not the blood, warm and sticky and coppery, that coated his hand.

Bile rose in Chase's throat. "I won't talk about it."

"Why not?"

When he didn't respond, a frustrated whine emerged from her throat. "Chase, please. If you don't tell me, I can't help you."

"No one can help me, Lana." It was true. There was no help, no cure, no moving past. He couldn't turn back the clock and choose not to get on that godforsaken helicopter.

"Then I can't fix it, can I?" Her voice sounded as broken as his heart. "I can't fix us. This won't work, will it? You will never forgive me."

"This isn't about you, Lana. I'll never forgive myself."

Her lips twisted. "It's a version of the old 'It's not you, it's me' line, isn't it? I've used it myself a time or two."

He didn't respond to that and a full minute ticked by. Then, a second minute. Chase couldn't look at her. He knew where this was headed, where it needed to go, but he was too much of a bastard, a coward, to broach the subject himself.

Finally, Lana spoke again. "Why didn't you tell me to stay in New York? Why let me come to Colorado?"

Chase still didn't speak, but by now, she didn't appear to expect it. She continued, "You don't care one way or another, do you? Not about anything."

Or maybe I care too much. You're a reminder. Of the crap that went down. Of the terrible choice I made.

"I've thought a lot about the mistakes I made in this relationship of ours. I do think that when we first got together, I was the right woman for you. My strengths supported your weaknesses and vice versa. We

244

made a good team. A great team. Life was fun and exciting — a wild ride. We were happy together, Chase. Do you remember that?"

"I do."

"When did it change?"

He didn't have to think about it. "When the show hit."

She nodded. "I began to find TV ratings more thrilling than the adventures we filmed. My focus shifted. Yours really didn't. It was always about the adventure for you, never the show, wasn't it?"

"I felt the life we had slipping away." He hadn't wanted that to happen. It had happened once before, and he didn't want it to happen to him again.

"So you asked me to marry you."

He'd never asked Lori. "I loved you."

"I loved you, too. Notice how we both used the past tense there? I see now that I put the show ahead of you and look what happened. I made a terrible decision that cost two good men their lives. I have their blood on my hands."

As do I.

"It's something I'll have to live with the rest of my life."

It was the crux of their problems. She had allowed ratings to rule their lives and she now had to live with it, as did he.

"You were right, Chase. I should have listened to you."

"Lana, I —"

"Let me get this out, Chase. I need to say this. I need to try to explain. When word came that you were missing, I spent a lot of sleepless hours thinking about you and about us. About our relationship. About the show. I realized that I rarely put your wishes and desires ahead of my own. That's not love, Chase. I swore to myself that if you came out of those mountains alive, I'd change that. I'd be the woman you needed me to be."

"An Eternity Springs housewife?"

"Sounds silly when you say it like that, doesn't it?"

"You'd never be happy here, Lana. It was stupid of me to suggest it."

"I don't know. It is a very nice little town. I think I could be happy here — under the right circumstances. These aren't the right circumstances."

"You're a big-city girl, Lana."

"Yes. And that's not who you need right now. Oh, Chase. Don't you see? I was the woman you needed for a time in your life, but I'm not the woman you need for the rest of your life."

He quelled a bitter laugh. "Don't take this wrong, but a woman is the last thing I need right now."

"I don't know about that," she mused. "Nevertheless, I'm going to keep my promise and be the right woman for you."

She slipped the engagement ring off her finger and held it out to him. "And being the right woman means knowing when to walk away. You belong here, Chase. You need to heal here. Amid the forests and mountains. I thought I could help you, but I see now, it's better for both of us if I head back to New York. That's where I belong."

"Lana, I . . ." Chase let the sentence trail off. She was right. He couldn't dispute that. He couldn't bring himself to ask her to stay, because in the end, he knew this was best — for both of them.

She took his hand, placed the ring in his palm, and curled his fingers around it. "You will always own a piece of my heart."

Then she pressed a kiss against his knuckles. "Good-bye, Chase. Take care of yourself. Promise me that?"

"I'll try." He shoved his hands into his pants pockets and watched her walk away. Just before she topped the rise that would take her beyond his sight, he called, "Lana?"

The tears on her cheeks sparkled like the

diamond in his hand. "Yes?"

"It wasn't your fault."

Her mouth lifted with a tremulous smile. "Thank you for that."

A hollow sadness for what could have been washed through him. "Take care of yourself."

"I will. You, too, Timberlake."

When she was gone, he shoved his hands into his pockets and started to walk back toward the yurt. He was tired. Exhausted. He wanted more than anything to crawl into bed and crash. So, that's what he did.

Chase took a three-hour nap. Upon awakening, he rolled from the bed and stumbled toward the bathroom where he took a long, steamy shower. Only after he dried off, wrapped a towel around his waist, and stood staring into the mirror contemplating a shave did he remember the dog. The last time he'd seen the puppy he'd been quaking like an aspen in autumn.

Well, hell.

Dark clouds rolled over Sinner's Prayer Pass and as thunder reverberated through the valley, Lori was reminded of one of Celeste's sayings about summer storms in the valley. *It's like being in Heaven's bowling alley.*

She sat in the wooden swing on her front

porch, a glass of excellent cabernet in her hand, the sound track from *Last of the Mohicans* drifting through the open window. The scent of rain mingled with that of evergreen arrived with a cool breeze that brought a smile to her face. Moments like this were what she'd missed during her time away at college. The Rockies sang to her soul, and she was ever so glad of her decision to return home.

She lifted her glass of wine and toasted the storm. "Despite my new neighbors."

She'd made progress on that front today. Chase seemed to be a little more upbeat than before. Maybe Eternity Springs was working its magic on him. If that were the case then she was glad for him. And, she was glad for herself. It hadn't been easy to be a friend today, but she'd pulled it off. As a reward, she'd decided to indulge herself with wine, a long soak in a hot bath, and a novel. First, though, she intended to enjoy the tempest.

The first wave of the storm had blown in from the west on a southeasterly path and skirted most of the valley, but sheets of rain headed her way now. Rainfall was a blessing. It had been an unusually dry spring and early summer. They needed the moisture.

The first patter of raindrops spattered against the sidewalk, blowing toward her. Green awnings on the houses up the street began to flap in the wind. Pedestrians hurried to beat the downpour.

The sky opened up.

At the corner, a lone figure turned onto her street. She recognized him immediately. Chase. Walking down the middle of the street in the middle of a thunderstorm.

Carrying his dog wrapped in the flannel shirt she recognized from earlier that day.

He wore no rain gear. Just a white T-shirt and jeans. He looked as if he'd been out in a storm for days. Lori set down her empty wineglass and rose from the swing to stand at the porch rail just beyond the splash of rain. "What in the world is he doing?"

According to his sister, Chase had not made a trip back to town since taking up residence in his parents' yurt. What would bring him down the mountain now? And why was he walking?

"Oh, no." She put the clues together and drew the obvious conclusion. The dog. The dog must have gotten hurt and Chase must have driven him to the clinic, probably in the jeep the Timberlakes kept garaged at the yurt. He couldn't call the number listed on her after-hours emergency sign because chances were he didn't have a phone. He must have decided the easiest thing to do would be to try her house. Someone — Caitlin, probably — had mentioned where Lori lived.

She took two steps toward her front door, thinking she'd grab her raincoat and boots since she wasn't equipped to treat an injured animal here at home. A glance over her shoulder brought her up short. The expression on Chase's face made her think that *he* was the injured animal, not Captain.

So, she waited.

Chase turned up her front walk. As he drew close, she was able to get a better look at him. She gasped a breath.

His T-shirt wasn't simply wet. It was grimy, torn, and bloodied. A raw slash on his left cheek looked like a scrape. He had an ugly bruise on his upper arm. His gaze met hers, his eyes dark with an emotion she couldn't name. He stopped at the top of the walk just short of the steps. "I can't do this, Lori."

She studied the pup. No obvious sign of injury. No sound of distress. He appeared to cuddle snuggly in Chase's arms. "Can't do what?"

"Keep him."

"Why not?"

Lightning flashed and a large boom of thunder shook the neighborhood. Lori and Captain both started. Chase climbed two porch steps then leaned over and set the puppy at Lori's feet. That's when a rip in his T-shirt revealed the bloody mess of his skin on his belly.

While she stood frozen, absorbing what she'd seen, he turned and headed back toward the street.

The puppy whimpered. Lori hesitated, her gaze locked on Chase's retreating form. "Don't let him go," she murmured to herself. He was hurt. She might not know how to treat his emotional pain, but she could darn sure do something about his physical injuries.

Even as she stepped forward, the dog took the matter out of her hands by darting back into the rain. *Yap! Yap! Yap! Yap!* A moment later, Captain was nipping at Chase's heels.

Chase stopped, scooped the puppy up, then turned around and started back toward Lori. When he drew close, she challenged him. "Why can't you keep him, Timberlake? He obviously wants you to."

"I can't . . ." His voice broke and he looked away. A moment later, he tried again. "I can't be responsible for another life."

Lori wanted to run to him and hold him

and comfort him, but she'd dealt with enough wounded animals to know that wasn't the response this moment needed. So she nodded and opened her screen door. "Bring him inside."

Chase hesitated. Obviously, he wanted to set the puppy down and bolt a second time, but didn't trust the pup not to follow him again.

Firmly, she added, "He needs to be out of the weather, Chase." *So do you.*

He dragged his feet up the porch steps and preceded Lori into her house. Lori followed close behind, crowding him to step forward when he obviously intended to set the dog down and retreat again. "The kitchen is through the door on the right. Carry him there."

He moved forward, and she shut both the screen door and the front door behind them, then made a quick detour into the bathroom to grab towels for both the wet animals in her house. She found Chase standing in the middle of the kitchen. Both he and the puppy shuddered visibly. "What happened?"

"I scared him. He hid. I couldn't find him. I need you to keep him."

No, I don't think that's what you need at all.

Lori might be a newly minted DVM, but

she had enough experience to recognize that the injured party in her kitchen walked on two legs rather than four. She also knew skittish animals well enough to know that she would need to approach this one carefully if she intended to doctor his physical wounds.

Lori draped one towel over Chase's shoulder, then held out the other and gestured for him to hand her the dog. She was a little worried that Chase might take off the minute his arms were empty of wet puppy, so in an effort to prevent it, she fired questions at him in rapid succession while she briskly dried the dog.

"Is he injured?"

"Not that I could see, but —"

"Has he been drinking plenty of water?"

"Sure."

"How's his appetite?"

"He eats like a horse."

"Sleeping?"

Chase hesitated. "The crate hasn't exactly worked out."

"Oh?"

"He cried."

Lori glanced up at Chase, whose brow furrowed as he frowned down at the dog. "Don't tell me you let him sleep with you."

"It was the only way to get him to shut up."

"Oh, for heaven's sake, Chase." Shaking her head, Lori set aside the towel. Captain romped a few steps away, stopped, and shook while Lori pulled a plastic bowl from her cabinet. After she filled it with water and set it down for the dog, she turned to her other visitor.

Chase hadn't moved. The towel still lay draped over his shoulder. Water dripped from his clothes onto her kitchen floor. "Oh, for heaven's sake," she repeated. "You're bleeding all over my floor. Take off your shirt and let me clean you up."

"I'm fine. I'll leave now."

"You are not fine, and you are not leaving until I look at those scrapes and cuts. All I need is for one of them to get a raging infection and then word would get out that I didn't treat you. You know it would happen. People talk. They wouldn't trust me. You'd ruin my vet practice before it barely got started. You might as well change out of your wet jeans, too. Devin left some clothes in the bureau in the guest room. It's the first door on the left. Go change."

"No. I'll just go," he insisted. Lightning flashed and thunder cracked on top of his words. The puppy darted back toward Chase.

Lori folded her arms. "And heaven has spoken. You are not going anywhere until the storm blows over." She shooed him toward the hallway. "And bring back your wet things. I'll throw them in the dryer."

When he disappeared down the short hallway to the bedrooms, the pup on his heels, Lori allowed her concern to show. A cursory visual examination suggested the puppy was just fine. Chase, on the other hand, had looked almost tortured. What had happened to the smiling man she'd seen just this morning?

She retrieved her glass of wine from her front porch, set out a second glass for Chase, then pulled a new bottle of red from her wine fridge. He returned to the kitchen carrying his wet clothes and wearing a pair of her brother's gym shorts. A black and purple COLORADO ROCKIES T-shirt hung over one bare shoulder.

And what a bare shoulder it was. Lori had to work to keep from ogling him. However, as much as the female in her wanted to stand there gawking at the masculine gorgeousness in front of her, the black and purple bruise on his other broad, bare shoulder required the doctor's attention —

as did the scrapes, cuts, and one long, deep cut that needed stitches.

"You look like you fell down a mountain."

"I took a careless step."

Frowning, she motioned for him to take a seat at one of the stools in front of her breakfast bar. She removed a basket of first-aid supplies from a cabinet as Captain settled down at Chase's feet. "It's not like you to be careless."

"The dog was crying. I thought he'd been hurt."

Lori gently cleaned the scrapes and scratches and rubbed cream onto the bruises, calling upon countless hours of training to keep her hands steady and impersonal as she touched him.

Memories floated like ghosts on the edge of her mind and it took all the self-discipline she possessed to hold them at bay. True, once or twice her fingers lingered on his skin, and a time or two a dab with a cotton ball lengthened to a dawdle, but nevertheless, she managed. It helped that the thorough soaking he'd received meant the only scent she could detect on his skin was that of the antiseptic she applied.

Throughout her ministrations, Chase sat as still as an oak. His mind seemed to be a million miles away.

"What caused this cut?" she asked as she began to tackle the deep slice across his rib cage.

His lack of response supported her theory that his thoughts were elsewhere. She raised her voice and repeated the question. His gaze jerked toward her and he blinked. "Dead tree branch."

"It sliced you like a knife."

"No. You hardly feel a knife slice," he said, his tone flatly matter-of-fact. "The tree branch jabbed and jerked."

Lori's gaze climbed to the pink scar across his collarbone and her stomach turned over. *What happened to you over there, Chase?* "You are lucky it didn't stab and kill," she observed, as she thoroughly cleansed the wound, then set aside the first-aid kit in favor of supplies from her medical bag. "I'm going to suture it."

"Are you licensed to do that?" he asked, eyeing the hypodermic needle with wariness.

"I have my defense argument ready," she said, speaking without thinking. "How many times did you confess to being a dog?"

His gaze shot up to hers, startled surprise giving his eyes a flicker of life. Satisfied to have elicited a reaction, Lori focused on the task at hand and tried not to think about the past. She failed.

"Sex. Sex. Sex. That's all you think about," Lori teased when Chase grabbed her hand *and increased the length and speed of his stride as they exited the parking garage headed for her apartment. They'd already made love twice that day, and she suspected that had she had any food in the fridge, they might never have left the apartment.*

"What can I say?" he fired back, his tone unapologetic. "I'm a dog."

It had become part of their couple's code. At one time, Chase's "woof" had been enough to send shivers down her skin.

But those days were long gone and he was now "woofing" for another woman.

Judging the wound sufficiently cleansed, Lori used a syringe to apply a local anesthetic. She stitched the wound without another word exchanged between them.

Finished, she affixed a bandage to his chest and stepped back, studied her handiwork, then nodded. She tossed him her brother's T-shirt and turned to pick up her wine. She spied the wet clothing he'd left on her counter when she'd ordered him to sit down. "Shoot. I meant to load the dryer before I dealt with your injuries. Open that bottle of wine, would you, please? The corkscrew is in the drawer directly beneath the bottle."

Without giving him the opportunity to voice a refusal, she scooped up the clothes and retreated to the laundry room. There, she opened the lid of the dryer, tossed in the flannel shirt, then frowned at the tee. Between the rips and blood, it was beyond salvage. She tossed it into the trash and turned her attention to the jeans.

Something bulged in the front pocket. His keys. She reached into the pocket, hooked her finger through the key ring, and pulled. Some other things came along with the keys and fell to the floor — a dime, two quarters, three pennies. And something else.

"Oh." Staring down at the object on her hardwood floor, Lori blinked.

The diamond glittered.

She recognized that ring. She'd seen it earlier that day on the left hand of the woman to whom she'd given a ride.

Holy Moses.

Did this mean what it looked like it meant? Was Chase and Lana's engagement off? Is that why he'd looked like his favorite dog just . . . got lost?

Her thoughts whirling, Lori absently checked the other pockets of his jeans then tossed them into the dryer. She turned the cycle dial, punched the on button, and debated what to do. She peeked around the laundry room door into the kitchen. Chase wasn't there. Neither was Captain. Neither was the bottle of wine and two glasses. So, probably, he hadn't left.

Lori scooped up the ring and went looking for him. Call her crazy, but she didn't think his current black mood was the result of a broken engagement. She'd score it as a contributing factor, but not the primary reason for his funk. This mood of his had a different vibe than one of rocky romance. She had personal experience in that particular area with this particular man, so she recognized the difference.

What had happened to turn the smiling, catch-playing man from this morning into the careless hiker who was ready to give up both his dog and his lady?

A friend would ask. *It's friendship, not being nosy.*

Yeah. Right. Liar, liar, pants on fire.

She found both of her visitors sitting on the porch swing. Chase had pulled on Devin's T-shirt and he sat with one bare foot propped against the railing. The dog lay snuggled against the man, his golden nose resting on Chase's thigh. Staring out at the steadily falling rain, Chase sipped his wine.

Lori lifted her own glass from the table

beside the swing and debated her next move. The ring in her left fist burned like a hot coal. Once upon a time, she'd dreamed of the moment she would hold Chase Timberlake's engagement ring in her hand. A little self-deprecating snort escaped her. She'd never quite imagined it like this.

Taking a seat beside him on the swing, she decided to ease into the subject of the ring. "Want to tell me what happened with Captain?"

For a long moment, he didn't respond. She was searching for something else to say when he finally confessed. "I forgot about him. I left him alone on the mountain. I really can't be trusted with him, Lori."

Sarcasm dripped like raindrops off the roof. "I can see that he's totally traumatized by your neglect."

"He has no sense whatsoever. I looked for him for over an hour before I found him. It was pure dumb luck that I heard him crying. I never would have seen him on that shelf otherwise."

"Shelf? What shelf? Did you climb to get him?"

"Not too far. About twenty feet down. Far enough that he could have been killed, though."

What about you?

"I'm not trustworthy, Lori. He was all but paralyzed with fear of the thunderstorm. That, after I scared him by shouting. He'd have been better off with a front-row seat for fireworks in town. Seriously, Lori. You need to find another foster home for him. Hell, if that dead tree hadn't stopped my fall, the poor little guy would still be up on that mountain."

Because you would be at the bottom of it? What is wrong with you? Lori stifled the urge to kick his foot off the rail.

But that wasn't the way to treat a skittish animal, and Lori knew better than to be fooled into thinking that he was seconds away from bolting. Instead, a tender, gentle wound-cleaning effort was called for.

Keeping her tone light, she observed, "I think perhaps today isn't the day to make that decision, considering."

"Considering what?"

She extended her hand toward him and opened her fist, revealing the engagement ring. "This fell out of your pocket."

"Oh." He left the ring lying in her hand, his manner one of total disinterest. "I forgot I had that."

Oh, wow. Lori honestly felt sorry for Lana. "That's a pretty expensive item to forget."

He shrugged, and judging by his wince,

263

that had tugged at his stitches. "I forgot the dog today, too. That's worse, don't you think?"

What she thought was that something pretty terrible must be occupying his thoughts for him to have forgotten so much.

"I don't have a use for the ring. Do you think one of the charities in town would take it as a donation?"

Lori was grateful for the shift in topic. After a moment's consideration, she visualized her refrigerator door where a dog's-paw magnet held an invitation in place. "Actually, I do. The Rocking L summer camp fundraising gala is this weekend up at Eagle's Way. The ring would be a great addition to the silent auction if it wouldn't make you uncomfortable."

"Why would it make me uncomfortable?"

"It's a recognizable ring."

He gave the swing an easy push. "Good. Maybe it will bring in more money that way. That camp does good work."

"Yes, it does."

The Rocking L summer camp was a project of the charitable foundation established by Jack and Cat Davenport in memory of their daughter, Lauren. Each summer at the camp up on Murphy Mountain, the Rocking L played host to children aged seven to fourteen who had suffered a significant loss. They welcomed children from all across the country, from all walks of life, for four weeks of traditional summer camp activities in a place that the Davenports — like so many other locals — believed promoted healing of troubled souls.

"Can you get the ring to whoever's in charge of the auction?"

Lori hesitated. The silent auction chairperson was none other than Ali Timberlake. "I can, but —"

"Do it. Please."

Lori licked her lips, then nodded. In the long run, that might be easier for both Chase and Ali. "I'm sure your donation will be very much appreciated. My mom says the Davenports have quite a crowd coming in for the gala. They don't open up Eagle's Way to outsiders very often, so invitations are coveted."

"Too bad Lana has already left town. An event like that is right up her alley. She could have talked up the ring and the breakup and probably boosted the amount it'll bring by ten thousand. Maybe I'll give her a call. She could send a video."

Lori studied him as she would a bug. She didn't understand this situation at all. How had it gone from wedding-gown purchase to good-bye so fast? "Jeez, Timberlake. That's a bit cold, don't you think?"

"You don't know Lana. She'd enjoy it."

"And you'd be okay having your personal business blabbered about?"

"It doesn't matter. None of it matters."

The hollow echo in his tone broke her heart a little. "What happened up there on the mountain today between the two of you, Chase?"

During the first minute of silence, she thought he actually might answer. During the second, she began to doubt. By the fifth minute, she'd accepted that he wouldn't respond at all, and she allowed herself to relax. There was something infinitely pleasurable about the combination of a swaying porch swing, gentle summer rain, and a softly snoring dog lying next to you. Chase's thoughts must have followed a similar path because as the swing's chain settled into a rhythmic squeak, she sensed the easing of tension inside the man sitting on the other side of the dog.

They sat in companionable silence until the rain stopped falling and the western sky began to clear. "Look," Lori said, smiling with delight. "A double rainbow over Murphy Mountain."

A faint smile hovered on Chase's lips.

"Well, Ms. Murphy, there must be a message in that."

"What sort of message?"

"What message would you like?"

Lori seriously considered the question, then spoke from her heart. "I don't know. I'll have to get back to you on that."

Chase nodded, then lowered his feet to the ground and stood. "I think that's my cue to head home. My jeans are in your dryer?"

"Yes."

"Stay where you are. I'll get them."

Captain gave his tail a twitch, but didn't lift his head as Chase disappeared inside. Once the screen door banged shut, Lori idly scratched him behind the ears as she took one more look at the ring in the palm of her hand.

The words "what if" drifted through her mind like a song.

She tucked the ring into her shirt pocket, lifted her wineglass in silent toast to the sunshine, and pushed with her foot to keep the porch swing moving.

The screen door hinges squeaked and Chase stepped outside wearing his jeans, his flannel shirt, and boots. Lori asked, "You found your keys?"

"I did."

He paused at the top of the porch steps as Captain roused himself, jumped down from the swing, and plopped his butt down at Chase's heels. The dog looked up and whimpered.

Chase looked down and sighed.

Lori stifled a smile.

Chase bent and scooped Captain up, cuddling him against his chest. "Ow," he muttered as the puppy nuzzled the wound on his side.

"Keep the wound clean and dry," Lori said, running her tongue around the inside of her cheek. "Change the bandage tomorrow. I'm sure your mom has a first-aid kit at the yurt."

"Yeah." Chase gave another long sigh, then stepped down the porch steps. When he was halfway down the front walk, he paused and glanced over his shoulder. "Thank you, Lori."

"For what?"

"I enjoyed our conversation."

"We didn't do much talking."

"Wasn't it great?"

Chase disappeared up Fifth Street. Lori raised her gaze to the west where a glorious explosion of crimson and gold marked God's signature across the masterpiece called Earth.

Then she shifted her focus to the east —
and the promise of tomorrow.

CHAPTER TWELVE

Mac Timberlake's Porsche 911 topped the summit of Sinner's Prayer Pass and began weaving its way down the hairpin curves toward Eternity Springs and home. He'd spent two nights at the Broadmoor in Colorado Springs while attending an Alternative Dispute Resolution conference in an effort to improve his mediation skills. As Eternity Springs's only resident lawyer, he was often called upon to assist in the settlement of disputes, thus avoiding the expense of going to court. The trip had been planned for months, and originally, Ali had intended to go with him for a pampering at the five-star resort. Chase's situation had changed all of that.

Mac downshifted and gunned the gas.

The stress of the past six weeks had been brutal, and he'd enjoyed getting away for a couple of days. He regretted that Ali had chosen not to come along. She needed a getaway as much, if not more, than he had, but she was in full Mother Bear mode. She believed that as long as Chase remained holed up at the yurt, one of them needed to remain close by at all times. Mac understood the sentiment, and if he harbored the tiniest bit of resentment about her unwavering focus on their son, well, he'd get over it.

He was worried about Chase, too. The boy had something more going on than grief for the loss of his friends and the breakup with his fiancée.

Chase wouldn't meet Mac's gaze.

Mac knew Ali hadn't noticed, because she would darn well have said something about it. Mac himself was in a quandary about what, if anything, he should do. Was he being an enabler by giving Chase a place to hide away from the world, giving him time and space to come to terms with whatever troubled him so much? Mac simply didn't know.

He reached the spot where the road widened with an exit to a scenic overlook with a view of Hummingbird Lake and the town beyond. Without making a conscious decision, Mac pulled his car into the overlook. He put the Porsche in park and exited the driver's seat.

His home . . . his heart . . . was straight

271

across the valley. His family was in crisis. Chase had been home almost a month now. What should he do? How did he make things right?

When Chase was missing, Mac had a mission with a certain goal. Find his son. Now, it was a different situation altogether.

Ali's father used to say that growing old was not for sissies. Mac would add that parenting adult children in this day and age required an extra set of balls.

Mac and Ali had been typical "involved" parents, though due to his heavy workload that was allied with his position at his father-in-law's law firm, she had been more involved than he. He'd coached Little League baseball a time or two. She'd been active in PTO at the children's schools. But they both had made a conscious effort to encourage independence in all of their children. They hadn't wanted to raise "snowflakes," and for the most part, they'd succeeded. If Mac thought the cell phone kept Caitlin tethered a little too tightly to her mother, well, he didn't think anyone would ever use the words "helicopter parent" to describe his wife.

And nobody would ever call Chase a snowflake.

From the very beginning, he had taken

independence to a totally new level. Always, the boy had itched to go and do. Never still, constantly trying new things, turning every-day events into adventures. Mac would never forget Chase's eighth birthday when he decided he wanted to explore the city of Denver. By city bus. The entire family had spent the whole day seeing the city in a brand-new way. The experience had been both educational and exhausting.

That's how life as Chase's parents had rolled.

Now, more than twenty years later, Mac struggled with the parent/child relationship like never before. Yes, Chase was an adult. It was his life to live, his choices his to make. However, some choices were different from others. His decision to continue working as a river guide after college graduation hadn't made Mac happy, but in the big scheme of things, Mac's opinion didn't matter. His choice to marry Lana — and then, not to marry her — did have a direct influence on the family, but most families had growing pains of one type or another. The Timber-lakes would adjust to new additions. Some adjustments might take longer than others, but the family would deal.

Chase's choice to go to Chizickstan was another thing altogether. That decision had come close to destroying the Timberlake family. It had been hard enough dealing with Chase's disappearance himself, but watching Stephen and Caitlin go through that misery had been a bitch. Seeing the pain that Chase's decisions had caused Alison damned near killed Mac. Had Chase vanished without a trace, Mac knew without a doubt that the family never would have recovered.

Mac was furious with his son. He was impotent to do anything about it. The days of grounding Chase and sending him to his room were long gone. Never mind that he was providing Chase a room. Shouldn't that give him some sort of stroke?

Yeah. Right. Like Ali would for a minute put up with throwing Chase out into the cold.

"Impotent," Mac muttered, returning to his car. A moment later he pulled out of the overlook and back onto the highway, taking the curves as tight as the car safely allowed — which was pretty damned tight. Almost as tight as Mac's nerves.

Those nerves went from tight to explosive when he made the turn to his home and spied Ali walking from the direction of the yurt, a foil-wrapped baking dish in her hands, and tears streaming down her face.

His heart pounding, Mac steered the

Porsche to intercept his wife. He shoved it into park, switched off the engine, and sprang from the driver's seat. "Alison, what's wrong? What happened?"

Please, God. Don't let him have hurt himself.

Ali swiped the tears from her cheeks with the back of her hand. "Mac, you're home."

"Why are you crying?"

"He breaks my heart."

"What did he do?"

"Nothing! He does nothing! He sleeps. He sits. I thought he was getting better. I know he went hiking and he played with the dog. Honestly, I took it as a positive sign when he and Lana called it quits. But that was ten days ago and still he sits and he sleeps and he doesn't eat. Look!"

She ripped the foil off the top of the baking dish and shoved it out toward him. It was a pan of her lasagna. Half a normal-sized piece was missing. "He had this for three days, Mac. Three days."

In a futile effort to make her feel better, he said, "Cool, I'm starving. All the more for me."

His comment only made her cry harder. "What are we going to do, Mac? We have to do something. He's not getting any better. I'm so worried about him."

Mac gazed helplessly at his wife for a long

moment, and then his temper blew. "We're not helping the situation. We've given him a place to hide. We're enabling him."

"What are we supposed to do? Kick him out?" Torment swam in her eyes. "He wouldn't care. He'd wander off and go sleep in a sleeping bag. You know he would. And it's not like we're supporting him financially because we're not."

"We're paying the light bill for the yurt," he defended, throwing out his arms.

"Like that's anything more than pocket change. I don't think he turns the lights on. I think he sits around in the dark."

Fresh tears welled up and spilled from Ali's eyes, and upon seeing them, Mac had had enough. "Okay. That's it. I might not be able to throw him out, but I'm a damned good poker player and I have an ace that can't be beat. I'm going to throw down the father card."

Chase leveled a stare at the dog. "You are totally in so much trouble. I am going to sell you to the first circus that comes along."

Captain trembled in his boots. Or at least, that's what he would have done if he'd been wearing boots instead of naked paws. At least, that's what Chase would have liked to believe the dog would have done. In reality,

Captain lay sprawled at Chase's feet, replete in an après-shoe-destruction coma. "Those were my favorite pair of sneakers."

They were his only pair of sneakers. "I can't believe you ate my sneakers."

Captain didn't answer him back, though one of his big floppy ears did twitch. Three times.

Chase swallowed a sigh. "Okay. Maybe I share some responsibility for this destructive tendency of yours, but seriously, you are such a pain."

Captain whimpered and whined and Chase shook his head. "Don't argue with me. I'm immune. I think —"

He broke off mid-sentence as he heard the sound of an approaching motorcycle. His family had warned away visitors at his request. Except for Lori, only one Eternity Springs resident had made the trip to the yurt. Celeste Blessing had come by once to drop off dog food. The purpose of a second visit was to invite him to join her on a motorcycle ride of the Alpine Loop. He'd been tempted to join her that time. Had it not meant retrieving his old bike from his parents' garage, thus risking running into a member of his family, he might have gone. The idea of a high-altitude road trip held some appeal to him.

Except, knowing his luck, a family member would insist on coming along. Probably worried he'd take a curve too fast and go sailing off a mountain. He couldn't blame them for worrying. He knew he acted weird when they came around. He wished he knew how to tell them that being around them made him feel worse instead of better.

Because he saw how much heartache he'd caused them.

Because he didn't want them to know what he'd done or who he'd become in the wilds of Chizickstan.

A coward. A killer.

A well and truly damned photographer.

Chase turned toward the sound and shielded his eyes from the sun in order to better see the rider zipping along the road. No helmet? That was stupid. That wasn't . . . couldn't be . . . "Dad?"

When had his father bought a motorcycle?

Captain darted into the yurt away from the roar of the approaching bike. Chase had yet to recover from the shock of seeing his father on a motorcycle when Mac pulled the BMW to a halt in the drive in front of the yurt. As soon as he switched the engine off, Chase snapped, "Where's your helmet? You should never ride a bike without a helmet, Dad."

"Oh, that's rich. Yeah, buddy. I get a safety lecture from you?"

As his father stalked toward him, Chase studied the motorcycle, the echo of dozens of paternal lectures on motorcycle safety floating through his mind. His parents had been antibike for as long as Chase could remember. They'd given him hell the day Chase had announced he'd bought his first Honda. "Does Mom know you have this?"

"We ride together."

"Mom? Seriously? Tell me she at least wears a helmet."

"Forget the damned helmet. You made her cry. I'm sick and tired of you making your mother cry."

If Mac had aimed a roundhouse punch directly at Chase's chin he couldn't have managed a more direct hit.

Chase felt the blood drain from his face. His throat tightened and he wanted to dig a hole in the dirt and crawl into it.

"Couldn't you at least pretend to eat the food she makes you? You know your mother, how much she invests in the meals she makes our family. And you turn up your nose at her lasagna? For heaven's sake, you could give some to the dog, you know, just to spare her feelings."

Chase shut his eyes. He wanted to explain

about his last conversation with Bradley, about the wager and the prize and how the sight of his mother's lasagna made him sick to his stomach. "Dad . . . I . . ."

"I may not have all the details, but I know that you went through a harrowing experience. I understand the need to hole up and lick your wounds and deal with your grief. I know that everybody grieves on his own timetable, but the way you're going about it isn't healthy. You need a reminder that you are not the only person in this world who is struggling. You need something constructive to occupy your mind and body. I have just the solution."

"Mom already gave me the name of a shrink, Dad."

"And I hope you'll talk to her, too. But that's not why I'm here. You may well have found your way out of that hellhole on your own, but Jack Davenport undoubtedly made it happen faster. He got intel from the government that even the Callahans couldn't have managed. He did you a solid. You owe him. Now you have the opportunity to do a little payback. Seven o'clock, tomorrow morning, you need to show up at the Rocking L camp on Murphy Mountain. No excuses. I don't care if you're too tired or too depressed or have a hair appointment or are on your period, you are going to show up tomorrow morning prepared to give swimming lessons to a group of children who have suffered their own kind of hell. Got it?"

Chase responded immediately and out of habit. "Yessir."

Mac had his mouth open to continue the argument, but the easy acquiescence took the wind out of his sails. "You'll be there?"

"I will." Chase paused a moment, then repeated, "Swimming lessons?"

"You can swim, can't you?"

"Well, yeah."

"Okay, then." Mac nodded once. "Good. Don't be late."

He turned and took four steps back toward the bike before coming to an abrupt halt. He whirled around and marched swiftly back toward Chase. He wrapped his arms around Chase, giving him a quick, fierce hug. "Dammit, son. We love you. Get some help."

Chase waited until after Mac had climbed back on his bike and roared away to respond. "Love you, too, Dad."

He returned to the yurt and crawled into his bed. He lay on his back, his arm flung across his eyes, as his father's parting shot echoed through his head. Get some help? If only it were that easy. There wasn't a therapist in the world who could erase the images haunting his mind.

Mac was right about one thing. Chase did owe Jack Davenport. But . . . swimming lessons? Seriously? How does a drowning man teach kids how to swim?

"Well, guess I'll find out at 0700."

Though only a small part of the work done by Lauren's Gifts, the children-focused charitable foundation established by Jack Davenport as a gift for his wife, Cat, the Rocking L summer camp program occupied a special place in their hearts. With the number of campers served kept small by design and in keeping with a "first-rate rustic" plan, the Rocking L boasted six log cabins that housed eight campers and two counselors each, a central mess and activity center, a stable, and a heated swimming pool. The number of campers served during the four-week session was kept small in order to give each child the individual attention he or she needed. While staff did include highly credentialed therapists whose talents were utilized as needed, the camp focused on fun.

Jack and Cat personally chose each camper who was awarded a spot based on applications submitted by friends, family, mental health professionals, and sometimes, the campers themselves. It was a heartbreaking job, but one they found infinitely rewarding. The lone criterion for becoming a Rocking L camper was having experienced a significant loss. The Davenports learned early on in the process that "significant" meant different things to different people, and thus afforded them a wide range of potential campers from which to make their selections.

Chase reported to the camp office where he met directors Shaun and Alisha Cummins. "I can't tell you what a blessing it is for us that you're able to join us," Shaun said, offering Chase a firm handshake. "We had a real run of bad luck when our aquatics counselor broke his leg three days ago. It's difficult to find qualified staff on short notice."

"I'm glad I could help. What exactly do you want me to do?"

Shaun outlined the daily schedule. Of the thirty-six campers due to arrive that day, only eight had elected to add swimming lessons to their activity schedule. Of those eight, five already knew how to swim and wanted to improve their skills. Three children — two boys and a girl — were afraid of the water.

Alisha handed Chase a thick binder containing detailed bios of all the campers with his swim students listed first. "It's confidential material and we'll ask you to respect that, but it's imperative that you know these kiddos' backgrounds. All of our staff needs to be sensitive to potential emotional triggers."

Chase eyed the binder with alarm. "I took three hours of psychology in college. I have no business attempting to counsel troubled children."

"No, of course not. All we ask is that you be aware. It's a case of if you see something, say something. The goal here is to give these kiddos four weeks of fun and adventure and time to be kids."

Because of the nature of his job Chase hadn't spent much time with children over the past few years. The first day he figured out that kids were a lot like puppies. They listened about as well, minded about as much, and if you didn't keep an eye on them, they peed where they shouldn't.

Spending time with them lifted his spirits.

By day two, he recognized that his three little non-swimmers presented a particular challenge. Seven-year-old Ava was terrified of water. Eight-year-old Trevor wasn't afraid of anything, but he didn't have the sense God gave a goat. Nicholas, also eight, touched a spot in Chase's heart that he hadn't known existed.

Blond and blue-eyed, wearing big dark-rimmed glasses, Nicholas Lancaster was a solemn little man. He listened intently to instruction and tried so hard to please. Too hard, Chase thought. No wonder, considering the horror the little guy's mother had put him through.

It was a grim story, one that left Chase shaken after he'd read it. What a selfish woman his mother had been. Another case of bad choices leading to horrific consequences. Poor kid would undoubtedly be scarred for life.

Nicholas proved to be a brave little boy. He approached the swimming pool with obvious trepidation, but he managed the first two days' lessons just fine. Chase's challenge with Trevor was getting the red-headed boy to slow down long enough to actually learn. Nothing like hauling off and jumping into the deep end before he learned to float.

Ava was a different case. The child's fear of water was a living, breathing beast and totally understandable since her significant loss was a twin sister who'd drowned. So far, Chase had been unable to coax her to so much as put a foot in the water.

However, the yearning on her face as she watched him work with Trevor and Nicholas made him determined to win this particular battle. Especially since Ava's parents had listed her learning to swim as the primary goal for her time at the Rocking L.

Chase tried everything he could think of to get her near the pool on the first two days of lessons, then last night as he'd fed Captain, he'd had what he hoped was a brilliant idea. On day three of camp, finished with the lessons for his group of five swimmers and waiting for the three Tadpoles — his nickname for Ava, Trevor, and Nicholas — to arrive for their afternoon lesson, he heard a familiar voice call his name.

He smiled as he turned around to see Lori approaching . . . with his dog.

"Okay, Timberlake," she said. "I'm here. With your dog."

"My *foster* dog," he corrected, accepting the leash from Lori. "Thank you for coming. And for running by my parents' house to pick up Captain."

"Want to fill me in on what this is all about? Your phone call last night was too cryptic."

"Not intentionally cryptic. The battery was dying on the cell phone. I didn't have time to explain."

"What important task have you assigned to a three-month-old puppy?"

"Afraid I'm mistreating my charge, Glitterbug?"

His use of the name caught them both by surprise. Color stained Lori's cheeks, but before she framed a response, the reason for Captain's presence at the Rocking L that afternoon came skipping out of the trees.

Little Ava's gaze settled on Captain and her eyes went round as saucers. "A puppy!"

She rushed forward, her expression alight with joy. "I love puppies!"

"Yes, so you said about a million times yesterday," Chase said with a grin. "He's my dog. He's only about three months old, and I don't think he's been in the water before. I thought he could take swim lessons with us."

Ava's eyes went round. "But he could drown! Aren't you afraid he'll drown?"

"No. Dogs — golden retrievers in particular — are natural swimmers. But they do need to grow accustomed to the water, and this little guy needs practice."

"Oh."

Chase reached out and gently tugged

Ava's ponytail. "Here's the deal, Little Bit. Think if Captain gets in the water then you can, too?"

Ava clasped her fingers together prayerfully. She sucked in a deep breath, then slowly nodded. "I'll try."

Chase grinned and his gaze slid past Ava to the two boys. Trevor went down on the ground beside the dog. His expression was almost as interested as Ava's.

Nicholas hung back. The little man had returned, his brow furrowed above his thick lenses, his lips pursed in a frown.

"He is so precious!" Ava went down on her knees in front of Captain and hugged and giggled as the pup licked her face and yipped and yapped. Trevor began peppering Chase with questions. "Is he a golden retriever? His name is Captain? Why did you name him Captain? Does he have fleas? Does he like bones? Does he play ball? Does he shed? My mom's cat sheds all over the house. And hawks up hair balls. Does Captain hawk up hairballs?"

Chase answered Trevor, but his attention focused in on Nicholas. The boy hadn't moved a muscle forward. *He's afraid. Great. Just great. Why hadn't his file mentioned that he was afraid of dogs?*

One afraid of water, one afraid of dogs.

288

One afraid of nothing. This little project had just got a whole lot more challenging.

CHAPTER THIRTEEN

Lori's heart melted at the sight of Chase with the children. The man standing in front of her now reminded her of the Chase she'd first met, the young man who had been so great with the children he'd led on horseback rides as part of his summer job at a local ranch. He used to tell her he worked hard to make each trip an adventure for the kids, one they would always remember. She'd thought at the time that he'd make a great father. It was good to see that aspect of his personality reassert itself.

"Nicholas? Everything okay?"

The casual concern she identified in Chase's voice had her looking sharply at the boy wearing the dark-rimmed glasses.

"Y-y-yes."

He doesn't look like everything is okay, Lori thought.

Chase shot a "help me" look toward Lori. "Maybe Captain isn't ready for swimming lessons."

"No!" the other little boy protested. "He's ready. I can tell."

"He's right, Mr. Chase." The girl wrapped her arms around the squirming puppy and begged. "Please let him stay. Please, please. Pretty please?"

Chase met Nicholas's gaze and arched a questioning brow.

"It's okay," the boy replied after a moment of thought. Bravely squaring his shoulders, he added, "He's just a dog. I'm not afraid of dogs."

He's had a bad experience with a dog, Lori thought. Poor little guy. He was the kind that stirred every woman's maternal instincts.

"You sure?" Chase asked.

"Yes."

"Okay, then. Everybody go sit in your spots," Chase told the children. The red-headed boy darted toward the bench at the side of the pool near the shallow end. Nicholas and the girl followed more slowly — and more warily. The girl's gaze shifted back and forth between the dog and the water. Nicholas's stare never left Captain.

"You have a bit of a mountain to climb, I think," she murmured as she handed Captain's leash over to Chase.

291

"Yep." He shook his head and grumbled, "Me and my great ideas. I trust you'll hang around for the fun, Dr. Murphy. Bail me out if necessary?"

"I didn't exactly come dressed for the swimming pool," she replied, gesturing toward her V-neck T-shirt and jeans.

"More's the pity," Chase murmured, earning a sharp look from Lori. He pasted an innocent look on his face before he added, "Let me officially introduce you to the three *amigos* here."

"I thought we were Tadpoles!" the redhead exclaimed.

"*Amigos* means friends," Nicholas said. "It's Spanish."

Chase frowned at his charges. "Zip your lips. Dr. Murphy, this is Ava, Trevor, and Nicholas. Kids, Dr. Murphy is a veterinarian."

"A dog doctor," Ava said, her brown eyes growing wide.

"Cats, too." Lori smiled gently at the little girl. Ava had eyelashes to die for. *She'll be a heartbreaker someday.*

All these kids tugged at Lori's heartstrings. As an Eternity Springs native, she knew the history behind the Rocking L summer camp and she wondered what losses had earned these three places at the camp mess table.

She'd have to ask Chase later.

Now, she gave Ava a wink and added, "And sometimes big animals — cows, pigs, and horses — though they are not part of my usual practice."

"Horses!" Ava clasped her hands in front of her. "I love horses, too!"

"I thought you might." In Lori's experience, most little girls did love horses.

"We get to go horseback riding every morning. My horse is spotted and her name is Rainbow."

"That's a stupid name for a horse," Trevor piped up. "My horse is Chief."

Nicholas remained silent, his cautious gaze still locked on Captain.

"How about you, Nicholas?" Lori asked gently. "What is your horse's name?"

"Lightning."

"Lightning is one of the Rocking L's biggest horses," Chase observed, watching Nicholas closely.

"He's very gentle."

But he looked at Captain as if he were a hound from hell. Wonder what the story was there?

"I am so in over my head here," Chase muttered before motion at the edge of the pool caught both his and Lori's notice. Trevor was up off the bench and chasing a butterfly. "Trevor, sit your butt in your spot and don't budge an inch. If you move before I give you permission I'll snatch you bald-headed. Dr. Murphy, would you tell the Tadpoles here about golden retrievers?"

"Snatch me bald-headed?" Trevor repeated. Then he giggled.

"I'm happy to tell you all about goldens," Lori hastened to say. "Only, where should I start?" She looked at Nicholas when she added, "I could talk about them all day. My family had two goldens when I was growing up — Daisy and Duke. I know the breed well."

"Do they like the water?" Chase asked.

"Oh, yes. As a rule, goldens love the water."

"But can a golden be scared of the water?"

"Of course. Dogs are individuals just like people."

"I'm not scared, Mr. Chase," Ava said solemnly. "I'm terrified." She blinked those heavenly eyelashes and explained to Lori. "My sister fell into the swimming pool at my granddad's house and drowned. I found her. She was my twin."

"Oh, Ava. I'm so sorry."

"Me, too. I don't like to be terrified. I want to be brave. It's just so hard."

"Being brave is terrifically hard," Chase

said, his tone as solemn as Ava's and filled with moral authority.

Nicholas finally jerked his gaze off Captain long enough to ask, "Does something terrify you, Mr. Chase?"

Chase met the boy's gaze. "Yes."

"What?"

Chase knelt down and scratched Captain on the ruff of his neck. Lori unconsciously held her breath until he admitted, "I have terrifying nightmares. They make me afraid to go to sleep sometimes."

"A person has to sleep," Ava pointed out. "They don't have to swim."

"You take baths, don't you?"

Slowly, she shook her head. "Only showers."

Trevor turned toward her, his mouth agape. "What about bubble baths?"

"I don't take bubble baths."

"That's lame." Trevor inched his butt toward the water. "Bubble baths are the best. Last week when the babysitter was over I talked her into letting me take my bath in my mom's tub and I dumped a ton of bubble stuff in the water and turned on the jets. The bubbles built and built and built and overflowed the tub and ran out onto the floor. It was like a volcano with white lava running down the mountain. It was so cool."

Chase dragged his hand down his chin. "I think I need to add something else to my frightened-of list. You scare me, Trevor."

The boy flashed a big grin and Lori laughed out loud.

"Okay, we've played around long enough. Time to get busy. Who wants to go first today?"

"I do! I do!" Trevor shouted.

"Of course you do. You went first yesterday and the day before. Nicholas or Ava?"

"Why don't you start with Captain?" Nicholas suggested. "You don't want him getting tired and being bad."

"All Captain does is be bad," Chase said with a sigh.

Dr. Lori couldn't let that one stand without comment. These children might be dog owners someday. "If that's so, it's your own fault, Mr. Chase. Captain is old enough to learn to follow simple commands. He's certainly old enough to understand the word 'no.' You must teach him and be consistent with your efforts. It's not fair to Captain if you're not."

"You're right," Chase admitted. To the children, he added, "She usually is right. I promise to do better from here on out. So, let's introduce Captain to the water, shall we?"

"How do we do that?" Trevor asked.

"This pool has a beach entry. We're going to take him there, remove the leash, and let him explore." Chase shortened the dog's retractable leash and held it out toward the little girl. "Ava, will you please take Captain to the pool?"

She didn't move, but scowled up at Chase. "You're making me go first."

Lori said, "Have you met Miss Celeste yet, Ava?"

The girl nodded. "She's wonderful. She leads story time — and she doesn't use a book! Her stories are the best."

"She's very wise. She once told me that for a person to be very brave, it helps to be scared down to your toes."

Lori felt the intensity of Nicholas's stare and knew she'd caught both his and Ava's interest. If Chase had been a little more forthcoming about today's events when he'd phoned last night, she'd have been better prepared to help today! As it was, she was flying blind.

"I don't get it," Ava said.

"Because it takes exceptional bravery to overcome extraordinary fears."

"Be exceptional, Ava," Chase encouraged.

"You can do it. You and Captain can do it together."

The little girl stood, but the swim shoes she wore appeared to have glue on the soles. "I can't."

Chase knelt down and offered the leash handle once more. "Just to the edge of the pool, sweetheart. You can do it. I'll go with you. Would that help? I'll stay right by your side."

"You won't leave?"

"Nope, I'll be right there."

That encouraging purr in his voice gave Lori the shivers. She had a flashback of memory to the first time she'd let Chase use his tongue on her.

"You'll like it, sweetheart," he'd promised. "Just say the word and I'll stop, but you won't want me to stop. You'll love it."

"I'm still scared!" Ava cried, yearning in her voice. "I don't want to be, but I can't help it. My sister wasn't scared and look what happened to her."

"Chase won't let anything happen to you," Lori said. "I promise. He will take excellent care of you."

Focused on the little girl, Lori was caught by surprise when little Nicholas squared his shoulders, stood, and marched toward

Chase. He took hold of the leash's grip. "I'll help."

Trembling like a stand of aspen in a gale wind, his complexion drained of color, Nicholas returned to the bench where Ava continued to stand frozen in place. He grabbed her hand and tugged her toward the pool's entrance. "C'mon, Ava. Let's get this done."

Chase moved forward, his intent to interfere if necessary obvious. But Nicholas's move appeared to be exactly what she'd needed because Ava allowed Nicholas to pull her along.

They stopped at the water's edge. Then Nicholas sucked in a bracing breath, squatted down, and unhooked the leash from Captain's collar.

What happened next was something Lori thought she'd remember the rest of her life.

As always, Captain's tail whipped back and forth nonstop. He dipped his nose into the water and then a paw. He backed up. Yipped at the water. Approached again. Sniffed again. This time the tips of his ears got wet. He dipped a paw and again backed away.

Ava's tremulous voice encouraged, "You can do it, Captain."

The pup looked up at the little girl, tail

wagging.

Ava took a single step into the water and Lori caught her breath. A second step, then a third. Chase shot a triumphant look toward Lori and she fired back a grin.

"C'mere, Captain. You can do it."

The pup followed Ava, and moments later, he was swimming — and Ava stood thigh-deep in water. Lori didn't try to hold back her cheer.

Not one to hold back, Trevor followed his fellow campers into the pool. Chase began moving the moment the boy did so he was already in the pool when Trevor, being Trevor, decided he was a natural swimmer like Captain and dove forward.

"Whoa, whoa, whoa," Chase said as he swept an arm around Trevor and deposited him on the side of the pool. "What did I say about keeping your butt planted?"

"Nicholas and Ava didn't stay planted."

"Don't worry about other butts. Worry about your own." Chase's gaze shifted from Trevor to Ava to Nicholas. "Nicholas, would you sit beside Trevor, please?"

"Yessir," Nicholas replied. A little color had returned to his cheeks and he didn't seem to be watching Captain so intently.

While the boys settled, Lori crossed to the bench and took a seat. A smile hovered on her lips as she watched Chase work with Ava. He really was good with children, maintaining the perfect balance between encouragement and teasing and teaching and discipline. Using Captain as an assistant, Chase managed to coax little Ava into the water waist-deep. When he dared the little girl to put her face in the water to finish out her turn, Lori honestly expected her to do it.

It might have happened, too, had Captain not exited the pool to investigate the beetle crawling across the ground and, in doing so, scrambled across Trevor's lap and onto Nicholas's.

The eight-year-old let out a shrill, terrified scream.

Chase watched the sun sink behind the mountains in the west and exhaled a sigh of profound gratitude. Thank God this day was over. Dealing with his own demons was challenge enough. Seeing them in eight-year-olds was a kick in the junk.

He sat on the swing on Lori's front porch, sipping from one of the cups of iced tea he'd purchased at the Taste of Texas Creamery along with a half gallon of Rocky Mountain Road ice cream and a package of cones on his way to Lori's. He'd arrived early. She'd warned him she wouldn't be home before eight-thirty, but he didn't mind waiting. Something about this porch, this swing, helped him unwind in a way that he'd never expected.

Lori's front porch was peaceful with the hummingbird feeders hanging from the rafters, the pots of red geraniums decorating the steps, and the scent of fresh-cut grass perfuming the air. Something about this place fed his spirit even more than being up on the mountain. He could sit here and relax and drink tea and not feel quite as . . . what . . . empty? Alone? Damned?

He dragged the toe of his hiking boot against the porch floor and sent the swing swaying. The chain squeaked. The scent of grilling steak drifted on the air from one of the neighbors' backyards. Stretched out beside him sleeping, Captain let out a little snuffle, and the tension that had hummed through Chase since the moment Nicholas let out his shriek slowly drained away.

The sight of Lori's SUV coming up the street had his pulse speeding up. He knew the moment she spied him on her porch because she abruptly applied the brake. He gave a little wave, and when Captain lifted his head, Chase scratched him behind the ears.

A moment later, she'd parked in her drive and exited the SUV. "Chase. What are you doing here?"

"You asked me to tell you how Nicholas was doing."

"I asked you to call."

"This is better. I brought ice cream from Taste of Texas."

That stopped her scowl mid-formation. "What kind?"

"Rocky Mountain Road. It's in your freezer. Brought some cones, too. They're on the counter." He reached into the sack at his feet and pulled out the cup of iced tea he'd brought for her. He hadn't forgotten that Lori always wanted something to drink along with her cone.

"You went into my house?" she asked, accepting the cup.

"You wouldn't leave it open and unlocked if you didn't want people going in and leaving you ice cream."

"True."

"I had to thank you for coming up to camp today. If you hadn't been there to watch the other two kids when Nicholas ran off, I'd have been in a bind."

"I was glad I could help. I want to hear everything. I hated having to leave before things settled down. First, though, how many scoops?"

"Two, please."

She nodded and the screen door banged behind her as she disappeared inside the house. A slow smile spread across Chase's face. He found it infinitely reassuring that some things . . . some people . . . didn't change. Lori Murphy might not be his lover anymore, but she would always be his friend.

When she joined him on the porch swing a few minutes later, she carried two ice-cream cones. She handed the large one to him and took a seat beside him. "Tell me what happened with Nicholas."

"Why don't we eat our ice cream first? The story will spoil your appetite."

"That bad?"

"I haven't had Taste of Texas ice cream in years," he said, avoiding the question.

Lori took the hint. For the next ten minutes or so, they ate their ice cream, rocked on the porch swing, shared the deepening twilight . . . and little, if any, conversation.

Chase was as content as he could recall being in a very long time.

When she popped the last bite of sugar cone into her mouth, she licked her fingers and all but purred. "What that man does with sugar and cream is sinful. You should see Michael when Mom and Dad take him to the creamery. Remember Cookie Monster on *Sesame Street*?"

"Om nom nom nom."

Lori laughed. "That's my little brother. Only it's not chocolate or strawberry or cookies-n-cream that sends him into orbit. The boy goes bonkers over orange sherbet."

"How's all that going these days? The family dynamics."

Lori shrugged. "Okay. For the most part, okay."

"What's the 'for the most part' part?"

"We're adjusting. This is the first time I've actually lived in Eternity Springs since Mom and Dad got married. Sometimes I'm not really sure where I fit in with their new family. Especially with Dad. He knows how to be a father to Devin and Michael. Sometimes, he's at a loss with me."

"I imagine that's the way most fathers are with their daughters. My dad is certainly that way with Caitlin. You're the beloved eldest child, the only daughter. You have a special place in Cam's heart."

"I know. I love him, too. It's just sometimes I'm sad for both of us that we didn't get to share my childhood. As much as I loved my granddad, I really would have liked to have had Cam with me at the school

Daddy/Daughter dance. But enough of this. I sound like a whiny girl. I have him in my life now and I'm grateful — especially when I hear some of the stories of our campers. So tell me, what's the deal with Nicholas?"

As Chase finished off his ice-cream cone, he recalled the moment that afternoon when he chased after the boy and found him with his arms thrown around the trunk of a tall pine tree, sobbing. He'd had to pry the boy away from the tree, and when the little arms came around him and the story began pouring from Nicholas's mouth, Chase had been horrified.

Slowly, he shook his head. "The poor kid. His file didn't say anything about his having a fear of dogs. I never would have asked you to bring Captain if I'd known."

"Of course not," she murmured. "But what I saw today isn't a normal fear of dogs."

"Wolves."

Lori's eyes went wide. "Wolves?"

"I knew the bare facts from his file. Nicholas added to them when I chased him down in the forest this afternoon. His parents had an ugly divorce, and it was his father's turn to have Nicholas for Christmas."

The memory of sitting outside his parents'

house and staring at the Christmas tree flashed through Chase's mind. He'd thought about the twinkle lights and ornaments and angel topper when he was alone in the mountains of Chizickstan. He'd found comfort in thoughts of faith and family and home.

What, he wondered, did poor Nicholas think when he saw a Christmas tree?

"The poor kid's mother basically kidnapped him," he said flatly. "She was in Idaho, driving through the mountains, and there was a storm. She wrecked the car and died at the scene."

"Was Nicholas hurt?"

"Not physically, no. But he was stranded with the body. The best guess is three days."

"Oh, no. Oh, Chase."

"When I chased him down today, he talked to me about wolves. Red eyes and gray fur. I guess they circled the car. Kept him trapped inside with his mother's body."

"That poor, poor little boy."

"Yeah. He was pretty shook up today. Captain took him by surprise. From what he told me, when the pup's sharp claws scratched him, it triggered a flashback. He tried to get out of the car once. Got one leg out and a wolf went after it. He has scars on his ankle, Lori. Dogs bring it all back.

Dogs and Christmas."

"Christmas?"

"Carols. I guess his mother played a Christmas station after she snatched him. She sang along. After the wreck, the radio kept playing until the battery went dead."

"Oh, no. How long would that take?"

"The file estimates eighteen hours."

Lori closed her eyes and shook her head. "These kids who come to the Rocking L . . . I don't know how Cat and Jack manage to wade through all the applications. Their stories are truly heartbreaking."

"I don't know how Nicholas will ever get over it."

Lori studied him for a long moment, and when she spoke, Chase knew she was talking about more than Nicholas. "He's lucky that he's found his way to Eternity Springs. This place . . . the people who live here . . . we can help him heal if only he'll let us. Look at the events of today. You helped him today."

"I scared him to death."

"You helped him face his fears."

"He screamed bloody murder."

"Sounds to me like his experience earned that sort of response. He verbalized it. Since it wasn't in his file, maybe he verbalized it for the first time. That's a giant step toward healing."

They both knew that Lori was talking about more than only Nicholas now. Defensively, he asked, "Are they teaching psychology in vet school these days?"

"Pets can't tell us where they hurt, Chase. We learn to read nonverbal cues."

"How about we leave that for another time and concentrate on swinging. I need me some porch-swing peace."

Lori shrugged. "Since you brought me Rocky Mountain Road . . ."

Neither spoke as the shadows lengthened, the only sounds the rhythmic squeak of the swing, the occasional snore from the dog, and the call of mountain cicadas hidden in nearby trees as twilight finally slipped into night.

Chase let out a long sigh. "Nicholas and I talked about the dog thing. He's okay with Captain now, but he's still worried about other dogs. Since our swim lessons are at the same time as your lunch break, we're hoping you might volunteer to join us two or three times a week and bring other dogs to visit."

She didn't answer right away and he found himself anxiously holding his breath. "Nicholas was on board with this?"

"It was his idea to begin with. He doesn't

want to be afraid. He liked dogs before the accident, but they do remind him. He watched Ava work on getting over her fear, and he wants to do the same. He just needs work. They all do."

"Okay, then. Yes, I can do that. Maybe I won't bring Dad's dog, though."

"That's probably a good plan. At least at the beginning. Mortimer is infamous. Has he slowed down at all in the past few years?"

"A little. He's still a challenge."

"Well, watching that little guy today . . . I think he'll do it. He's gutsy. I'm gonna bet right now that when camp is over and his father comes to pick him up, the first thing he's going to do is ask for a dog."

"I like the way you think, Timberlake."

"Maybe the thing to do is save Mortimer for a final exam. If Nicholas can give that crazy dog some love, I think it'll be safe to say that he's conquered his fear of dogs."

"That will be a nice summer's work," Lori observed.

"Wish I could think of something to do about Christmas."

Acting instinctively, Lori reached out and laid her hand atop his. "Healing occurs in stages, but the process is a dynamic one. It's critical to remember that it's not linear. Wounds can progress both forward and back through the phases depending upon internal and external forces at work within the patient."

Chase turned his hand over and threaded his fingers with hers. "What are you trying to tell me, Dr. Murphy?"

"Don't forget you're in Eternity Springs. It takes longer for some than for others, but I have yet to run across a broken heart that has failed to heal."

"Are you talking about me or about a little boy who is afraid of dogs?" Immediately, Chase wished he'd kept his big mouth shut. He didn't really want to go there.

And yet, Lori was the one person he thought he could possibly go there with.

Lori smiled and stretched out a leg and gave the swing a push. She didn't respond to his question, and Chase was relieved.

Especially since she didn't pull her hand away from his, either.

Eventually, Captain stirred and hopped down from the swing, and Chase knew he'd better go. He had to be at the Rocking L early in the morning. "Thanks for sharing your porch swing," he said, giving her hand a squeeze.

"Thanks for bringing me ice cream."

As they stood, Captain managed to wrap himself around Lori's ankles and she stumbled forward. Chase's hand shot out to catch her . . . steady her. He caught her around the waist and pulled her against him.

"Time stood still" might be a cliché, but that's damned sure how it felt to Chase. As if time *had* stood still. For just a moment, with Lori in his arms, he felt young again. Clean again. Innocent again. Though in truth, little he'd felt for Lori could be termed innocent.

Which was why it felt as natural as sin to lower his head and kiss her.

CHAPTER FOURTEEN

Lori's heart fluttered like a hummingbird's wings when Chase's arm slipped around her waist and they somehow ended up plastered against each other. *Home. It's like coming home.*

Only you don't live there anymore!

Jerking away from him before she could make a fool of herself and lift her face for his kiss — *his kiss? Holy moly. Had he been about to kiss her?* — Lori said, "Whoa. Sorry about that. Clumsy of me. I'll . . . um . . . see you . . . um . . . not tomorrow. Probably not tomorrow. The day after."

She would need a day to recover from this.

"G'night." She fled. Ran like a Heisman trophy running back heading for the end zone. The screen door banged behind her before he'd taken two steps.

His voice, soft and a little gruff, floated in from the porch. "Good night, Glitterbug."

Like any woman in similar circumstances,

she went straight for the freezer and the Rocky Mountain Road. She went to bed that night feeling just a little sick to her stomach.

She slept fitfully and awoke the following morning to a bluebird summer sky and an appointment book filled to overflowing — of which she was glad. She didn't need to obsess about last night's interlude on the porch swing. Or the moment when it ended.

She woke up telling herself that Chase was her friend. That she shouldn't worry about a momentary reaction. Muscle memory. That's all it had been, right?

"Right."

And the temperature would crack the century mark on New Year's Day in Eternity Springs, too.

Lori did her best to put the events of last evening behind her as she went about her work the next morning, but off and on throughout the day, thoughts of Chase itched like a bug bite. She tried to distract herself with an inner debate over which of Eternity Springs's canine residents she should take to the Rocking L and in what order. She decided to start with small and stylish — Sage Rafferty's Snowdrop — and she made arrangements to pick up the bichon frise from Sage's art gallery, Vistas, at lunchtime the following day.

With that decision behind her and the potential lineup settled, her thoughts kept straying back to Chase. Her distraction must have been obvious, too, because that evening when she joined the Callahan clan on the patio at Murphy's Pub for a live music performance by a Callahan family friend, a singer/songwriter named Shaky Wells, she noticed that Brick kept giving her narrow-eyed looks.

She did her best to ignore him and have fun. The Texas-based contingent of the Callahan family had begun arriving for their annual summertime visit to Eternity Springs earlier in the week, and Lori appreciated the opportunity to catch up on family news. She liked Nic's in-laws very much, having gotten to know them well while visiting their ranch during her undergrad years at Texas A&M. While they waited for the entertainment to begin, Brick's aunts caught her up on recent events in Brazos Bend. At intermission, his father managed to quiz her subtly about his son's life in Eternity Springs.

"I think he's very happy," she told Mark Callahan. "He speaks often about how much he likes the challenge of building something from the ground up. I think once

315

word gets around about Stardance, he'll be wildly successful."

"But do you think —"

"Enough, Dad," Brick interrupted as he moved up behind Lori. "Lori came here tonight to enjoy the music, not to be interrogated. Here." He pulled out her chair. "Let me rescue you. I want to introduce you to Shaky."

He cut her away from the herd as smoothly as a working cowboy.

"You shouldn't have said that to your dad," she scolded. "That was no interrogation. You should hear my dad. For a man who had no experience parenting me until I was in college, he can fire off nosy questions like nobody's business."

"It was just an excuse. My family has monopolized you and I wanted to get you off by myself," he said, once he had her cornered by the side gate. "So what has you wound tighter than a corkscrew tonight?"

"I'm not wound tight."

"Yeah. Right. And my grandfather's favorite meal isn't chicken-fried steak with cream gravy and fried okra."

"Oh, wow. Cream gravy and fried okra. Sometimes I really miss Texas."

"Branch still eats it twice a week."

"He must have wheedled the location of

the Fountain of Youth out of Celeste. My mom swears our resident angel knows where it is, and your grandfather seems to get younger every time I see him rather than vice versa."

Brick wouldn't be distracted. "Enough about Branch. Back to you. What has you so twitchy?

"I'm not twitchy."

"I've heard rumors in town. It's Timberlake, isn't it? Is he giving you trouble?"

That depends on your definition of "trouble." She scowled at him over the top of her pint of beer. "Why would you think that?"

"Word around town is that his woman flew the coop. The wedding is off again. For good this time."

"They've broken their engagement, but I don't know that I'd put money on it being permanent."

"Speculation is that the two of you might take up where you left off. He's been seen in town — on your front porch."

Lori closed her eyes and groaned. *Welcome to Eternity Springs — where everybody knows your business before you do.* It was the very worst part of small-town living. "Where did you hear that?"

"Well, let's see." He dragged his hand down his cheek. "I heard it when I bought a box of nails at the lumberyard. Got a whiff of it when I put gas in my truck at the Fill-U-Up. Margaret Rhodes about wore me out about it when I dropped off a sackful of donations for the library book sale."

I'm so toast. "It's a blessing that my parents are on vacation."

"When are they due back?"

"A week from Saturday."

"So you've got a little time to come up with a story for them. On the other hand, as your friend and the person who listened during a certain late-night drunken sobfest on a recent trip to Durango, I want an answer now. What the hell are you doing, Murphy?"

She tossed back a sip of beer as if it were a shot of rotgut whisky. "I thought you were going to introduce me to the singer."

"I will. Later." He pushed open the gate and ushered her outside. "I didn't spend three hours letting you cry on my shoulder to ignore this."

"I didn't cry on your shoulder."

"Trust me. After the second bottle of wine, you absolutely did."

She scowled at him. "Whatever."

Brick slung his arm around her shoulders and led her around to the side of the building and down the street to the garden area outside of the Catholic church and the park bench that offered a nice view of Sinner's Prayer Pass. "Allow me to quote you. 'It's all my father's fault. If he hadn't run off, then I would have trusted that Chase would wait.' Now, I'm not exactly sure what all of that was supposed to mean — your sloshed little self wasn't making tons of sense — but I can connect the obvious dots. You're vulnerable to him and I know your history, so I'm concerned for you. I care about you."

"I care about you too, Brick, and I appreciate your concern. But you don't need to worry because here's the bottom line. Chase is my friend. He's in a bad place right now, and I won't let our past stop me from being the friend he needs, but I would have to be an idiot to let myself fall for him again."

"Why's that?"

"Well, gee. I don't know." Sarcasm dripped from her voice. "Maybe I don't like the idea of being rebound girl?"

Brick shook his head. "You're not. The TV chick was the rebound girl. Hasn't he been with her since the two of you broke up? Technically, you'd be the bounce-back girl. You're the one who got away."

Lana had said that to her one time, too. Lori didn't believe it then, and she didn't believe it today.

"So what's the problem?" Brick continued. "Are you scared off because Timberlake has gone crackers?"

"He hasn't gone crackers!" Lori was quick
to defend him. "He's mourning his friends
and recovering from a horrible experience
and he's probably dealing with some depres-
sion and maybe even post-traumatic stress.
If he comes and sits on my porch swing, it's
just because he finds some comfort there."

"I'll just bet he does."

"Come on, Brick. It's totally innocent."

"I think the lady doth protest too much.
Therefore, I intend to nurse my broken
heart with another beer. You want one?"

"Oh, stop it, Brick. You're not in love with
me."

The teasing light in his eyes faded, and a
new note of sincerity cued Lori to the fact
that he spoke the truth. "No, I think it could
have gone that way, but I knew better than
to let myself fall. I didn't want to be rebound
guy any more than you want to be rebound
girl. Been there, done that. It sucks."

Brick had told Lori enough about his
relationship history to know that he'd had
his heart stomped by a woman before moving to Eternity Springs.

"At any rate, I haven't been in a rush. I

figured it didn't hurt to wait around and see what happened with you. I thought once Timberlake actually settled, you might have been ready to move on and we might have a chance."

Lori placed her hand atop his and gave it a squeeze. "I appreciate the thought, Brick, but despite what you like to tell yourself, my confusion about Chase hasn't been the only thing keeping us apart."

"Oh?"

"You pay lip service to moving on, my friend, but this is a pot/kettle situation. You're still in love with your ex."

Now it was his turn to scowl. He glanced over his shoulder as if to make sure that his family hadn't overheard. "You're one to talk."

"No, I love him, but I'm not in love with him. I'm not 'involved' with him."

"Yet."

"No 'yet' about it. Maybe I could take that fall, but I'd be stupid to let it happen. I'm his friend and friendship is all it can be."

"Why?"

"Because the problem that broke us up before hasn't gone away. I have roots. Chase has wings. They might be a bit beat-up and broken right now, but as soon as he heals, he'll fly away. That's what he does."

Brick studied her for a long moment. "Seems to me that you're jumping the gun. So the guy wanted to see the world. He's done that. Maybe he's ready to settle down now. It happens, you know. Hell, he's camped out in a yurt and from what I hear, he's not inclined to leave it."

"He will. He always does."

"Maybe not this time."

"Yes, well, I'm not ready to roll that particular pair of dice." She'd survived being in love with Chase Timberlake once. She wasn't at all certain she could do it a second time. "So, your third degree is almost reaching Cam Murphy status. Let's go back to the patio, shall we? I still want to meet the songwriter."

Brick held her gaze a long moment, then nodded. They returned to Murphy's, but just before they reached the gate, she added, "Thank you for caring, Brick. And maybe you'll listen to one piece of advice I have? If that slipknot you tied hitching your reins to your past is actually a square knot, sometimes the only way to get on down the road is to take a second run at the knot."

"Lori Murphy, I think you've been spending too much time with Celeste Blessing. And I'll see your advice and raise you. Real honest-to-God second chances don't come along often in life. Don't squander yours just because you're afraid."

"Now who has been spending too much time with Celeste." Lori went up on her tiptoes and kissed his cheek, then followed him onto the patio where he introduced her to Shaky Wells. It was the last they spoke about anybody's past that evening.

Late the following morning, Lori picked up Snowdrop from the Raffertys' and made the trip up to the Rocking L summer camp on Murphy Mountain.

Snowdrop was a hit with the children. Sage had dressed the dog in a fairy princess outfit and Nicholas did just fine with her. "Who can be afraid of a dog wearing fairy wings," he explained.

Time passed and Lori's days stayed full. She adjusted her work hours — opening early and staying late — to give herself time for an extra long lunch. One of the perks about being her own boss, she told her mother.

"Is it . . . smart . . . for you to spend so much time up at the Rocking L while you are getting your practice established in Eternity Springs?" her mother asked. "Someone else could take dogs up to visit that poor little boy."

Lori recognized the question as not-so-subtle mother-speak that really asked, "Do you know what you're letting yourself in for where Chase is concerned?"

As much as Sarah Murphy had wanted Chase and Lori to tie the knot once upon a time, she now harbored serious doubts that they should take up where they'd left off. She'd shared that viewpoint with Lori shortly after news of the broken engagement reached her ears. Lana's words and actions toward Chase had made a positive impression on the Timberlake family friends following Chase's return to Eternity Springs. Sarah wasn't certain that this wedding postponement was permanent, and after having witnessed her daughter's meltdown when Chase was missing, she feared that Lori would end up brokenhearted — again.

"I'm careful not to overextend myself, Mom," she'd replied. "This session of summer camp will be over before we know it, Nicholas will go home, and I won't have a reason to return to the Rocking L." Daughter-speak for "I'm protecting my heart, Mom. Don't worry."

Her words mollified her mother somewhat. It didn't help that Chase continued to come down out of the mountains more evenings than not to spend an hour or so on her porch swing. Lori knew tongues were wagging all over town, but she didn't care. Chase seemed more at peace each time she saw him. If spending time on her front porch helped his heart to heal, that's all that mattered.

And if she got a bit of a hormonal buzz every time she saw him interact with the Tadpoles or heard the creak of the porch swing then, well, that was her problem, wasn't it? Chase certainly didn't seem to be bothered by a similar reaction. In fact, so totally . . . companionable . . . was he that she began to understand that she must have misread the almost-kiss the night he brought ice cream.

Obviously, Chase thought of her as a friend. So much for Brick's talk of second chances. Lori told herself that it was only natural for her to long for a time when the evening would have ended with a kiss between them. That was an old, familiar pattern. A comfortable pattern. That's all. They weren't the same two people who'd met at the Trading Post and carried on a secret affair in their early twenties. He was a friend. Just a friend. Period. She was glad that Chase didn't have romance on the mind.

She almost believed it.

Chase dreamed of fireworks.

The thundering boom as a rocket launches. A high-pitched whistle rises, fading to a whir as the glittering trail of sparks climbs higher and higher. Anticipation builds. Tension grows. The pinprick of light has now all but disappeared.

Yearning . . .

The sky explodes. A dazzling starburst of colors burn brilliant and beautiful. Spears of red and orange and gold and silver slice across the midnight sky.

Ahhhhh.

In the heavens, beams soften and slowly begin to fall. A waterfall of color, luminescent and glowing. Now green.

Green, Lori's eyes.

Chase lifted his head from his pillow. He blinked once. Twice. *Well, sonofabitch.* Damned if he didn't have a morning hard-on. A serious morning hard-on.

Huh. Well. That was a good thing, wasn't it? His libido had been nonexistent for weeks now. Hell, it had been months. He hadn't had sex since the Valentine's Day vacation — and, he hadn't missed it. Sad comment, there, on how the state of his relationship with Lana had been even before the whole Markhor Pass question surfaced. The fact that he'd had a sex dream about fireworks was a little weird, but not completely beyond understanding. Today was the Fourth of July and this was the day that Lana had chosen as their rescheduled wedding day.

However, Chase didn't even want to begin to speculate about why the dream had ended with Lori's green eyes. At least, not before he'd taken a cold shower.

He rolled from his bed and began his day — without touching the hot water spigot. Either one of them.

Chase pulled into the parking lot at the Rocking L a full hour before his usual arrival time because today was Family Day. Hearing the sound of a motorcycle approaching, Chase turned to see Celeste drive up on her Gold Wing. He slowed his step while she guided the bike toward her parking spot near the camp's main entrance and waited while Captain darted forward to receive his pets and scratches and coos and cuddles.

"Happy Fourth of July," she said when she finally lifted her attention away from his dog.

"Happy Fourth of July, Celeste. I'm surprised to see you here today. Don't you have a full day of activities at Angel's Rest?"

"We do. But the nature walks I do here are such a lovely part of my week that I didn't want to skip it. These children take hold of my heart and don't let go. Don't you agree?"

"I can't argue with you."

Celeste reached out and touched Chase's arm. "One of the lessons spending time with these little ones teaches me is that a brush with tragedy can affect us in two different ways. Either we can lose hope and descend into the darkness, or we can use the challenge to find our inner strength and make our way into the light. The easier path is to sink. The struggle to strength is a lesson these children live and display day after day."

The struggle to strength.

Her words stayed with Chase as he entered the camp where staff and campers scurried about like ants making final preparations before visitors descended. It was, he thought, a rather profound thought in a handful of words.

"My swimmers tell me that you tell the best stories on your nature walks, Celeste. I've been tempted to tag along on them myself."

"You are welcome anytime, Chase."

"Thank you. I might just do that. Though I'm not sure I could keep up with you. Lori says that you are the Energizer bunny of

Eternity Springs."

Celeste laughed. "That Lori. She's one to talk. I'm amazed at all she manages. Is she bringing a dog to camp today?"

"No. Not with all the events on today's agenda. We have lots to accomplish before it's time to load up the buses for the trip down to Hummingbird Lake."

"I think it's lovely that the Callahans have invited our campers to their holiday picnic."

"They are good people. And, they have the best fireworks viewing spot on the lake."

Saying the word "fireworks" took Chase's mind in a direction it shouldn't have gone. He had no business walking around a children's camp with a boner. What happened next didn't help his situation one bit.

He and Celeste walked into the admin building to find Lori already there, visiting with Alisha and Shaun and wearing a form-fitting, sleeveless sundress in flag red.

"You look like a million bucks," he told her.

She dipped her head, accepting the compliment, and showed him a smile as bright as the summer sunshine. "Thank you. I'm giving a presentation to guests about tourist activities and places of interest in the area to visit. I was feeling especially patriotic when I opened my closet this morning. It's nice to wave the flag from time to time."

She definitely managed that. Only instead of the Stars and Stripes of the good old U.S. of A., Chase's thoughts went to the bullrings of Seville. He wanted to snort and paw the ground and charge the red flag in front of him.

Yep, the old sex drive had definitely come roaring back.

Except, maybe it wasn't just testosterone finding its way back into his blood. Maybe it was Lori.

It's always been Lori.

"So, are you ready for the watermelon scramble?" she asked.

The question distracted Chase, and he pulled his gaze away from her shapely bare legs. He was not looking forward to that part of the day. "No, I'm not. Whoever decided that it'd be a good idea to grease up a watermelon with Vaseline and throw it in a swimming pool for kids to wrestle over, anyway?"

"It's a Callahan family tradition," Celeste said. "I'm looking forward to it. It's so much fun to watch."

"Unless you're the person responsible for swimmers' safety," Chase grumbled. "Or the one dealing with bruises and busted lips after it's over." To the camp directors, he added, "The legal liability makes me shudder. Are you sure you want to keep it on the schedule?"

"The Davenports suggested it," Alisha replied. "That and the money scramble."

"Don't fret, Chase." Celeste patted his arm. "Kids need to be kids. A little roughhousing doesn't hurt as long as it's at the proper time and in the proper place. Besides, these children here have already faced trial by fire of one sort or another. Our campers aren't snowflakes."

No, they weren't, and it was one of the reasons Chase enjoyed his time here at the Rocking L so much. He'd always respected grit. These kids had grit and then some.

"Relax, Chase," Lori said, her green eyes glowing with amusement. "As I recall, you love watermelon. Play your cards right and you'll be able to bum a slice or two from the winners. I was the courier for the prizes this morning. Picked up two huge ones and a smallish-sized one they'd set aside for us at the Trading Post. They look gorgeous."

"Three? We have to do it three times?"

"Three different age groups."

"Great. Just great." But the spark in Lori's eyes was so damned appealing that he couldn't help but smile in return.

The morning passed swiftly. At the Rock-

331

ing L, the "family" part of Family Day meant that every camper had someone special there just for him. Not all visitors were blood related. In fact, seven of the campers had visitors whom they'd never even met, but whom they'd listed as "family" choices. These visitors included professional athletes, an actress, teachers, and even two members of a popular boy band.

Jack Davenport had connections like nobody's business.

The watermelon scramble went off with only a couple of bruises and a few scrapes, and without any eye gouges. The kids had an amazing amount of fun. His little Tadpoles didn't participate in that activity, but when it came time for the money scramble — bags and bags and bags of coins — to be thrown into the pool for the kids to dive for, Trevor and Nicholas stood at the ready.

But first, Ava and Chase had prepared a surprise for her parents.

Rows of white folding chairs had been lined up around the pool and visitors invited to sit. Children sat cross-legged on the pool deck, faces and hands red and sticky with juice from their watermelon prizes. Lori stood across the pool from Ava and her parents, a camera at the ready.

Chase met Ava's gaze and arched a questioning brow. The little minx grinned and attempted to wink, though she did it with both eyes.

Chase smothered a grin and stepped forward. "Before we begin our final aquatic event today, I want to thank you for coming. The kids have been excited and looking forward to sharing this day with you. The Rocking L is a great program, a fabulous place, and I'm so glad I've had the opportunity to be part of it. We should all have a chance to go to summer camp. Believe me when I say that it's good for the heart. Everyone's heart."

"And watermelon is good for the tummy, too!" Trevor shouted out.

The crowd laughed. Chase sighed and shook his head, then continued. "Now, since we do lessons here at the pool, one of my students and I decided we'd give a demonstration. Ava, want to join me?"

"Yes, please, Mr. Chase." The little girl sat tall, smiled up at her mom and dad, then rose and walked regally to stand at his side.

"Wonderful. So, everyone, if we can have your attention, my assistant and I will show you how this next event is going to work."

At the base of the lifeguard stand, Chase picked up a canvas bag and one of the dozen pails that the Davenports had delivered earlier that day.

"I've always loved a good treasure hunt," he began, stealing a glance toward Lori as he spoke, the memory of their treasure hunt anniversary date a quick flash through his mind. "Ava, please explain to our guests how this one will work."

Like the hostess on a daytime TV game show, the little girl gestured toward the pool with a flourish. "Imagine please that our beautiful blue swimming pool is the deep blue sea. A gallon gets in a pirate fight and sinks."

"Galleon," Chase corrected, stifling a grin.

She clapped her cheeks with her hands. "Galleon. I *always* mess that up."

After the visitors' laughter died down, she continued. "Treasure spills across the ocean floor."

She waved a hand toward Chase who reached into the pail, removed a handful of silver coins, and tossed them into the pool at about the four-foot depth marker. "And, our treasure hunters will take their booty bags —" She held out her hand toward Chase. He passed over a small mesh pouch from the canvas bag. "And dive to collect their treasure."

Then Chase's little fearful Tadpole took

her bag, held her nose, and jumped into the water.

Her parents audibly gasped and rose instinctively to their feet. After a few seconds underwater, Ava's head popped from the water followed by her hand. She held a gleaming silver dollar high for everyone to see. "Ta-da!" she called, and a wide grin split her face.

Her mother started to cry. Her father grinned even bigger than Ava.

Satisfaction flowed though Chase like a river. And as he met Lori's warm and approving gaze, so did another emotion he'd never thought to experience again — joy.

CHAPTER FIFTEEN

"That was a lot of fun," Lori said as she watched the children carry their newfound treasure off to their cabins to change clothes and prepare for the day's next event. Campers and their Family Day visitors were slated to be special guests of honor at the Callahan family's place on Hummingbird Lake where they'd have the best seats in the house for the annual Eternity Springs fireworks display. "I don't think I've ever seen a little girl quite as proud as Ava today. Good job, Chase."

"Thanks. I was pretty darn proud of her. She was a little ham, wasn't she?"

"You've done a great job with your three little Tadpoles. Did you see how much money Trevor raked in?"

"Kid is destined for Wall Street, I'm telling you. Nicholas didn't do too bad, either."

"I just wish that Nicholas's dad had been able to make it. I know he was a little down about it."

"His grandparents are very nice, but I know they don't fill a dad's shoes."

Chase turned his head and studied her. "You still have wounds on your heart about growing up without your dad, don't you?"

She shrugged. "No, a little bit of a scar, maybe, but that's not a bad thing. After all, scar tissue knits together the wound and makes you whole again."

"You really are working on filling Celeste's shoes, aren't you?"

"No one will ever fill Celeste's shoes. That said, I'd better get moving or I won't have time to change into jeans and my sneakers before I toddle along to the Callahans tonight." She hesitated a moment and tried to tell herself that her pulse didn't increase when she asked, "Are you planning to come down to the lake for the fireworks?"

He hesitated. "I don't know that I'm up to running that gauntlet. Everyone in the county will be there." He licked his lips, then added, "I have a better idea. Why don't you come up to the yurt for dinner? There's that spot up the creek that overlooks the lake. You'd see the fireworks from a different perspective."

If her pulse had raced before, now her heart started pounding.

"I don't have hot dogs and potato salad," Chase continued. "I do have a couple of nice steaks I could grill."

He has wings, Murphy. He will fly away again.

"C'mon, Lori. Help me grow that scar tissue. Say yes."

"Help you grow scar tissue? I don't know that anyone's ever said that to me before."

"Being with you helps me. You're my Dr. Glitterbug."

That one proved irresistible. "Okay. I need to go home first and change my clothes."

"I can come pick you up."

"No, don't do that. I'll drive up. Do you have everything you need for dinner?"

"Maybe bring up some ice cream?"

"I can do that." The Taste of Texas Creamery was open today. She'd stop by and get a gallon of peppermint. It had always been his favorite.

She second-guessed herself all the way to town and that's even before she called her mother to tell her not to expect her to join the family at the Callahans' that evening. "Do you know what you're doing?" Sarah asked.

"It's just dinner, Mom."

He called me Dr. Glitterbug.

"All right, honey," Sarah said with a sigh.

"Be careful."

"I will."

She remembered her mother's words of caution as she stood before her closet and debated her choice of tops. She'd planned to wear the flag T-shirt and jeans out to Hummingbird Lake. It would be cooler up on the mountain. She should wear a sweater. She should wear her flag T-shirt with a cardigan over it.

Somehow, though, instead of a cotton tee, she left the house dressed in a clingy cashmere V-necked sweater in bright fire-engine red.

Appropriately enough, as she started up out of the valley, the satellite radio station she listened to played Marvin Gaye's "Ain't No Mountain High Enough." *Dr. Glitterbug, you're setting yourself up for heartache.*

She knew it, but she couldn't seem to stop herself.

Captain ran out to meet her as she climbed out of the car at the yurt. She spent a couple minutes petting him, cooing at him, and scolding him for jumping.

"He's going to get dog hair all over that spectacular sweater, Lori."

"That's okay." *Maybe you can brush it off later.*

339

She mentally kicked herself. *Stop it! Just stop it!*

"I'm a vet. I not a stranger to dog hair."

He smiled at her. "Come on inside. Dinner's about ready."

She handed him the bag containing the ice cream and followed him into the yurt. He'd set the table using chargers, napkin rings, and linen napkins. He'd even fashioned a centerpiece out of a Mason jar and red and blue bandanas. His mother's influence, Lori knew. "The table is festive."

He lifted his shoulders. "My mom has all kinds of decorating stuff here."

"It's definitely the best-equipped yurt I've ever seen. Although I think some of Brick's tents might give it a run for its money. I know your dad showed him this place when Brick was getting started."

Chase frowned as he poured Lori a glass of wine. "So what's the deal with him? Are you still dating him?"

"We're friends. Good friends, but just friends."

"He's building a camp of some sort?"

"It's called glamping — glamorous camping. It's basically what your folks have done here."

"Huh. I'll bet he does pretty well with it. People do like their creature comforts."

"I know I do." She took a sip of her wine, then posed a question. "So did Thrillseekers bring in trailers for their stars like they do on movie sets?"

"Not hardly. We were lucky to get Porta Pottis most places."

"Tell me about your job, Chase. The good parts. Not what happened in Chizickstan."

For a long moment, she didn't think he'd answer. Finally, he said, "It was exciting. I got to see parts of the world I'd probably never have visited otherwise. I loved the work. I really loved the work."

"I haven't seen you with a camera since you've been back."

Another long pause followed that, and when he finally spoke, he changed the subject. "Tell me some of the good things about being a vet in Eternity Springs."

She took the hint, and while he cooked the steaks, they talked dogs and cats and cattle, family and free time. Dinner was delicious and Lori enjoyed herself. As they left the yurt to make their way to the overlook where they would watch the fireworks, she thought that Chase was as relaxed as she had seen him since his return.

He'd prepared the spot prior to their arrival by placing a quilt atop a couple of sleeping bags for padding. A red filtered flashlight sat ready for use along with a blanket and a cooler. Chase reached into the cooler and pulled out a couple bottles of water. Handing one of them to her, he said, "We're early. Fireworks probably won't start for twenty minutes or so. There are lawn chairs if you'd be more comfortable."

"No, thanks. This is great."

And it was. They sat side by side, not touching, but definitely a little closer than the nights she'd joined him on the porch swing. Close enough for her to detect the heat from his body. She'd been right about it being cool up this high and she was glad she'd worn her sweater. Otherwise, she might have snuggled right up against him.

Looking for a distraction, she leaned back on her elbows and gazed up at the sky. As the last glow of light faded in the western sky, stars popped like diamonds shimmering against black velvet. "It's so beautiful up here. Daytime is great, but there is something about looking at the stars when you are this high and away from the ambient light of town. Up here, I see . . . dreams."

"What sort of dreams?"

"I don't know. Possibilities. New worlds. This world in ages past. I think about Galileo and Carl Sagan having a beer with Han Solo and Chewbacca."

Chase laughed softly and the sound of it made her heart sing. A month ago, he wouldn't have done that.

"What do you see when you look at the stars?" she asked.

"From here?"

"Is it different here than from other places?"

"Literally, yes, it's different here than in other places. For instance, here you don't see the Southern Cross in the night sky above Eternity Springs. But what I see when I look at the stars . . . from here and anywhere — everywhere — else I've been in the world . . . I see home."

"Home? Really?"

"Yeah."

"It's not a connection I'd ordinarily make."

"I think it's because the stars are so distant. No matter where I was on Earth, I was closer to home than I was to the nearest star."

"Ah . . ."

Silence fell between them, but it was a comfortable silence not unlike those they shared on her porch swing. Then Chase rolled over onto his side and went up on his elbow. Though the shadows of the night hid his face from view, she tangibly felt his gaze.

"I missed home," he said, his voice a little gruff. "Lori, I missed you."

And then he leaned down and kissed her.

Her heart turned over. This was coming home. At the touch of his lips to hers, the years melted away. He tasted of peppermint and the past. She forgot the hurts and the heartache, forgot the promises she'd made to herself when she built her walls against him. Memories of young love, first love, came roaring back.

When he ended the kiss and lifted his mouth from hers, Lori said, "Chase, I can't . . . I don't think . . ."

"Don't think," he murmured. "It's working for me."

He lowered his head and kissed her again.

The first *boom* of fireworks echoed across the night. At least, Lori thought it was the sound of fireworks. It could have been the rockets going off in her head.

Chase must have heard them, too, because he chuckled against her lips. "Some things never change. Lori and fireworks. You two just go together."

"I think maybe it's best that we watch them instead of make our own."

"Why?"

"Well, for starters, you were going to marry someone else. Today."

He rolled onto his back with a sigh. "Lana and I are over. We've been over for months. It doesn't say anything good about me to admit this, but I agreed to the July Fourth wedding date because, at the time, it was easier than sending her away."

Lori sat up and silently watched the sky above Hummingbird Lake explode with peonies of purple, chrysanthemums of gold, and horsetails of red, white, and blue.

After a time, she said, "When I was doing my practicum someone brought in a hawk with a fractured wing. The avian specialist we had on staff stabilized the wing to allow it to heal. Bird's bones heal relatively fast, and after a month with our local wildlife rehabber, he was ready to be released. I went over and watched. It was lovely to watch when he unfurled those wings and flew away."

Chase sat up. "You think I'm going to leave again."

"You are not going to live in your parents' yurt forever. You are an adventure photographer. It's not just your job. It's your calling. You can't make a living as an adventure photographer in Eternity Springs."

He didn't protest, and as the minutes dragged by, Lori's heart sank. *You knew it.*

Better to do this now before you get in any deeper.

Deeper? Ha. Like that could happen. She'd taken the dive in high school and she'd never made her way back to the surface. She'd been swimming on the bottom alongside little Ava's galleon for years now.

Below them, the grand finale of the fireworks show filled the sky with explosions one on top of the other. When the *booms* and *whees* and *cracks* faded and the faint sound of cheering reached their ears, Chase said, "You are right. I won't stay in my parents' yurt forever, but neither will I go back to my job. I need to find something else to do."

"I get not wanting to work with your ex, but Chase, you're incredibly talented behind the lens. I'm sure you could get another job in a heartbeat."

"You don't understand. This isn't because of Lana. I don't want to, I'm done with photography."

"I don't understand. Why say that?"

"This has been a great evening and it's not a pretty story. Let's save that for another day."

"But you will tell me?"

"If I ever tell anyone, it will be you, Lori.

It will be you."

In the days and weeks following the Fourth of July holiday, Chase knew a lightening of spirit that added a spring to his step, put a smile on his face, and brought his appetite roaring back. He thrilled his mother by regularly stopping by the house for supper and delighted his father, who was nursing a strained hamstring, by volunteering to sub for him at the weekly softball game. He even managed a hit off ace pitcher Brick Callahan that earned him a free beer at Murphy's courtesy of Coach Rafferty following the game.

That his father's slot was in center field playing behind Lori's second base was a bonus. The woman looked really fine bending over in tight white baseball pants.

Lori's visits to the Rocking L for the work with Nicholas continued to be the highlight of his day, while more evenings than not had him headed for her porch swing. After dark, he always managed to steal a few kisses.

He wasn't sure where their relationship was going. Lori was as skittish as a yearling filly, and he couldn't blame her. What intelligent woman would want to hitch her wagon to a head case like him? However, he also recognized that Eternity Springs was working its mojo. He knew he'd never entirely get over the events in Chizickstan, but he was beginning to put them behind him. He'd even made an appointment to speak with a counselor in Gunnison during the weeklong break between the first and second sessions of camp at the Rocking L.

Tomorrow was the last day of Session One. With Nicholas's father due to arrive to pick up his son, Lori and Nicholas had planned a special event. Tomorrow, she was bringing one last new dog to camp. Chase could only hope that it didn't prove to be a disaster.

Chase woke up early, so he stopped by his parents' place and wheedled waffles out of his mother on the way to camp. He arrived at the Rocking L with a full stomach and a light step. The morning was reserved for awards and he had a stack of certificates to pass out. Then, after lunch and a little ceremonial sing-along, parents, friends, and guardians were slated to pick up their children and take them home.

Chase had volunteered to oversee the departure of his Tadpoles. Ava's father and mother arrived first and the girl started talking from the moment she saw them and didn't stop. Trevor's parents showed up about midway through the designated two-hour window for departure, but Trevor was in no hurry to leave so it took them over half an hour to get loaded up and away.

Time dragged by as Nicholas watched the clock. At quarter of two, the boy murmured just above a whisper, "He's doing it again. He's not coming again. He always breaks his promises."

Chase and Lori shared looks of concern. She held a leash in her hand and Mortimer sat quietly at her side. Two o'clock came and went and Nicholas suddenly started to cry. Big, racking sobs that involved his whole body. Lori stepped forward. "Oh, Nicholas."

"I'll go check at the office. Maybe they can give him a call."

Chase marched toward the admin building with anger fueling every step. If he happened to run into Jax Lancaster at this particular moment, he'd whip his ass.

He strode into the admin building and saw . . . Jax Lancaster. At least, he guessed this man was Jax Lancaster. He looked just like the photograph in Nicholas's file. Lancaster knelt on one knee beside Trevor. Both man and boy were covered in blood. Words burst from Chase's mouth. "What the hell happened?"

"I was whittling a stick and my knife slipped, Mr. Chase. We hadn't gone far so my dad turned around to get help. Nicholas's dad gave me stitches!"

"Where did you get a knife?"

Trevor hung his head and didn't speak. Suddenly, Chase got a bad feeling. "Trevor?"

"I wanted a souvenir."

At that moment, Trevor's parents exited the office with Alisha Cummins. Alisha held a folding knife in her hand — one that Chase recognized in an instant. "You went through my pack?"

Trevor's dad grimaced and said, "He's in so much trouble. He'll be disciplined severely. In our family we don't lie, cheat, or steal, or tolerate those who do. Son, apologize to the man."

"I'm sorry, Mr. Chase. It's just . . . I love you and I wanted something to remember you by."

The kid was a real piece of work. "Trevor, I will never forget you."

Alisha spoke up. "Mr. Lancaster, there's a restroom off my office in which you can wash up. And since your shirt is stained, you are welcome to change into one of the camp T-shirts."

"Thank you," Lancaster said, stepping

toward the office. "I'm anxious to see Nicholas."

When he returned a few moments later, Trevor's mother said, "I can't tell you how much we appreciate your help. I'm afraid I just panicked when I saw the blood."

Chase could relate.

"You kept such a cool head," Trevor's father added.

"Training kicked in. I was glad to help. Now, if you all will excuse me, I need to find my son."

"I'll take you to him," Chase volunteered, as he tried to recall what sort of training Nicholas's dad would have had. "Are you a doctor?"

"I'm Navy. We learn lots of useful things."

Oh, yeah. Now Chase remembered. So much of the boy's file had to do with the incident with his mother, facts about the father hadn't made a huge impression with him. "I'm Chase Timberlake, by the way. I gave Nicholas swimming lessons."

"How did he do?"

"Great. He has the basics mastered. He needs to have the opportunity to use the skills he's learned."

"I'll see that he does. His mother didn't like the water, but I want more for Nicholas."

"Swimming isn't the only skill he's worked on. Your son has the heart of a lion, Mr. Lancaster. He's been working on conquering another fear, and he has a surprise prepared to show you. I don't want to ruin it for him, but it doesn't hurt to give you a heads-up. You'll want to react with appropriate encouragement."

Lancaster's brow furrowed and he gave a hesitant, "O-kay."

"Also, when you were late arriving, he thought you weren't coming to get him. He's pretty upset."

Lancaster muttered a curse beneath his breath. "I was afraid of that."

"Why don't you hang back about five minutes and give me a chance to explain things. It'll make a difference. His cabin is along this trail about three minutes ahead."

Lancaster halted and checked his watch. "Okay."

Chase picked up his pace and returned to find Lori sitting beside Nicholas on his bunk, stroking his head like he'd seen her do innumerable times before with an animal of one sort or another. For the first time in a long time — since he quit carrying the ring he'd intended to give her in his pocket — he pictured her as a mother. *To my child. Whoa. Getting a little ahead of yourself*

352

there, aren't you, Timberlake?

He cleared his throat. "Good news, Nicholas. Your dad is here. He wasn't even late." He gave them a brief rundown of Trevor's shenanigans and how Jax Lancaster had stepped in to save the day.

"That boy," Lori said with a groan.

Nicholas lifted watery eyes filled with hope toward Chase. "He's here? Dad's really here?"

"Yep. On his way right now. If you and Miss Lori are going to do your thing, better get ready."

"He's here. He came." Nicholas blew out a heavy breath, swiped the back of his hand across his eyes, and scrambled off his bunk. "Miss Lori?"

"Are you ready, Nicholas? You have this, don't you?"

"Yes. Yes. I can do this."

"All right, then. I'll go get my part of this show and meet you outside in five."

"Okay."

Chase and Nicholas exited the cabin just as Jax Lancaster emerged from the trees. If Chase expected father and son to go running toward each other, arms extended and joyful greetings spilling from their lips, he was sadly mistaken.

Nicholas shoved his hands into his pants

pockets as he walked toward his father. Damned if the dad didn't mimic the gesture. His smile looked forced, too. "Hello, son."

Nicholas shrugged. "Hey, Dad."

"I think you've grown a foot since I saw you last."

"You haven't seen me for a long time, but I've only grown two inches this year."

"It's been eighty-two days." Lancaster briefly closed his eyes, then checked his watch. "Six hours and about twenty minutes. I've missed you, son. Is it okay if I give you a hug?"

Nicholas shrugged, but Chase didn't miss the yearning on the faces of both Lancasters when the father wrapped his arms around the boy's shoulders.

The movement Chase spied along the side of the cabin would be a welcome distraction for them both. "Nicholas, Dr. Murphy is here."

The boy wiggled away from his father and turned to face Lori. "Oh, wow."

"What in the world is that?" Ross Lancaster asked.

Chase couldn't help but grin. Mortimer could easily star in one of those ugly-dog videos on the Internet.

"That's Mortimer," Nicholas said, his voice a little wobbly. "Dr. Murphy warned me he was scary looking. Dr. Murphy is the vet, Dad."

Lancaster's gaze flicked toward Chase's. With a look, he asked, *Is this the surprise?*

Chase nodded and sent up a little silent prayer that this went as well as the rest of the introductions she'd made during the past few weeks. Though the Boston terrier had slowed down since Cam Murphy rescued him from threatened euthanasia his first summer in town, the dog still had plenty of spunk left in him — as evidenced by the fact that Lori mentioned he'd escaped the Murphys' backyard the previous day and chewed up a water sprinkler before Sarah chased him down. The years hadn't improved his looks, either. Mortimer had two different-color eyes that bugged out, more scars than Frankenstein, and an underbite that made dentists see dollar signs.

"That is one frightening dog," Lancaster agreed.

Nicholas said, "I haven't met him before."

"Okay."

Nicholas exhaled heavily, squared his shoulders, and started walking toward Lori.

"Dogs?" His father asked softly. "This surprise involves dogs?"

"Yep."

"He's deathly afraid of dogs!"

"Yeah, you probably should have mentioned that in his file. Nevertheless, look at what he's accomplished in his time at the Rocking L."

The next few minutes were even more rewarding than those when Ava put on her July Fourth treasure-diving show. The look on Jax Lancaster's face when he watched Nicholas follow Lori's instructions and extend a hand to the Devil Dog to sniff made Chase want to give Lori a high five. And the fact that the tall, tough naval officer blinked away tears from his eyes when Nicholas actually laughed while giving Mortimer a treat made Chase feel like a million dollars. As father, son, vet, and monster dog interacted, Chase's thoughts drifted back over the past few weeks. His father had done him a favor when he sent him to the Rocking L. Working with these kids had been a great experience. He was sorry it was over.

Although, he didn't guess it had to be over. Another, shorter session started week after next.

The sound of Nicholas's unbridled laughter distracted Chase from his thoughts and had him doing a double take. "Who took Mortimer off his leash?"

"I did!" Nicholas said, giggling.

"Wow. Just wow."

Jax Lancaster wore a huge smile as he sauntered back toward Chase. He handed him his phone, saying, "Do me a favor? Would you take our picture, please?"

Chase stood frozen, staring down at the phone in his palm. It was open to the camera app. He broke out in a cold sweat. His hand started to shake.

"Sorry. No. I've got to go." He shoved the phone back at Nicholas's dad and fled.

Chased by the hounds of his own personal hell.

And Lori calling his name.

CHAPTER SIXTEEN

Lori spent the next few minutes doing damage control with Nicholas and his dad, making excuses for Chase's behavior that she pulled out of thin air. "One of the reasons Mr. Chase relates to the campers is that he's mourning the loss of some close friends earlier this spring. Sometimes he flashes back."

"I know what that's like," Nicholas said solemnly. "Tell him I said sometimes it helps to pinch yourself."

"I'll do that."

Or maybe she'd just pinch him herself.

After she saw the Lancasters off, she loaded up Mortimer and took him back to her dad. Cam invited her over to dinner that night — he planned to grill steaks in the backyard — but she begged off, telling him she already had plans. It was the truth.

She had a blockhead to pinch.

She screeched her car to a halt in a cloud

of dust in front of the yurt and she yanked open the door and marched inside without bothering to knock. The blasted man was standing in front of the open refrigerator door. Channeling responsible women everywhere, she snarled, "Don't just stand there with the door open. You're wasting energy!"

"It's not a good time, Lori."

"Not a good time? Well, bless your heart. I guess when you call Nicholas to apologize for being such a jerk you can tell him it just wasn't a good time. Shut the refrigerator door!"

"Dammit!" He grabbed a beer and slammed the door and whirled on her. "You are not my mother!"

"No, I'm damn sure not. But neither am I a doormat for you to wipe your feet on."

"What? What do you mean?"

"You drag me into this dog-introduction business and then you leave me hanging? Ten minutes, Chase. You needed ten minutes to see it through."

"I know. I'm sorry. Dammit, I'm sorry!"

The torment in his expression served to bank Lori's temper. "What happened? Why did you throw Mr. Lancaster's phone at him?"

"I didn't throw his phone."

"Yes you did. What's the deal, Chase? You

can't keep it all inside. You have to talk about it."

"No I don't," he fired back, his eyes closed, standing with his hands clenched at his sides and breathing as if he'd just finished a marathon. "I damned well don't have to talk about anything. I have all I can handle living with the pictures flashing through my mind."

Lori's heart went out to him. He looked so tortured. "Talk to me, Chase. Tell me what hurts you so."

Before she quite realized he moved, he advanced on her two solid steps. "No. No. It's ugly, Lori. So black and evil and ugly. Not for you. Never for you. You are . . . clean. Clean and white and . . . ah, Lori. As much as I have to remember them, want to remember them, I want to forget it. All of it. I need to forget. Please help me forget."

Chase backed her against the yurt's wall and kissed her. It was a desperate kiss, full of pain and loneliness and guilt. His hand lifted to her breast, cupped her, kneaded her. His thumb flicked her nipple and sent electric shivers racing up and down her spine. Chase moaned into her mouth. "Lori. My Lori. Where have you been?"

She tore her mouth away from his. "You left me, Chase. I waited . . . I waited for you. You gave up on me."

"I'm sorry. I'm so, so sorry."

Then his hand was in her hair, tugging, exposing her neck. His teeth nipped and tugged as he unerringly found those sensitive spots he'd learned eons ago. Sensitive places he'd discovered a lifetime ago. Places no man had found in quite the same way during the years that had followed.

Chase.

She'd missed him. Dear heaven above, she'd missed him.

So she kissed him back.

Her response seemed to release whatever dam held him back and he devoured her mouth with lips that ravaged. His tongue plunged and plundered and took. His hands moved across her body, delved beneath her shirt, and made her shudder and shiver and want. Oh, how she wanted.

He held her pinned against the wall, the evidence of his need hot and hard and huge against her belly. The familiarity of it coaxed a whimper from her throat.

At the sound, he tore his mouth away from hers. He gazed down at her with molten-chocolate eyes that stared straight into her soul. In a voice rough with arousal, he demanded, "Say yes."

She couldn't speak. She wished he hadn't

asked. It would be so much easier if he hadn't asked.

His hands gave her shoulders a shake. "Lori!"

"Yes!" she cried, her voice a little wild. "Yes, Chase. Yes."

Triumph glittered in his eyes. He lifted her and carried her to his bed where he stripped her naked and made love to her with an intensity that was both familiar and new. She moaned, she thrashed about. As he nibbled and licked his way down her body, when he pushed her thighs apart to allow him access to her core, she threaded her fingers in his thick dark hair and surrendered to the pleasure. As the first climax slammed into her and sent her soaring, Lori sobbed out his name.

When he filled her, when her body clenched around him and gripped him hard, when his thrusting stoked the cinders of her desire back into flame, Lori wondered how she had survived without him.

And as they lay entwined together in the aftermath of passion, her body aching deliciously, the hum of satisfaction singing in her veins, she asked herself the more immediate question.

How would she survive if he left her again?

Long minutes of silence ticked by. She had

yet to come up with an answer when Chase's voice rumbled beneath her ear.

"When I left Eternity Springs the last time, I thought I was headed for Tibet to raft the Hidden River Gorge. It's the one ride a river rat dreams about."

Lori went still. She knew about the Hidden River Gorge. His mother had cried on her mother's shoulder about the trip last January. Lori had looked it up. "The Hidden River Gorge is your Everest."

"Yeah."

He rolled over onto his back, keeping her tucked against him as he told her about floods and fears and feuds. He spoke of ignoring his intuition and making a fateful decision to climb onto a helicopter for an unnecessary trip. He spoke of Bradley Austin's skill in crash-landing the helicopter and David Whitelaw's youthful confidence in the people back at camp. He painted a vivid picture of the landing zone and walked through the decision to leave it to scout out a campsite that offered some shelter from an approaching storm.

"I picked up my pack and camera bag out of habit. I carried it everywhere. The grass was dense. I hiked for ten, maybe twelve minutes before I started climbing. Needed the vantage point of height."

Lori waited, her mouth dry, tension zinging on her nerves. It seemed like an hour passed before he continued, though she suspected it wasn't more than a minute.

"They came up from below and surrounded Bradley and David. Ten men. Armed to the hilt. They were not like the locals who'd worked with us. They looked different. Foreigners, as much as me. I watched them through my long-range lens and for a few minutes, they just talked. I began to think it might be okay."

He paused again and Lori wanted to tell him never mind. She didn't want to hear any more. But she knew she had to hear it. She knew Chase had to tell it.

"Then they set the helicopter on fire. Bradley lost it and started yelling. This little short guy took the butt of his weapon and slammed it into his gut. Bradley doubled over and David . . . well . . . the kid went Rambo. Tried to wrestle the gun away from the little SOB. Didn't get the gun but he got in a few good licks. I thought for sure they'd shoot him right then and there." He sucked in a breath and exhaled a heavy sigh. "Better if they had."

Chase continued the story, explaining how he had trailed the men and their captives for days, always on the lookout for an opportunity to effect a rescue. "By the third day, I was having trouble keeping up. Staying awake. One time it caught up with me and I slept hard for hours. When I woke up, they were long gone. I picked up their trail easy enough, but I'll always wonder if I missed my chance to rescue them then. It was the last chance, because when I caught up with them, they'd joined a larger group. It was a training camp. Instead of being outnumbered ten to three, they had us by forty."

Lori wanted to lift her head and look at him, but she sensed he wouldn't welcome it. The only movement she dared was to splay her fingers wider across his bare chest.

"Still, I hid and I watched. I'm good in the woods, but I'm still surprised they didn't sense I was out there. I know that Bradley and David never mentioned a third man. They never gave me up. Otherwise, the bastards would have started looking for me. They'd have found my ass. I hadn't tried to hide my trail because I figured someone on the side of the good guys would come looking for us. I have to live with that. I escaped and they were loyal to the end. And nobody came. I hoped. I prayed." He paused a long moment, then in a tight, raspy voice repeated, "Nobody came."

He rolled away from her, sat up, and grabbed his boxers from the floor where they'd fallen. Standing, he pulled on his shorts and padded barefoot across the room to the sink. He filled a glass with water, drained it, then repeated the action.

Lori sat up and kept the sheet clasped to her chest. She was trying to decide whether to speak or keep silent when he finally spoke again in flat, rapid words.

"They chained them to a post. They beat them. Every single day, they kicked them and clubbed them and beat them bloody. I watched. I couldn't do a damned thing about it, but I stood witness for them. And . . . I took pictures. I wanted evidence to show when our rescuers arrived, and besides, it was second nature to me. Taking pictures is what I did. I kept clicking the shutter. Click. Click. Click. I hear it in my sleep now. It was a death knell."

Lori covered her mouth with her hand. She sensed what was coming.

He stretched out his arms and gripped the counter, his muscles flexing with the force of the action. "The third day in camp, they unchained Bradley and David and stripped them naked. Gave them soap and a pail of water and told them to wash. I thought it was good news. I thought someone was coming for them. I thought maybe the good guys had pinpointed our location by satellite and worked out a deal and there would be a prisoner exchange or something. Those things happen, right?"

For the briefest of moments, he met her gaze. His mouth twisted bitterly. "In the movies, maybe. Not in real life."

Oh, Chase.

"In real life I was trying to figure out a way to get rescued with them without putting my own ass in the wringer. But then the little son of a bitch from the first day set up a tripod and mounted a video camera on it. They tossed Bradley and David something orange. Jumpsuits. The moment I saw that they were jumpsuits, I knew. Bradley and David did, too."

"Oh, dear God," Lori murmured. Because it didn't feel right to be naked now, she scooted out of bed and pulled on his T-shirt.

He turned around then, his tortured gaze seeking hers. "I don't know why I didn't set down my camera. I even changed the lens so I could get closer shots. I took the pictures, Lori. I did it instinctively. I took photos of the bastard as he pulled on a black face mask and spouted some long diatribe in a language I didn't know."

He closed his eyes. "I took photos from

beginning to bloody end."

Tears running down her face, Lori crossed the room to him. She wrapped her arms around him.

"So much blood," he said, his voice cracking. He stood so stiff and still that he could have been another boulder on the mountain.

"I will never forget it. I will never forget them. They were brave, Lori. In the end, they were so brave. And I was such a damned coward, hiding in the rocks. Watching. Taking . . ." — his voice broke on a sob — "pictures."

She murmured soothing sounds, stroked her hand across his back, patted him as she would a child.

For a long moment he stood, silent and shaking. When finally he cleared his throat and continued his horrifying tale, anger fired his words. "They burned the bodies. The little SOB kept the camera rolling for that, too. When it was . . . over. Finally, over . . . the leader had a long talk with the cameraman. Obviously giving him instructions. He packed the camera in a backpack and he and one other guy headed out of camp. I knew what I had to do. I couldn't let them upload that video onto the Internet and use my friends for their ungodly cause. I couldn't let that happen."

"Of course you couldn't."

He shook her off then and began pacing the room like a tiger. "I followed them. I stalked them. I figured I'd have to ambush them. I decided to wait until they were asleep and sneak into their camp and kill them. I had the knife I carry in my pack — the knife Trevor took — so I was going to slit their throats. Turn the tables on them. I imagined it. I pictured every move. I was cold-blooded and ready to kill."

Lori's heart ached for him. Tears welled in her eyes and spilled down her cheeks.

"But . . . I couldn't do it. I'm not an Army Ranger or a Navy SEAL. I'm a lousy river rat. When the time came, I was too much a coward to do it. A sorry, yellow-bellied coward."

No, Chase. You're not a cold-blooded killer.

"I still couldn't let them get away with the video, though, so I went for the camera. Got sloppy about it and made noise and then the bigger guy was on me with his knife."

Unconsciously, his hand lifted to the scar across his collarbone. "I got the knife away from him, and I was damned lucky that the little a-hole was slow to wake up because it allowed me to fight them one at a time. I couldn't have taken two of them at once. I remember . . . I remember the little guy's laughter. His partner was dead and we were rolling on the ground and I had sixty pounds on him at least. He laughed. Craziest sound I ever heard. I still hear it in my sleep. He laughed . . . until he stopped."

Thank God.

"At that point, it all blurs for me. I went a little crazy, Lori. I threw their bodies off a cliff and I took a rock to the camera and smashed it to smithereens and threw it after the bodies. Then I did the same to my camera. It made me sick. I puked my guts out. It all made me sick. It still makes me sick. I don't ever want to pick up a camera again."

"Oh, Chase." Lori went to him again and wrapped her arms around him. This time, he accepted her embrace and returned it, holding on to her hard. "That's the most horrible, terrifying, devastating story I've ever heard. My heart breaks for your friends and I am so sorry this happened to you. But I am also overwhelmed by gratitude that you survived. That you triumphed."

"My hands are bloody, Lori. I'm not proud of that part."

"And I can't feel bad for them. I am sorry you carry the weight of it, but you killed them in self-defense, Chase. And thank God you did. You absolutely had to go for the camera. You're a photographer. You know better than most the power that images have, and I'm sure that's why you realized how important it was to prevent those images from seeing the light of day. Those men were your colleagues. Bradley Austin was one of your best friends. You couldn't allow their lives . . . their deaths . . . to be turned into propaganda. Of course you had to do everything possible to destroy those horrific images. I'm so glad you did and you need to be glad, too. Think about their friends and families and all the people who loved them. You saved them such heartache. Oh, my God, Chase. If I put myself in their place . . . it would have killed me. And your dad and mom . . . Ali seriously wouldn't have survived it."

Lori stepped back and lifted her hand to his cheek. She waited for his gaze to meet hers, and then she spoke with quiet intensity. "You saved their families, Michael Chase Timberlake. You did that for your friends. You were strong and brave and —"

"I wasn't brave," he interrupted. "I was scared shitless."

"And you acted in spite of your fear. That is true courage, my love."

His eyes grew watery. His jaw hardened as he clenched his teeth and swallowed hard.

"It was the most awful thing."

"I know, baby. I know. Here . . ." She took hold of his hand and pulled him back toward the bed. "Lie down with me again. Let me hold you. I need to hold you."

And, she thought, he needed to be held.

For the longest time, that's what they did. All they did. And in that silent embrace, they both sought and found comfort. Then, sensing that it was something his spirit needed, she told him of the love and support offered by the people of Eternity Springs to his family during the time that he was missing. She touched upon her own heartache and then described in detail the all-encompassing joy that filled the Timberlake home and soon the entire valley at the news that their prayers had been answered and Chase had been found. "You are loved by many, Chase."

He rolled up on his elbow and studied her intently. "Does that include you, Glitterbug?"

She reached up and tenderly pushed a lock of dark hair away from his eyes. "I never stopped loving you. God help me, but I never could stop."

"I know the feeling," he said. "We were idiots to let it go so easy."

"Yes."

"I won't do it again," he vowed.

As he lowered his mouth to hers in a honeyed kiss, Lori's hand stroked up and down his back.

Feeling for his wings.

CHAPTER SEVENTEEN

Chase drifted gently toward wakefulness the following morning, well rested, sated, and warm. He opened his eyes, blinked twice, and smiled. Nothing like waking up with a naked woman snuggled against you.

He'd spilled his guts to her yesterday. Just opened his mouth and let the whole hideous story pour out. Saying the words had been hard and yet cathartic, and for the first time in longer than he could recall, he'd slept without being haunted by nightmares. She'd listened and she'd supported him. She hadn't turned away from him when he'd admitted the ugly truth.

Then she'd spoken words that applied salve to the wounds on his soul. *You saved them such heartache.* And, *You absolutely had to go for the camera.* She'd understood and she hadn't thought him a monster.

The burden he'd carried for months wasn't quite as heavy today as it had been the day before.

He woke her by making sweet love to her, cooked her bacon and eggs for breakfast, then sent her off with a kiss to begin her day of vaccinating cats and doing blood tests on dogs. He told her he'd see her that evening on her front porch and asked her what she'd like him to cook for dinner.

Then he turned his attention to slaying his personal beast. It wasn't easy. It took him a while to work up the nerve. But finally, surrounded by the peace and privacy of the yurt with memories of last night fresh in his mind, ignoring hands that shook and the cold sweat running down his spine, Chase used his phone to snap a photograph of Captain.

It was lousy, blurred, and beautiful to him.

By the time he went down to Eternity Springs to shop for supper and wait for his date on her porch swing, he had a couple shots of the dog worth framing. Later that night, he took a picture of a sleeping Lori, her hair a midnight waterfall across her pillow, her lips still moist and swollen from his kisses. He knew he'd treasure the photograph forever.

It set the tone for the following week. He'd retrieved the replacement camera Lana had given him from the closet where he'd stashed it out of sight, and when campers arrived for the second session of the Rocking L's summer season, Chase met them at the entrance to snap shots of their smiles.

The children invited to the second, shorter camp session were all return campers, so they all knew how to swim. Chase didn't have any Tadpoles to introduce to the water, but he did end up offering to teach a basics-of-photography class for the older kids. Upon hearing the news, Jack and Cat Davenport sent over age-appropriate cameras for every child in camp.

Chase was taking photos of kids and horses at the camp corral when he heard Celeste call his name. "Good morning, Celeste."

"It is a glorious morning, isn't it? I was wondering if you'd do me a favor in a bit."

"Anything for you."

"My nature walk begins soon. I've asked Lori to join us today to talk to the children about the wildlife we see. Would you tag along and record the moment in photographs?"

"I'd be happy to do that."

Her blue eyes twinkled. "I thought you might. Meet us at the trailhead in twenty minutes."

"I'll be there."

Chase took a few last shots as the horse-back riders set out on their morning ride, then he wandered toward the trailhead to wait for his woman.

His woman. That's how he thought of her. He wasn't quite as certain that she thought of herself that way or that she'd consider him to be her man — never mind that they slept together almost every night.

The woman was skittish. No surprise there. The Lori he'd always known and never stopped loving moved slowly and deliberately more often than not. She was still dipping her toes in the waters of their relationship. Chase believed that the best way to get wet was to dive right in.

So he was making plans to push her.

She arrived with Celeste wearing jeans, hiking boots, and a V-neck FRESH BAKERY T-shirt in a green that matched her eyes. She looked relaxed and lovely, and Chase had to restrain himself from kissing her hello. She wasn't ready to go public with their relationship, she'd told him just last night.

He wondered just who she considered to be the public. From what he could tell, everyone in town already knew.

Chase's mother had asked him if he wanted to bring Lori up for supper next

Tuesday night. Her brother Devin had made a smart-ass remark about Chase's jeep being parked in her driveway overnight.

Cam Murphy had given Chase the stink eye when he went into his sporting goods store to purchase a new fishing license that very morning. When Chase caught Cam gazing from the bows and arrows behind the counter to Chase's chest and back to the bows and arrows, he quickly handed over his credit card. Cam rang up the sale, but when he handed back Chase's credit card, he didn't let go of it. "Got your act together?"

"Getting there."

"Huh. Well, I'm keeping my eye on you."

Chase slipped the card back into his wallet, grabbed his license, and hightailed it out of Refresh. And to think Lori regretted Cam's having missed out on playing "Dad" during her high school years.

The campers arrived and they headed out on their walk. It proved to be a good wildlife day. They spotted deer, a pair of marmots, a pine marten, a weasel, and more squirrels, chipmunks, and birds than he could count. The prize of the day was an elk across the creek and some fifteen yards away.

Celeste's voice interrupted him. "Well, I think this does it. I sensed the time had come, but this gives me undeniable proof."

He glanced over to see Celeste staring at her phone. She looked up at Chase and beamed. "Don't you agree?"

She held up the phone and he saw that while he'd been occupied taking photos of Lori lecturing about elk to the excited group of campers, Celeste had turned her phone's photo app toward the photographer and recorded a thirty-three-second video. Chase watched it, watched himself snap photos of the campers and Lori, and said, "I don't get it. What are you trying to show me, Celeste?"

"Your camera isn't pointed toward the elk. What were you taking pictures of, Chase?"

"Smiles. I'm taking pictures of smiles."

"And look at your face."

Chase wore a grin as big as any of the children.

"I have something for you," Celeste continued. She reached into the pocket of her jeans and pulled out a pendant on a silver chain. Recognizing it, Chase felt his throat go tight. "You're giving me Angel's Rest wings?"

"Our official healing-center blazon, awarded to those who have embraced healing's grace. You've earned it, my dear Chase."

He accepted it. Smiled down at it as wonder and gratitude rose within him. "When you started handing these things out, I never thought I'd be in the market for one. Never wanted to be."

He glanced toward Lori. "I thought she'd be the one earning her wings, what with all the to-do over her dad coming home."

"Yes, well. Our Lori still has a little work to do, you see. She's not quite ready to take that leap of faith that her parents took. But with encouragement . . ." Celeste glanced pointedly down at the pendant in his palm. "She's competitive."

Chase's lips twisted in a grin. "I like the way you think, Celeste."

He stepped forward, calling, "Hey, Lori. Look at what I just got."

As Lori dressed for her date with Chase to the annual Eternity Springs Arts Festival, Lori told herself she was glad that Celeste had awarded Chase the Angel's Rest blazon, and for the most part, she meant it. Chase was almost back to his old self now. The frequency of both his bouts of brooding and nightmares that jerked him from sleep had decreased substantially. That pleased her and relieved her, and if at the back of her mind she began to wait for him to start flapping his wings in prep to fly away, well, he hadn't died on a mountain in Chizickstan, had he?

She heard him knock on her screen door and call, "Lori?"

"C'mon inside. I'll be right out." She dragged the brush through her hair one more time, touched up her lip gloss, then exited her bedroom. Chase waited for her in the front room. Admiration shone in his eyes when he saw her. "Hey, Glitterbug. You look spectacular. Love the dress."

"Thank you." She spread the full skirt of her floral sundress and made a little curtsy. "Nic sent it over to me. She said she was online shopping the end-of-season sales and thought it looked like me."

"She's right. It's perfect for you. So how is she doing?"

"Mama and baby are both doing well, she tells me. The baby is due in about six weeks."

"My sister is coming in for the baby shower."

"Oh? I hadn't heard that. I'm glad. I've missed Caitlin this summer."

"I talked to her this morning. She likes her job, but she misses Colorado. Personally, I don't think she'll stay in New York past the first of the year."

A sound at the door caught Lori's attention. "You brought Captain?"

"Yeah. He's still a little damp from his bath so I left him on the porch. He has a date with Sage to have his puppy portrait drawn."

Lori chuckled and picked up her purse. "Good thing she draws fast."

"I know. I warned both Claire and Sage."

"Claire? Claire Branham?"

"Yes."

Claire Branham owned the newest retail establishment in Eternity Springs — Forever Christmas. Delight spread through Lori as she put the clues together. "She chose Captain to be one of her models?"

"The Twelve Dogs of Christmas. He's going to have his own ornament and everything."

Chase sounded like such a proud papa that she couldn't help but laugh. She thought that she'd keep the news to herself for now that Mortimer had been chosen for the honor, too.

They left the house and started toward Spruce Street where white canvas tents lined both sides of the street. The Summer Arts Festival was Eternity Springs's biggest tourist event, having grown in both size and reputation each year since its inception. The juried show brought in local, regional, and national artists and featured work in a wide variety of mediums from sculpture to jewelry to woodwork to paintings, from the dramatic to the whimsical. Local featured artists included glass artists Gabi Brogan and Cicero, and painter Sage Rafferty. Savannah Turner's homemade soaps were a hit, as were the delectable edibles available in Lori's mother's bakery's booth and that of Chase's mom's restaurant. The festival saw every available room for miles around rented and kept merchants' cash registers ringing.

"I love the arts festival," Lori said upon reaching Spruce.

Chase grabbed hold of her hand. "As long as nobody plays John Denver, I'm okay with it."

Lori recognized his reference to the festival the summer when she'd been struck by a bullet. She recalled what he'd said during their middle-of-the-night discussion last winter. *I was afraid we'd lose you. Afraid I would lose you. That's when I knew I was in love.* And, *What happened to us, Lori? Why wasn't love enough?*

That made this summer's arts festival an anniversary of sorts. She stole a look at Chase. Why hadn't love been enough? Had anything really changed?

He might have read her mind, because he lifted her hand to his mouth and pressed a kiss against her knuckles. "Let's go make some good memories, shall we?"

"Sounds fine by me," she replied.

"In that case, follow me."

He led her first to the Vistas Art Gallery booth where Sage sat with sketchpad in hand. "There's the pooch of the hour," she said, smiling brightly at Chase, Lori, and Captain. "I've been wondering when you'd show up."

"Are you ready for us?"

"I am. Have a seat. There's a basket of dog toys beneath that chair. See it?"

"Yes," Chase replied.

"Give him something to play with. Don't worry about keeping him still. That's not what I need. Just hold the leash and let him roam around the booth."

"Seems like you picked a strange time to do this drawing, Sage," Lori said.

Sage picked up a piece of charcoal and went to work. "Not really. I always do drawing demonstrations during the arts festival. I really liked the idea for this particular drawing."

Lori watched her work for a couple of minutes. Sage's talent always amazed her.

Captain's face was coming to life right in front of her.

From the corner of her eye, she saw Chase frown and reach into his pocket. He checked his phone and said, "Hmm. My mother is asking for my help with something. She says it'll just take a few minutes."

"Lori, you can hold the leash," Sage said without looking up from her drawing.

"Okay." Lori stepped forward as Chase stood.

"Thanks, Glitterbug." He kissed her on the cheek. "See you in a bit. Have fun."

Have fun? Holding his dog? That was a bit weird.

Sage distracted her with a comment about the other drawings she'd done for the Twelve Dogs of Christmas. They talked about the project and then the Christmas store and how Claire was quickly becoming part of the fabric of the town. "It's such a fun project," Sage said. "It's nice to have new ideas for chamber of commerce fundraisers. I think this one will be a hit."

"Me, too. I think — Oh, hi, Devin."

"Sis. I've been looking for you."

"Oh?"

"I'm supposed to take care of the dog."

"What? Why? I don't understand."

"Here, sweetheart," Sage said, tearing a

page out of her sketchbook. Her eyes sparkled and her lips twitched as she handed the paper over to Lori.

Two things hit her immediately. First, the artwork around the edge of the page was that whimsical style that defined Sage's work — dogs and roses and angels and hearts. Lots of hearts. The handwriting and what that handwriting said was all Chase.

Roses are red,
Dogs are tame,
Tell me, Lori my love,
Do you have game?

1. Hard to soft, salt to sweet,
Puppies love this sticky treat.

"It's another treasure hunt," she murmured. Her heart went pitty-pat and a grin tugged at her lips. Staring from Devin to Sage, she accused, "You both knew about this?"

Two identical shrugs of innocence had Lori rolling her eyes. Her mind had moved on to the riddle. She knew the answer, of course. Peanut butter. Peanut butter meant one of two places. Either the Taste of Texas Creamery with its peanut butter cup ice cream or her mother's peanut butter cookies. Since Lori couldn't picture Chase using her mother for the first stop in this treasure hunt, she decided to try Taste of Texas. She all but skipped to their booth.

"Do you by any chance have something for me?" she asked the owner, Jared Kelly.

"As a matter of fact, I do." He pulled a frozen treat out of the freezer. She unwrapped a piece of fruit on a stick. The pineapple slice had been cut in the shape of a dog and dipped in white chocolate. A note tied with a ribbon dangled from the stick.

2. Mirror Mirror on the wall
Who doth sparkle for them all?
Angels sent with scented slab.
Lori, my love, find one to grab.

Lori grinned like a maniac, bit the head off the pineapple dog, and put her brain to work. The thing to remember when solving his riddles was the KISS principle — keep it simple, stupid.

So . . . hmm . . . mirror and sparkle. Could he mean makeup? The only place to buy makeup in town was the drugstore. No, that didn't feel right.

Angels could be Angel's Rest. Scented slab could be the spa. Was he sending her to choose a treatment at the spa? Maybe. Unless . . . Angels sent with scented slab. Angels scent could be Heavenscents, Savannah Turner's handmade soap shop. Scented slab — a bar of soap. That sounded like a better fit. She'd try Heavenscents first.

Sure enough, at the shop a delighted Savannah handed over a darling tote bag that held a bar of heavenly scented soap. "Oh, I love this," Lori told her when she lifted the bar to her nose to sniff it. "I can't put my finger on the oils. Lavender? But there's a tinge of spice, too."

"It's a new fragrance," Savannah told her. "Specially commissioned for you. It's supposed to smell like summer and puppies, new beginnings and children's smiles."

Lori's heart melted.

The riddle tucked in with the soap sent her off to Fresh where her mother had a cookie baked especially for her and another riddle. For the next hour, she visited the Callahans' kitchen, Ali's restaurant, the *Eternity Times* office, the sheriff's office, the Christmas shop, the taxidermy collection at the school, Cicero's art glass gallery, and Gabi's shop, Whimsies. She'd filled up the little tote bag she'd received at Whimsies and, for that reason alone, hoped she was reaching the end of the hunt.

The riddle at Whimsies sent her to Murphy's Pub where she found a single red rose, a sparkling glass of champagne, and a handwritten challenge.

The past is out of the pocket
The future waits where it began.
The question is in the can.
What will be your answer?

Whoa. Lori took a long sip of her champagne. Liquid courage? She didn't get the first line, but the next three were pretty clear. Was the question the question she thought it might be?

She wasn't ready. She really wasn't ready for that. The man had been rushing her from the very first. He was born to rush. Born to fly. And she was born to sink roots and roost.

Leave it to Chase to force the issue.

Too soon.

They'd only been together a few weeks. They were still getting to know the people they'd become in the intervening years.

And yet, excitement sparkled in her veins like the champagne dancing on her tongue. She finished her drink, picked up the rose and riddle card, and made her way to the place where it all began. The Trading Post grocery store. At one time, the family business. It's where she'd been stocking the shelves the fateful moment that Chase Timberlake first walked into her life.

He waited for her in the canned vegetable aisle. In front of the corn.

When she saw him, Lori's steps slowed. Her memories flashed back to that first moment she'd seen him. Not love at first sight, but definitely crush at first sight. He'd been her crush for weeks and months. She hadn't experienced a single blinding moment when she'd tumbled into love. For her, falling in love — into true love — was more a gradual thing.

So falling out of love took a very long time to manage, too. In theory, anyway. Lori wasn't sure she'd ever pulled that one off.

"Hello, Glitterbug. Fancy running into you here."

"A treasure hunt, Timberlake? And you involved our friends and family?"

He grinned. "I was tired of the questions. They were straining themselves coming up with ways to ask that didn't seem too nosy. I figured we might as well put them out of their misery by going full-out public with our relationship."

"You've done that."

"Do you like your gifts?"

"They're treasures. Each and every one of

them. I especially like the angel from the Christmas shop. I hadn't been in Claire's angel room before. It's spectacular."

"I know you're a little jealous that Celeste awarded me my wings."

"Yeah, well. Let's not go there. This was fun, Chase. Thank you. You've changed the way I'll look at the Summer Arts Festival forever."

"Good. I like the idea of replacing bad memories with good, and good memories with better ones. So, Glitterbug, are you ready to solve the last riddle?" He gestured toward the shelf of canned vegetables.

Her heart thundered. The prize was obvious. One can of Del Monte corn was mixed in with the row of Libby's. She inhaled a deep breath and reached for it. As expected, it was lightweight. A diversion can safe. Slowly, she unscrewed the lid and turned the can over.

A black velvet ring box fell into her hand.

"Oh, Chase."

"I bought it when you were in college. I carried it in my pocket for months. The time was never right to give it to you. Now, it is."

Lori's throat went tight with emotion. The pressure of tears built in the back of her eyes. Chase took the box from her hand, went down on one knee and opened it. Held it up.

A simple solitaire on a plain gold band sparkled up at her. "Lori Elizabeth Reese Murphy, I love you. I've always loved you. I want to live with you and love with you and grow old with you. I want you to have my children. Glitterbug, will you marry me?"

She closed her eyes. So long. So long, she'd dreamed of hearing those words.

And yet, she licked her lips and met his gaze. "I'm scared, Chase. I'm scared to say yes. It hasn't been that long. What if you get bored here again? What if I'm not exciting enough for you? What if once your spirit has completely healed you realize this is all a mistake and you're ready to fly off to Zambia or Brazil or Yap!"

"Yap?" His brow furrowed. He came up off his knee. "Where's Yap?"

"It's an island in the South Pacific. You have wings, Chase. I sink roots. That hasn't changed."

"My wings brought me home to you, Lori. Home to my family. I'm not a migratory bird." His warm brown eyes remained solid and steady with promise. "I'm home to stay."

"I want to believe that." Big fat tears spilled from her eyes and rolled down her cheeks. "In my heart, I think I do believe it. But I'm afraid. I'm like Nicholas. My head knows you are not a danger to me, but my heart . . . my heart fears you'll rip it out if I let you close."

The man actually laughed. "So am I a bird or a wolf?"

"You're a hawk, Chase, and I watched that hawk's broken wing heal and then he flew away."

He reached out and touched her cheek. "Do you love me, Lori?"

"Yes. I do. I love you with all my heart."

"And I love you with all my heart. That's our bottom line. We can build from there."

"But we tried to do that before! We failed."

"That's because we didn't trust each other enough. We didn't trust that we could overcome the obstacles we faced. I made a mistake when I didn't give you this ring years ago. I'm correcting that now. Trust me, Lori. Trust us. We don't have to set a wedding date now, but I want you to wear my ring."

"No wedding date?" The idea intrigued Lori. Maybe that's the way she could do this. Be engaged, but wait until she was sure. Until she was ready.

"No wedding date for now. We'll figure out a way to introduce you to the idea. Give you time to get used to it. I predict that before long, you'll be ready for the Mortimer test."

She blinked away her tears and let out a short, soft laugh. "What's that?"

"I don't know. Probably something to do with our mothers. Shopping for a wedding gown."

"Yeah. That would certainly be a Mortimer test. Mom and Ali would love it."

He took it from the case and held out his left hand palm up. "Wear my ring, Lori. Promise to be my wife someday. Say yes."

The word spilled from her lips like a love song. "Yes. Yes, Chase. I'll marry you. Someday."

He slid the ring onto her finger and took her in his arms and kissed her long and lovingly.

It was only when they broke apart and turned to go that Lori saw the heads peeking around the aisle end caps. Mom. Ali. Nic. Celeste. "I should have known we'd have an audience."

"No way around it. This is Eternity Springs, after all."

CHAPTER EIGHTEEN

"Two weeks." Sarah Murphy breezed into the kitchen at Angel's Rest and set an empty tray down on the counter. Guests were due to arrive for Nic Callahan's baby shower shortly, and as one of the hostesses, Sarah had just transferred two dozen cookies onto a plate in the dining room. "She's been engaged two whole weeks and still no word about a wedding date. The girl is so hard-headed and stubborn. She drives me absolutely crazy."

"Now, Sarah, don't be so hard on her," Cam said, following his wife into the kitchen with a second tray empty but for bread crumbs. He'd just unloaded a platter of sandwiches onto a table in Angel's Rest's front parlor, now utilized as a media room. Today's baby shower was a couples event, but it was also the opening weekend of the college football season.

Lori's dad continued, "She comes by her

stubbornness naturally. Remember your father?"

"She's just like him. But now she's totally upped her game. I swear she's channeling his ghost to tap him for added stubborn strength. Chase has the patience of a saint."

Ali Timberlake laughed and checked the hors d'oeuvres in the oven. She was relaxed and happy — just like her younger son had been of late. "Chase loves Lori and he's confident she'll come around sooner rather than later."

"Well, she'd better," Sarah groused. "I've been looking forward to planning her wedding all her life, and this refusal to name a date is putting a real kink in my plans."

Judging that the coffee had finished brewing, Sage Rafferty began to fill the antique silver coffeepot Celeste had brought in from its display spot on the dining room sideboard. "Maybe we should roll out one of our interventions," Sage suggested, a teasing note in her voice.

Entering the room with his daughter, Caitlin, Mac Timberlake observed, "You might be onto something there. You've had an excellent success rate with your interventions."

"What are you talking about?" Caitlin asked.

The older women shared a look and a laugh. Celeste said, "It started with Nic and became somewhat of a tradition with us."

Sarah shot Caitlin a grin. "Sometimes, some of us needed a little . . . well, I'd call it encouragement from our girlfriends when it came to our seeing the truth about our romantic relationships."

"Encouragement?" Celeste scoffed. "Honey, we were outright buttinskys. And it's a good thing we were, I will say. It worked, didn't it? Every time. Cam, would you get a bag of potato chips out of the pantry and fill that wooden bowl on the butler's pantry? It's for the media room."

"Consider it done," he replied with a wink toward Celeste.

"Well, Lori doesn't need an intervention," Ali said. "She has good reason to question the steadfastness of Chase's decision to make his home in Eternity Springs. She doesn't need us to tell her she's being foolish, because she's not."

Sarah whipped her head around and stared at Ali, her eyes widened with alarm. "You think he'll leave Eternity Springs?"

"No. Not at all. But we're not the ones to convince her of that. It's Chase's job and he will do it. His mind is made up, and once that happens, he doesn't give up. That's why we called him Terrier when he was a little boy."

"I don't know, Mom," Caitlin said. "He gave up on her before, didn't he? He got engaged to Lana."

Celeste shook her head. "No, Alison is right. He did that before he earned his wings. Lori is still working toward winning hers. You can't rush the girl. Remember how she was when it came to accepting Cam?"

"Like I said," Sarah grumbled. "As stubborn as her grandfather."

"You're talking about me again, aren't you?" Lori said as she walked arm in arm with the guest of honor into the kitchen.

"They are talking about doing an intervention," Caitlin said.

"I know about their interventions." Lori gave an exaggerated roll of her eyes. "Don't do that, please?"

"We need to do something," her mother said, her violet eyes snapping with frustration. "Each and every person here loves you. Each of us thinks you're making a huge mistake. You have a chance at a second chance, Lori Elizabeth. And you're still young! Do you know how much I'd have given to have a second chance with Dad at your age?"

"Mom, I love you, but I'm not you. Chase

isn't Dad. The situations are totally different."

"Then why are you treating him . . . treating the situation . . . like he is your father? Don't hold Cam against Chase. Don't blow it."

"I don't hold Cam against Chase," Lori protested, but a note of doubt had crept into her voice.

"Yes you do. And it reminds me of something you need to hear." Sarah shifted her gaze toward Celeste. "Celeste, do you remember what you told me when I was afraid to trust Cam? About taking a leap of faith?"

"Of course. I told you to leap like a lunatic."

"Exactly!" Sarah snapped her fingers triumphantly. "That's what I did. I leaped like a lunatic and look what I have now — a wonderful husband, two fabulous sons, and a beautiful, accomplished, granite-headed daughter who needs to take a leap so we can get the church reserved!"

Lori turned a long-suffering glance toward Nic. "Make them stop."

Amusement lit Nic's eyes. "Honey, you can shut them up with one little word. Well, I guess it's two words."

"Like . . . December twenty-fourth?"

Sarah rolled out.

"I'm not getting married on Christmas Eve, Mother."

"Okay, then when *are* you getting married?"

"That's not the date we're concerned about today," Chase said in a placating tone as he strode into the kitchen and went to stand with Lori. "The date that matters today is the one when the next Callahan man joins the world."

He reached into his pocket and fished out a twenty-dollar bill. "I call dibs on September twenty-seventh. Four-fourteen P.M."

Nic beamed with pleasure. "Why, that's a full week before my due date. Chase, my man, I like the way you think."

"I'm going to win the baby pool this time. I'm due." He winked at Lori and added, "Besides, I'm feeling lucky."

Just then Colt Rafferty arrived carrying a cooler full of drinks. "These go where, Celeste?"

"The parlor."

"There are fruit drinks in there for the kids, right?" Sage asked. "Not just beer?"

"I have another cooler for the kids. Chase, it's in the bed of my truck. Would you grab it?"

"Sure." He returned a few moments later

400

carrying a white cooler. "Water and juice boxes here. Where would you like them, Celeste?"

"Hmm . . ." Celeste tapped her index finger against her lips. "The front porch, I think. You know how the children always congregate in the front yard."

"Best place to play hide-and-seek in town." As Chase carried the cooler through the house, he called over his shoulder. "Gabe's brothers just pulled up. I hope we smoked enough ribs. Those Texas guys like to eat."

"We have plenty of food," said Ali. "Everything from jalapeño poppers to petits fours to serve with tea and coffee."

"It's a strange mix," Lori observed as the front doorbell chimed. Her mother went to open the door for the first shower guests. "Football and baby showers and free play time for the children."

Chase returned to the kitchen in time to snag a sausage ball from the plate his mother carried toward the parlor, which earned him a slap to the hand. He grinned and popped the meat into his mouth. "It's football and friendship. A perfect mix. A perfect compromise for this afternoon. Laid-back and easy. I love that about this town. I love how people pull together. They appreciate established traditions, but they don't mind change when change is needed. They identify a problem and figure a way to fix it. They treasure friendships that have existed for a long time, but they don't hesitate to make room for new ones. This town has the perfect mix."

A half-dozen more cars pulled up and the party got started. For the most part, the men gravitated to the media room and the women to the library where Nic was opening baby gifts, but there was also a good bit of back-and-forth between the two rooms.

It was a fun afternoon. One time Lori wandered into the media room and saw Celeste and Sage high-fiving over a touchdown by Air Force. She then drifted into the library to see Colt Rafferty and Zach Turner grinning like fiends as they held up onesies that touted their favorite college team. Minutes later, seven-year-old Meg Callahan wandered by holding Michael's hand. "Have you seen your mom, Lori? Michael needs a new diaper."

Lori wrinkled her nose. "Yes, he certainly does. I'll take him."

He chattered like a magpie as she carried him upstairs to do the deed, but just when she finished the odorous task, the sound of cheering children out on the lawn snagged both her and her little brother's attention. Lori toted him to the window where she saw Chase with a blindfold tied around his head playing blindman's buff with a gaggle of young children.

He had a grin on his face as wide as the Rio Grande, and watching him, Lori felt her heart swell. This man had parasailed off a mountaintop. He'd ridden a kayak over a waterfall. Someday, she imagined, he would surely tackle his Everest and ride the Hidden River Gorge. Chase Timberlake was an adventurer.

"Well, so am I."

"You're what?"

She turned to see her mother standing in the doorway, smiling at her. "Happy."

She set a freshly diapered Michael down and the boy padded over to his mother. Sarah picked him up.

"I'm happy, Mom. For you and Dad and Devin and Michael. For our family. We've figured it out."

"Yes, we have, but it will always be a work in progress. That's the way families are. The way relationships are. They change, they grow, they adapt. They have bumps along the way. As long as you love and trust in that love, you'll do just fine."

Lori went to Sarah and wrapped her arms

around her. "You've always been my hero. I've apologized before, but I need to say it again today. I'm sorry I was so hard on you when Dad came back to town. I didn't understand second chances."

Sarah smiled tenderly and kissed her daughter's brow. "Now you do?"

"Now I do. Mom, I'm ready to leap like a lunatic. Right here, right now."

"Go for it, girl."

Lori flashed her mother an impish grin and opened the door that led out onto the balcony. "Hey, Chase," she called. "Come over here. Stand below me."

"Lori!" Her mother moved forward, concern clouding her eyes. "What do you think you are doing?"

"October fifteenth, Mom. That's the big day. You can go give Ali the scoop."

"Lori Elizabeth Reese Murphy. You are not going to jump off that balcony!"

"I'm going to leap like a lunatic and earn my wings, Mama. But don't you worry. Chase is gonna catch me."

THE WEDDING

Around town, citizens of Eternity Springs remained on their guard. Today their own Lori Reese Murphy would marry another they claimed as theirs, Chase Timberlake.

At least, that was the plan. This was the third wedding date the boy had scheduled in the same year, so public opinion held that a little concern was justified. If this one didn't go off, folks feared for his mother's sanity.

If the worst happened and the reason the wedding didn't go off could be laid at the groom's feet, well, Lori's daddy did sell guns at his outdoors store, Refresh.

"He'll refresh that boyo with a twelve-gauge," the town's former mayor, Hank Townsend, declared.

Those parties with skin in the game, so to speak, had total confidence that the wedding would begin with all parties present at two o'clock that afternoon at St. Stephen's.

However, to a person, they spent a nervous morning.

Nic Callahan had missed her goddaughter's vet school graduation, and she had every intention of sitting at the front of the church behind Cam, Sarah, Devin, and Michael with her husband, daughters, and two-week-old bundle of joy, John Gabriel Callahan, Junior. But she had awoken this morning with an uncertain stomach, and the girls had mentioned that three classmates had stayed home from school with a virus yesterday.

"I can't get sick," Nic told Gabe as she rummaged through the refrigerator looking for a bottle of sparkling water. Maybe the bubbles would settle her stomach. "I cannot miss Lori and Chase's wedding. It would break my heart, and Sarah and Lori's hearts, too."

"You'll be fine," Gabe told her, as he lifted his son to his shoulder to pat his back and coax up a burp after his morning nursing. "I don't think you're getting sick. I think you're nervous on your best friend's behalf."

"Maybe. You have to admit that Sarah has had a stretch of bad luck where this wedding is concerned. Seriously, Mortimer is lucky to be alive after yesterday."

"Well, it turned out okay in the end.

Celeste is a magician with needle and thread. You said yourself you couldn't find the tear in her mother-of-the-bride dress once Sarah put it on." He paused and mused, "I wonder if she really did make Cam sleep outside with the dog like she threatened."

The answer to Gabe's question was no, though as Lori's brother sneaked some Lucky Charms into recently-turned-three-year-old Michael's bowl of boring Cheerios, Devin would have added that it had been a touch-and-go moment here at wedding central. "You keep these Lucky Charms just between the two of us, little man," he warned. "We don't want to do anything to set Mom off. And for the sake of all of Colorado, don't let Mortimer out of his crate today."

"Bad Morty," Michael said solemnly. He shoveled another spoon of cereal into his mouth.

Life was chaotic in the Murphy house this morning, and Devin already had made three trips to the community center at Angel's Rest where the reception was being held. What did brides' families do if they didn't have a brother available to serve step-and-fetch-it duty? he wanted to know.

He wondered if Caitlin was facing similar

issues with her crew up at Heartache Falls. Had organized and efficient Ali Timberlake managed to maintain her calm or had she finally lost her cool?

Had Devin picked up the phone and called the groom's sister, he'd have learned that no, Ali Timberlake wasn't the Queen of Calm on this bright October morning. She'd been such an emotional mess, in fact, that Mac Timberlake had called in the big guns first thing that morning.

In her kitchen, because it was what Ali did, she'd begun putting together a red sauce. The big gun summoned by Mac had arrived on her Gold Wing twenty minutes ago and now sat at the kitchen table stirring a teaspoon of sugar into her coffee. "Of course you're nervous, dear," Celeste said. "It's only natural."

"It's ridiculous. I didn't expect them to honeymoon in Eternity Springs and the circumstances this time are totally different. It's just that the thought of him leaving the valley, the idea that they're going so far away, it terrifies me. I think that —"

She broke off abruptly as the groom himself sauntered into the kitchen. "Good morning, Celeste."

"Happy wedding day, Chase."

His grin flashed. "Thank you." Displaying

the calm his mother had apparently misplaced, he sniffed the air and veered his course to the silverware drawer. Removing a spoon, he sidled up beside his mother and dipped it into the sauce pot.

Ali slapped his hand. "Michael Chase, you stop that!"

He grinned wider and brought a spoonful of sauce to his mouth, closed his eyes, and gave a reverent moan. Then he leaned over and kissed Ali's cheek. "Delish as always, Mom. I'll see you later."

"Where are you going?"

"Fishing."

"But . . . but . . . it's your wedding day!"

"I know. Isn't that great?" Beaming, he winked, waved, and walked out of the house.

Ali harrumphed. "I'll bet they're not fishing at the Murphy household."

At that particular moment, Sarah actually *was* fishing — her phone, out of the upstairs commode. "It's ruined!" she wailed. "Michael Cameron Murphy! What possessed you? What made me ever think that three-year-old boys would be less destructive than devil dogs? What am I going to do? We have flowers being delivered. We have chairs being delivered. We have food being delivered! I cannot not have a phone today!"

"You can use mine, honey," Cam offered,

smiling helpfully.

Sarah whirled on him like Cujo. "The vendors don't have *your* number. They have *my* number. I need *my* phone."

"It's okay, Mom," Lori soothed, sweeping into the room. "Your SIM card should be fine. I'll switch yours with Dad's and you won't miss a beat."

"Okay. Good. That's good." Sarah patted her hand over her heart then turned the evil eye toward Cam. "You are in charge of your son from this moment until the time we leave for the church. Do you understand me?"

"Absolutely." Cam turned his head and called. "Hey, Devin? Mom says I'm in charge of you."

Sarah balled up her fist, punched him in the gut, then marched out of the bathroom. "Too soon, Dad," Lori advised. "Too soon."

As she removed the SIM card from her mother's phone, her own phone rang. The bride smiled serenely and answered her groom's call.

Three and a half hours later, Mac Timberlake took his wife's hands in the vestment room of St. Stephen's church, extended her arms, and gave her a slow once-over. Admiration gleamed in his eyes, and he gave a low-pitched wolf whistle. "Alison, you look divine."

"You look pretty fine yourself, Judge Timberlake. The gray of that suit matches your eyes."

"I'm glad Chase decided to go with suits over tuxes."

"Our groom made a number of excellent choices where this wedding is concerned, beginning with his choice of bride."

"Amen to that. Along those lines, his former fiancée did make it. She's sitting about halfway back with other crew members from the show."

"That's nice." Ali peered around the doorway into the church. "I'm so glad he and Lana managed to come out of this as friends. She's a nice woman."

"Yes, she is. Chase has done himself proud."

"He's done us proud."

"Yep. I told him that on our way to the church." Mac cupped Ali's chin and said, "I'd so kiss you right now if I didn't know better."

"You mess up my lipstick and I'll —"

"I know. I know. But I want to kiss you, Alison. I want to kiss you and tell you how blessed I am that you are the mother of my children. I want to tell you that you are our family's heart, and that as long as you stand beside me, I know we can face anything life has to throw at us."

"Let's hope life is done chucking things for a while."

"Amen to that."

Mac leaned forward and carefully, cautiously touched his mouth to his wife's. "I love you, Alison."

"I love you, too, MacKenzie."

"I'm so glad you found your way — that we found our way — to Eternity Springs."

"Go check on your sons, Mac. I'd better make sure our bridesmaid daughter is ready for her trip up the aisle."

"Don't say it like that, Ali. That's too close to making my little girl sound like a bride."

"Little girl," Sarah said, fluffing the net of her daughter's wedding veil so that it hung properly. "You make a magnificent bride. You couldn't have chosen a more perfect dress." With an A-line silhouette, Queen Anne neckline, and chapel-length train, the gown was traditional, but unique. "The lace overlay suits you and embellishments add the perfect amount of sparkle."

"Thank you, Mom. I absolutely love the dress. Yours is perfect, too. Shantung silk looks gorgeous against your skin and the violet shade couldn't match your eyes any better. You're pretty hot for an MOB. Don't you think, Dad?"

Cam gave Sarah a long, studious look, then made a tiger's growl. "If we had five extra minutes, I'd trap her in the closet for an up-close-and-personal inspection."

"Cam!"

"Daddy!"

"Hey, you started it."

"No. You started it," Sarah argued, an amused gleam in her eyes. "Back when we were in high school."

"Those were the days," Cam said. He reached out and snagged Sarah's hand and brought it to his lips. "I despised those days when I was living them, but if I'd known then that those lousy times would lead me here today, living the life I have today, I'd be happy to relive every one. In slow motion."

Then he caught hold of Lori's hand and kissed it the same way he had her mother's. "My girls. My fabulous, spectacular girls. I love you both more than words can say. Thank you for letting me back into your lives."

"God was watching out for all of us when I won that trip to Australia."

"God and Celeste," Lori added.

"Lori and I are pretty danged lucky ourselves," Sarah said, blinking away more of the tears that had been a constant threat all day. "You didn't give up on us, and we didn't always make it easy on you."

"You never made it easy on me," Cam corrected.

"Mom and I are stubborn that way." Lori tugged a tissue from the box on the vanity and handed it to her mother.

With feeling, Cam said, "Tell me about it."

Lori shot him an unapologetic grin. "Like they say, 'All's well that ends well.' You and Mom and Chase and I both got our second-chance romances."

"That we did." Sarah shared a warm look with her daughter. "All we had to do was leap like lunatics."

A quick knock sounded on the door, then it opened and Devin stuck his head in the door. "Mom, it's time to escort you up the aisle."

"Okay." Sarah went up on her tiptoes and kissed Cam swiftly on the mouth. "Be careful. Don't step on her train. For heaven's sake, don't cry or else I'll cry and ruin my makeup for the pictures and I'll never forgive you."

"Yes, ma'am."

Sarah smiled into Lori's eyes, then gave her a quick, hard hug. "I loved having you all to myself all those years. It's hard to share you. You're the best daughter a mother could have. Now, go be the best wife a man can have."

"I will, Mom. I've had an excellent role model."

Then Sarah was gone and it was just Cam and Lori waiting for their cue. For the first time all day, a little bit of nerves fluttered through Lori. To combat them, she rubbed her thumb over the Angel's Rest blazon that she'd wrapped around the grip of her bridal bouquet when Celeste awarded her her wings earlier that day.

"Nervous?" Cam asked.

"A little. It's a big step."

"It's the best step."

The organ sounded those first announcing notes of Wagner's "Bridal Chorus" and Cam drew in a deep breath. "I've dreamed of this moment since the day you were born, Lori."

"I love you, Daddy." The doors opened. "Let's go do this thing."

On her father's arm, her heart singing with joy, under the loving gazes of family and dear friends, Lori Reese Murphy walked forward toward her past.

The Honeymoon

"Would you put down the blasted camera?" Lori said to Chase, frustration filling her tone. "I look like a drowned rat."

"You look gorgeous, Mrs. Timberlake. Absolutely breathtaking."

Lori rolled her eyes and pointed toward the mountains surrounding them. "That is breathtaking. Tibet is breathtaking. The Hidden River Gorge is breathtaking. I'm tired. I'm cranky. My shoulders ache from all the paddling yesterday, and I have a bruise the size of a baseball on my butt."

"Hey, this wasn't my idea. I booked a honeymoon trip to Tahiti. You're the one who hijacked it by getting Jack Davenport to pull his strings."

Lori frowned and pursed her lips in a pout. "I wanted to give you your Everest for a wedding gift."

"Oh, my love." Chase set down his camera, took hold of his wife's arms, and pulled her to her feet. "I said it before, and I'll say it again. Thank you. It was a spectacular surprise. The ride through the gorge with the guides y'all arranged was a dream come true, for me. A bucket-list check. It was the best wedding gift ever."

"I don't know. Your surprise was pretty darned awesome. I've always wanted to be married to the new executive director of the Rocking L summer camp."

"That wasn't your wedding gift. Your wedding gift was the new ultrasound machine for your practice."

She sighed happily at the thought of it. "I love that you know me so well."

"Right back at you. The trip this morning with you on the gentler water is a memory I will always treasure."

"And in case you forget, you have about a bajillion photos," she groused, though her lips twitched with a smile.

Chase leaned in and kissed the twitches. "God bless digital technology. Imagine how much you'd have cost me in film."

She sniffed with disdain.

Chase laughed. "I'm sorry you're wet, tired, and have a bruise the size of a baseball on your butt. This has been the most awesomely, wonderfully spectacular honeymoon, Lori, but I have to correct one misconception."

"Oh? What's that?"

"You didn't give me my Everest when you arranged for this trip. You gave me my Everest when you stood at the altar in St. Stephen's and repeated your wedding vows to me. Even if you did leave out the word 'obey.' "

Her slow, sweet smile made him weak at the knees. Chase took her in his arms, pulled her tight against him, and answered her smile with a slow, sweet kiss.

Finally, he lifted his head and stared down into those warm, loving eyes the color of a mountain in springtime. A beautiful, gorgeous Colorado Rocky Mountain. He spoke past a lump of emotion to say, "I love you, Lori Timberlake. Thanks for a perfect honeymoon. Thanks for bringing me to Tibet. But now, I'm ready to go home."

"That sounds really nice." She blinked back tears. "Let's go home, Chase. Home to Eternity Springs."

In a lush, picturesque mountain valley halfway around the world, he rested his forehead against hers and repeated, "Home to Eternity Springs."

In a dry, wry tone, he added, "It'll make our moms deliriously happy."

ABOUT THE AUTHOR

Emily March is the *New York Times* and *USA Today* bestselling author of the heartwarming Eternity Springs series. She was nominated three times for the prestigious RITA award. In 2009, the American Library Association named her romantic suspense novel, *Always Look Twice*, as one of the top ten romances of the year. A graduate of Texas A&M University, her real name is Geralyn Dawson.

The employees of Thorndike Press hope you have enjoyed this Large Print book. All our Thorndike, Wheeler, and Kennebec Large Print titles are designed for easy reading, and all our books are made to last. Other Thorndike Press Large Print books are available at your library, through selected bookstores, or directly from us.

For information about titles, please call:
  (800) 223-1244

or visit our Web site at:
  http://gale.cengage.com/thorndike

To share your comments, please write:
  Publisher
  Thorndike Press
  10 Water St., Suite 310
  Waterville, ME 04901